Freeze Frame: Murder

Skye could hardly wait to get a glimpse of the photographs. Excitedly, she unwound the negatives and wiped them off. Smiling in anticipation, she held the pictures up to the light for a look.

It appeared to be a woman asleep. Her position was awkward and her face puffy.

The sense of fun vanished, was replaced by a dull dread. Moving with mechanical precision, she set to work developing the photos.

In minutes she pulled out the eight-by-ten contact sheet, and stared at the woman's image come to life. Her heart began a dull thudding in her ears and she sat on the stool, breathing deeply.

"My God," she said aloud. "It can't be. It just can't!"

DARK ROOM

D. F. MILLS

CHARTER/DIAMOND BOOKS, NEW YORK

DARK ROOM

A Charter/Diamond Book / published by arrangement
with the author

PRINTING HISTORY
Charter/Diamond edition / August 1990

ISBN: 1-55773-370-8

Charter/Diamond Books are published by The Berkley Publishing Group,
200 Madison Avenue, New York, New York 10016.
The name "CHARTER/DIAMOND" and its logo
are trademarks belonging to Charter Communications, Inc.

PRINTED IN THE UNITED STATES OF AMERICA

10 9 8 7 6 5 4 3 2 1

The one who has overcome his own fear has conquered the beast.

—Glenn Clark

For Kent,
who helped me conquer
my own
beasts.

Acknowledgments

ALTHOUGH MY NAME appears on the title page, no fewer than a dozen people contributed their time, expertise, and encouragement in seeing that this book presented an accurate picture of the psychopathic mind, the criminal investigation, and the world of child pornography. I am deeply grateful to them all, and even though I've thanked them profusely already, I think they deserve a little recognition here.

The book could not have been written without my dear friend Dallas police officer Donna (D.K.) Lowe. She made a crisp blue uniform come to life for me in a way few civilians are privileged to see. I'll always owe her a debt of gratitude.

My deepest thanks go to several fine officers on the Dallas police force: Deputy Chief Richard Shifelbein, Tactical Division; Sergeant Charles Layer of Physical Evidence and Fingerprinting; Sergeant Bill Turnage of Vice, and Investigator David MacDonald of Youth, for taking time out of busy schedules to answer hours of questions. Sergeant Layer was famous for saying, "You want TV or the truth?" I wanted the truth, and they all gave it to me.

I will always be grateful to Patrick E. Besant-Matthews,

M.D., former Deputy Chief Medical Examiner for the Southwestern Institute of Forensic Sciences in Dallas, for revealing to me the fascinating world of forensic investigation and giving superb assistance with this book.

Kudos go to my friend Ron Lepard, a licensed professional counselor with many years' experience at the Rusk State Hospital and the Big Spring State Hospital of Texas for enabling me to crawl through the labyrinth of the psychopathic mind. Thanks also to Dr. Eliana Gil for her expertise on the adult abused as child, and her fine book, *Outgrowing the Pain: A Book for and About Adults Abused as Children*.

Bouquets for Ray Robbins, professor of criminal justice at Western Texas College and author of *The Texas Peace Officer*, for offering expert guidance and warm friendship.

My gratitude to Harley Bynum, who demonstrated to me the secrets of the studio photographer's craft (and made me look pretty damn good for the inside photo in the process); and love and thanks to John and Sammie Jarrell for showing me the mysteries of the darkroom and asking for each new chapter before it was finished.

I'd also like to thank the following organizations for their prompt and generous responses to requests for information: the National Center for Missing and Exploited Children, Childfind of America, Inc., and the Adam Walsh Child Resource Center.

I couldn't have made it without the following ragtag group of cronies: Karen Rinker, Barbara Wilkerson, Rebekah Thornton, and Pam Ravell Readell. They thought I could do it long before I did.

To Robby Trevey: a kiss for making me laugh.

To my mother: thanks for assuming, from the day I was born, that I could do anything I set my mind to do.

To my dad: *Semper fi*.

To my husband, Kent (my love, my life), my deepest appreciation for never letting me quit, and for sharing the vision.

To Dustin and Jessica, love and kisses, because even though their mother would rather read a book on serial killers than bake cookies, they love her anyway.

And as they say, last but not least my deepest thanks and affection for my agent, Anita Diamant, for believing in me long before anybody else did; and my editor, Ginjer Buchanan, for her patience and guidance.

Although the Dallas Police Department is a very real place, which I have tried very hard to depict accurately in policy and procedure, none of the officers or other characters in this book are meant to resemble anyone, living or dead. Nor will you find, upon visiting Dallas, 115000 Preston Road, Preston Haven Shopping Center, Preston-shade Road, or Skye Meredith Studios. All other locations and places in and around the city are real and true.

DARK ROOM

‖Prologue

HE'D NEVER KILLED anyone before and he wasn't sure how to go about it. Planning for something and then being faced with the reality of actually going through with it were sometimes two different things. Still, it had to be done. He had to protect the children. If he didn't, who would?

For a moment, when she first opened the door to him, he was tempted not to go through with it. She had such a friendly, open face, with a nice smile and smooth dark hair that touched her shoulders. Then he remembered. Smiles were deceiving. They were always nice and friendly. It was part of the game. It made you trust them. Everyone always trusted them. Except him. *He* knew better.

"Good evening," he said with a smile, extending his hand. "I'm Ralph Thompson of Play-Learn Toys, International, makers of educational toys even grown-ups enjoy. You might have seen some of our products, such as the Krazy Kube and the Stack-a-Block?"

"I, er . . ."

"We make toys exclusively for the preschool child, offering them what we like to call Fun Challenges, puzzles and building toys which present a challenge that is fun to meet. I'd be happy to show you our catalogue and some samples."

He clutched his arms in the raw February wind and peered over her shoulder. "May I come in?" Better be careful. Keep alert. He couldn't show her that he knew the truth.

She hesitated. "Well, you really need to speak to my supervisor about this, but she left already."

He knew full well when her supervisor had left. He'd waited, shielded from the waist up by a phone booth at the 7-Eleven store across the parking lot, watching, until all the children were gone. Until she was alone. And now it was dark, and cold, and most of the stores had closed. Just as he planned.

But she was smart. She wasn't going to let him in.

"Tell you what, it's late, and I have some samples in the trunk of my car," he said, straightening his tie and shifting his briefcase slightly. "I'd be happy to leave them with you. Why don't we just get them from there, and then we can both leave? I'll call another day. I'm tired, anyway," he added, catching her eye with that "we're just a couple of working stiffs" look.

The sigh, the nod, the shrug, and the flicker of a change across her face told him that she had decided to trust him, after all. "I'll get my purse," she said, and his heart started to pound.

She was back before he had time to react, shutting the door firmly behind her and locking it. She headed out into the parking lot. "Where's your car?"

"I feel so dumb." He lifted his hands and the briefcase apologetically. "I drove into the exit of the parking lot instead of the entrance. I'm parked around here." Gesturing vaguely toward the rear of the building, he started striding purposefully in that direction. He stopped and looked behind him. "You coming?"

She glanced around the near-deserted parking lot.

"Oh, for heaven's sake," he said, allowing just the right note of irritation into his voice, "I've had a long day. If you don't want the samples, then fine. We can just forget the whole thing. You seemed interested . . ."

"I'm sorry." She moved toward him. "It's just . . . I thought it would be better if we looked at them with the supervisor, that's all."

He headed around the building. "So, you can show them to her tomorrow. You can talk about them without feeling pressured by a salesman. And I'll call you in a few days, okay?" They had arrived at his car, parked in shadow at the side of the building, near the alley.

To keep his hand from trembling, he gripped the handle of the briefcase and opened the trunk, concentrating on keeping the key steady, thinking: *She's still alive and vital. I can walk away right now.* The temptation was powerful, but he had to think of the children.

He couldn't forget the children.

‖Chapter One

LATE AFTERNOON SUN caught dust motes in the open door and made the old house seem darker than usual. For a moment, Skye thought she saw someone—Tommy, maybe?—standing in the hall by the stairway, but as she blinked her eyes into focus she found that she was quite alone. The slow, rhythmic tick of the grandfather clock in the sitting room reassured her.

Good. The last thing she needed was a confrontation with Tommy. She had already tangled with him once, before work. He was bound to be around someplace, this close to the dinner hour, mooching another meal off his mother. There was a time she would have run lightly up the stairs on the balls of her feet to avoid seeing him without tiring or making a sound.

Instead, she braced the left side of her body and the grocery sack on the mahogany railing, and placed her left foot and the cane, which she held in her right hand, on the first step. Suppressing a groan, Skye heaved her body and right foot parallel with them and waited a second, positioning her body and cane for the next step.

She stopped for a rest on the stair landing, bathed in the crimson glow of the stained-glass rose that served as a window. Halfway there. No sweat. It might even be getting a little easier.

With a slight grunt, she finally reached the top of the stairs. Two doors led to her apartment. One door opened to her bedroom, but the one closer to the stairs led to the living room, so she let herself in there.

Long experience had taught her the wisdom of wearing a shoulder bag on the right, which hung at hand-length and had a side pocket from which she now slipped her keys. Opening the door, she moved as quickly as possible across the polished hardwood floors, set groceries down on the small bar that separated living area from kitchen, and sank gratefully onto the beige linen sofa.

Burying her face in a sofa cushion her mother had embroidered for her in a bright floral pattern, Skye moaned softly. The day's accumulated exhaustion swept over her, and she gave herself the luxury of giving in to it. Her legs cried out from the abuse they'd taken from the stairs, the supermarket, the studio, and beyond. It was time for aspirin, a meal, and a hot bath. But for now, all she wanted was rest and refuge.

Her mother's voice seemed to emanate from the cushion: "Why do you have to push yourself so hard? Must you open your own business? And why does it have to be in Dallas? You'd be surprised how much business you could drum up in a small town in West Texas, especially for children's portraits."

And the unspoken question: *Why do you insist on being so alone?*

There was a hint of movement beside her, a soft thump, and a delicate brush against her face. She reached out and caught the furry body to her and was rewarded with a loud, husky purr.

"Well, Bartholomew, how was your day? Catch any intruders? Slay any dragons?" She giggled as the scrawny pumpkin-colored tabby patted her face. "I think you're too tenderhearted to be doing your job properly, or you wouldn't be so skinny." She stroked the cat, who stropped himself against her hand, sending out little sparks of electricity. Then he curled up beside her, pressed close to her body, and Skye felt comforted.

She lay there for a while, allowing the pain to wash over her and then subside, as it often did when she rested. Before long the chill of early evening set in, and with a little squeal she remembered there was milk to put away. Struggling to her feet, she limped into the kitchen, using furniture for support, taking care not to trip over Bartholomew, who yowled at her feet. She dropped a handful of dry cat food into his dish.

A few things had spilled out of her purse where she had dropped it on the bar, including the roll of film she'd received that day in the mail. Curious, she hefted the film in her hand. There was nothing particularly different about it. It was a standard, commonly used type that required no special chemicals or devices to develop.

Someone—perhaps Maggie—must have taken a roll of photographs as a prank and sent them to her to develop. Something silly, to make her laugh.

Resisting the temptation to head straight for the darkroom, Skye perched on a barstool and made herself a salad, poured a glass of wine, and watched the evening news. She sat through a half-hour of murder, mayhem, and a report on a child molesting trial in California before reaching for the remote control and turning off the set. Vivaldi would be better.

As the sounds of Spring filled the air, she rinsed her few dishes, poured some more wine, and started toward the darkroom, feeling lighthearted with anticipation. It was a rare feeling, these days, and she didn't want to lose it.

Darkroom work was Skye's one salvation. It took the blackness of night and turned it into a creative force, the stuff of life itself. There, godlike and solitary in her dim-lit womb, Skye could watch an image come to life that previously had existed only in her mind's eye. What fun it would be to watch an unknown unfolding.

Most studio photographers had little patience or energy left for darkroom work at night. Most of them wanted to get away from the business for a while, be with their families. Most of them *had* families.

The work Skye did in her studio was her *job*. In order to develop those full-color portraits to the satisfaction of paying clients, Skye would have needed equipment worth tens of thousands of dollars and a setup far more elaborate than the converted laundry room she used.

But the black-and-white photography she did in her spare time was *fun*, and took much more skill than expense to develop. With her camera, Skye was free to play, and the darkroom was her playground. The split-second timing required total concentration. Hours flew past . . . unlike the evenings she spent drowsing in limbo on the sofa or crying softly in her empty bed.

Not to think about that tonight. Tonight was going to be all right. As always, Bartholomew tried to follow her into the forbidden room, and as always, she pushed him gently out with her foot and closed the door. Once, his curiosity got the better of him and he jumped onto the cabinet, deftly flipping a tray of developing fluid onto the floor. He'd been banished in disgrace, but like most cats, felt no guilt. Sometimes, as she worked, she could hear him scratching on the door or mewing in frustration. More than once she'd pushed open the door with his weight pressed securely against it.

Flicking on the overhead exhaust fan, Skye took three shallow eight-by-ten trays from the wall cupboard and placed them on the clean cabinet top, along with some plastic containers of chemicals. The darkroom was arranged like an open-ended tube, with one door opening into the kitchen and one leading to the bedroom. On the wall flanking the bathroom was a long Formica cabinet that ended in a specially made, rectangular, shallow sink, about six inches deep, three feet long, and two feet wide. Cupboards lined the wall above and below the cabinet. The opposite wall had another, shorter cabinet, which ended in an adjustable shelf. Mounted above the shelf was a tall photograph enlarger and printer. The shelf could be lowered if necessary, in order to make very large prints.

The room was spotless and windowless. The cabinets were wiped clean and there was no clutter in sight. In the darkroom she used to share with Paul, he would tease her about it, saying, "Oh, no, I think I just saw a dust mote!" But it was the way Skye liked to work. It was the only area of her life where she felt in complete control.

There was a stool in the corner, but oddly enough, Skye only used it if she wanted to hang negatives to dry on the line above. More than once, while cleaning up after spending hours on her feet, Skye realized that her legs never seemed to hurt in the darkroom.

From a large plastic container she poured developer into a small stainless-steel can and placed the can in a tray of warm water. After plunking a thermometer into the can, she double-checked instructions on timing and exposure from a film company which she kept taped to the inside of a cupboard door, although long experience made the habit unnecessary. In front of her she arranged a bottle opener, a funnel, the film, and a sprocketed spool. When the temperature of the developer was right, Skye turned out the light.

Sometimes in those moments of absolute blindness, Skye fancied that she felt Paul's hands resting lightly on her waist, or his breath on the back of her neck. She would stand very still, listening, waiting, almost believing . . . But the feeling always passed. Still, she loved the soundless blackness, the total cessation of noise and people and movement. For a few moments she could gather her fragmented strength and draw on it. But only for a moment. There was work to be done.

Tonight, Paul's ghost slept, and Skye busied herself prying open the lid from the film roll with the bottle opener, shaking out the roll, tearing off the crooked edge, and threading it through the intricate sprockets of the spool, working the complicated maneuver with experienced fingers. Once the film was completely wound, she dropped the spool into the can of developer, placed a tight lid on the can, and set the dial of a timer whose clockface glowed incandescent green from a corner of the cabinet. She had seven minutes.

By the dim amber glow of a safety light, Skye slowly upended the can, back and forth, to keep the chemicals "active," and wondered again what might be on the film. There was no telling what Maggie and Tony had in mind, and she was sure they were responsible. Maggie Venatucci, her "transplanted Yankee" friend from Brooklyn, and her loud and loving husband, Tony . . . Without them, she'd never have managed the move from Paul's house to this apartment. She'd never have managed, period.

A soft *ding* reminded her that the seven minutes were up. She poured the developing fluid down the sink from a small hole in the top of the can's lid and flooded the can with water through the funnel, then added film-fixing solution and waited another four minutes, still rocking the can gently. Only then did she turn on the overhead light and remove the spool.

Almost done. Skye felt a little thrill of curiosity as she plunged the spool into the film washer, which worked like a tiny hot tub, and as she waited impatiently for five more minutes, she ran imaginary film strips through her mind of what she would find. Maggie in a clown suit, or Tony in cowboy clothes, cigar clamped firmly between his teeth. Afterward she placed the spool in a tray of cleaning fluid for another minute.

She could hardly wait to get a glimpse. Excitedly she unwound the negatives from the spool and wiped them off with a pair of sponge-covered tongs. Smiling in anticipation, she held the negatives up to the light for a look.

It appeared to be a woman asleep. Her position was

awkward and her face puffy. In fact . . . it wasn't what Skye had been expecting, but then, what *had* she been expecting? With a slight feeling of uneasiness, she prepared to make a contact sheet, an eight-by-ten page which contained all the photos from the negatives in the same size as the negatives. That way she could see the entire roll at a glance, choose the best one with the aid of a magnifying glass, and enlarge it.

With agitated movements, Skye took a hair dryer and worked over the negatives, shortening their drying time from twenty minutes to under three. Somehow it seemed to take longer.

Hurriedly she prepared a solution of print developer, one part chemical to two parts water, and filled a tray with it. Into another tray she placed the deadly acidic stop bath, poured directly from the bottle marked with skull and crossbones. A third tray held print-fixing solution.

As Skye filled a round tub with water and started the water moving in a counterclockwise motion, she tried not to be too disappointed. After all, it was hard to tell much from a negative.

Darkness again. Skye turned on the safety light, suffusing the room in its dull golden glow, a color she always associated with life, warmth, and safety. Fumbling a little now, she removed a piece of print paper from a light-tight box and took out a printing frame, a glass-topped box lined with a spongy material. Putting the paper "emulsion side up"—the slick side—she placed the negatives against it, dull side down. Carefully closing the glass top, Skye situated it underneath the enlarger, focused it as if it were a camera, and "flashed" it.

The sense of fun had vanished and been replaced by a dull dread. Moving with mechanical precision, Skye pursed her mouth. She removed the paper from the printing frame, placed it in the developing tray facedown, flipped it over with tongs, and slowly agitated the tray for a few seconds. Then into the print fixer for a couple more minutes.

As the woman's image came to life, there was very little Skye could tell by the dim, fuzzy glow of the safety light. Immersing the print into the washer, she snapped on the overhead light and watched, hypnotized, as it spun round and round.

With two fingers she pulled out the contact sheet and stared at it. Her heart began a dull thudding in her ears and she sat on the stool, breathing deeply.

"My God," she said aloud. "It looks like a woman's body. A dead body. It can't be. It's just too sick. It can't."

The unknown photographer had "bracketed" his photographs, using a variety of lighting exposures on the identical subject, in hopes of getting one ideal shot. There was something . . . unnatural . . . about her face. Over and over the woman grimaced from the page with never a change in expression. A whole roll of film, and not so much as a blink.

There had to be some logical explanation. Maybe if she enlarged one, she could see something she was missing, and it would all make sense. The only thing she could be sure of at this point was that Maggie and Tony had nothing to do with these photographs.

With a practiced eye, Skye selected the best negative and fitted it into a negative carrier, an implement that framed the chosen negative.

Inserting the negative carrier onto an "easel," underneath the enlarger, she set it for a five-by-seven print, moving the machine up and down above the shelf until the square of light fit the proper paper size. Focusing the enlarger, she hit the exposure, timing the precious seconds by instinct and experience.

She wouldn't think about the woman. Only the job at hand. Frowning in concentration, Skye dipped the print into the developer exactly as before, into the stop bath, and into the fixer, dreading what she thought she saw taking shape in the murky yellow light. Then, with a feeling of finality, she turned on the overhead light.

The woman's face was dark and swollen, with a raw scrape along one cheek, as if she'd been struck, or had fallen. There was a narrow line of bruises around her neck, with long streaks making little crosses through the bruises. Her long dark hair was matted beneath her. A few strands stuck to her face.

The photograph revealed the woman only from the waist up. She seemed to be lying down, but her head was cocked at an unnatural angle from her shoulders. She was wearing a winter coat, and attached to the lapel of the coat was a small pin—such as what a child might wear—a pin of a cat's smiling face. It looked as if she were lying on carpeting, the flat, indoor-outdoor kind. Some deep, primeval instinct told Skye that the woman was not asleep.

A bone-racking shudder overtook her and she dropped the print into the washer as if it had burned her. She couldn't seem to stop shaking. Clutching her arms close to her chest, Skye collapsed onto the stool, rocking slightly back and forth.

"What a terrible, terrible thing to do," she said. "What a sick joke for someone to play."

When she felt a little more controlled, she took the photograph out and looked at it again. A cold pit of nausea settled in her stomach. With a sudden righteous fury, Skye grabbed the print, contact sheet, and negatives and shoved open the door, almost falling over Bartholomew.

Taking a book of matches and a trash can in the other hand, she limped into the bathroom—her legs were starting to hurt again—put the trash can into the bathtub, threw the photographs and negatives into it, lit a match, and tossed it in.

There was a dull thud, and acrid chemical smoke rose to the ceiling. Skye stood and watched until it burned itself out.

Only then did the shaking stop. Only then did she feel safe.

* * *

From underneath the jabbing shadow of the trees, he could see her moving around in her apartment. On a dark night like this, when her lights were on, he could sometimes see her framed behind the sheer white draperies in those large bay windows in front of the house.

She would know now. She had to know. The film should have arrived in the mail today. He'd been watching her apartment all night, and for a couple of hours she hadn't been visible. She must have been developing the film then.

It was cold, but he had long since ceased to feel it. The dark, though, that bothered him. Streetlights helped, but he could handle it better outside, where he could breathe. Little dark rooms, that's what he couldn't take. There was a word for it, he'd heard. Clauso-something. Something.

He had actually done it! He could hardly contain the power of it, the joy of it. Now the children were safe, at least for a while. He took his fists out of the pockets and blew on them. Now she would know someone was on to her. Surely, now that she could see the consequences of her actions, she would learn a lesson. She would stop hurting the children. And he, *he,* would be their savior.

For a moment he was tempted to tell someone and share his excitement. He'd be in all the newspapers and on all the talk shows. Maybe the President would give him a medal. But not yet. It was too soon. There was still so much to be done. Like, wait for her to make the next move.

The house across the street was still, the bottom half dark. Even the old lady was in bed. He wondered what she would think if she knew what her precious tenant was up to. She'd learn not to trust the smiling faces of strangers. Just as he had learned.

He placed his hands under his armpits and looked toward the windows of the second floor. Then it dawned on him, as clear as if God Himself had told him, that it wouldn't matter. No matter what she did about the warnings, it wouldn't make any difference. The evil was in *her,* and she would just continue doing the same things, no matter what.

And the others would continue to help her. Even if she moved, they would find her and help her. But who would help the children?

It was clear to him then. He had to find the others—all those who helped her. He'd send her the evidence, just enough to let her know that he was closing in, just enough to torture her with her own terror (he liked the way that sounded—"torture her with her own terror"—maybe someday he would write a book and use that phrase). She would know that there was nowhere to run, nowhere to hide. Then he would kill her.

The light went out in her bedroom. She was in bed, then. He wondered how she would sleep tonight. Were the eyes watching her in the dark?

He shivered. He would find them all. He would ferret them out, like the rodents they were. He would find them in their rat holes, and he would destroy them.

It would serve as a warning, to all the evil vermin like them in the world, that they would not go unpunished. And he, *he,* would be the avenger.

The children would be safe. Everybody would want to see him, ask his advice, talk to him. They would be so grateful, and they would bring their children to him for his blessing.

Turning the frayed collar of his old leather coat up, he crossed the street and walked right past the house, looking up once to smile at the darkened window.

Chapter Two

SHE HAD JUST locked her door and stuffed the key into the side pocket of her purse when, pivoting on her cane, Skye saw him standing on the stair landing, shafts of morning light from the stained glass masking his face, half in crimson, half in shadow. She felt the floor sway beneath her while pinpricks of shock jolted through her body. In the next instant she flung the cane away from her and watched it tumble, end over end, in slow motion over the hallway stair banister to the floor below.

The distance from her door to the landing seemed to float past as she hurled herself down, clasping him to her so tightly that she had trouble breathing.

"They told me you were dead," she murmured into the familiar starchiness of his shirt. "I thought I'd never see you again. I've missed you so much." She wept, her body trembling.

Yet even though his body was firm against hers, he seemed strangely aloof; *he* was not holding *her,* she was holding *him.* Raising her head, she looked into his eyes, but it was hard to read the expression in them, shadowed as they were by the scarlet flush of light.

A loud jarring buzz startled her, and he started to pull away. She clutched at him.

"I must go," he said.

"But why?"

"It's the timer. It's time. I have to go now."

"What timer?" she cried, reaching for him as he stepped back. "Please don't leave me again. Please." She put her hand to his cheek and pulled it away. Blood dripped from her fingers.

She screamed, but the sound died in her throat and she struggled to get it out. The buzzing grew louder and he began to fade in front of her, vanishing into the shadows behind the bloodred light. Choking, she tried once more to scream, and as the strangled cry emerged from her she opened her eyes and saw her own hand reaching toward the alarm clock. She hit the button, and was enveloped in silence.

Heart thudding against her eardrums, Skye fell back on the damp pillow. Bedclothes were wadded and rumpled all around her. Her head ached. Squeezing her eyes shut, she rolled over and buried her face in the pillow, sobbing raggedly. Many times she had dreamed of seeing Paul again, and each dream opened the jagged edge of the wound inside, but never had a dream been so powerful, so horrible.

It was the film. She never should have touched it. She'd lain awake half the night, seeing the woman's face in front of her, trying to reassure herself that it was a prank, a sick joke, telling herself not to worry. Then the dream.

She didn't want to get up. She didn't have the strength to face another day. Bartholomew came to her, trilling little soft noises of concern. As he threaded his way through the things on the nightstand, an inexpensively framed snapshot fell with a rattle to the hardwood floor. Skye reached for it and lay back on the pillows, looking at it as if she'd never seen it before.

Her dark hair was shorter then, the natural curls tight and springy around her chin. Tugging absently at a shoulder-length strand, she stared at the picture as if by sheer force of will she could *become* that person again. Her fair complexion had burned slightly pink that day, and more freckles had popped out across the bridge of her nose. Sunglasses hid eyes the color of the water and sky, her namesake. She was blushing when the picture was taken, a natural rosy flush that suffused her cheeks whenever she laughed or felt self-conscious. Oddly enough, she hated having her picture taken.

Skye touched the face of the man in the photo. Deeply tanned that summer day, the lines around his eyes crinkling in the sun, the gray at his temples shone silver when the wind whipped his thick hair. Scorning sunglasses, his brown eyes squinted at the camera. They were both laughing.

The photo blurred. So many tears these days. Where did they all go?

"Oh, Paul," she sobbed, "I can't go on. I can't play the game anymore without you."

At last the tears subsided, leaving an anvil on her chest and splitting pain in her head. If only she had an assistant, someone who could call off her appointments for the day.

She staggered into the bathroom, clinging harder than usual to the furniture, and splashed cold water on her face. The shock felt good. Rooting around in the medicine chest, she found some aspirin and took three. Then she slipped out of Paul's pajama top—she'd started wearing them when they were married—and climbed into the shower.

For a long while she leaned into her hands, letting the hot stream cascade down the back of her neck, then switched the water to cool. It helped to dull the pain.

At last she toweled off, pulled on an oversized sweater and jeans, and made her way with Bartholomew into the kitchen for coffee and toast. Paul had always risen before she did and made breakfast. Now she could never make coffee in the morning without thinking of him.

The pain finally lessened from piercing intensity to a dull grinding ache that made her eyes feel grainy.

She felt vulnerable.

Whoever sent the film to her had done it maliciously. They had sent it to her business address. Maybe they would come in today and ask her about it.

Moving as if her ankles were weighted, she gathered her things and headed out the door, stopping for a moment to stare at the crimson shafts of light filtering across the stair landing.

His own cries awoke him, and he rolled straight out of bed, sitting up on the edge and groping his way from the nightmare to the shadows of his apartment. The dream wasn't clearly imprinted on his mind—not like that other dream that came so often—but left more of an impression, a feeling, than a clear image. It was the feeling that someone was watching him.

Rubbing his hands over his face, he listened to the muted early morning traffic noises and looked around the room. If someone *were* there, he would know it soon enough.

As he awakened more fully, he became aware of more noises from the apartment complex, a baby crying, doors closing in the hallway, cars starting up in the parking lot. Most of his neighbors were decent working people, but he knew a few individuals who lived on the left-handed side of the law. He liked it, though. Nobody bothered him. Nobody asked anything of him.

A loud buzz from the alarm caused him to jump. Quickly he turned it off. He felt hung over, although he'd had nothing to drink. He never drank alcohol. Booze only fuzzed up a person's brain, made him lose control. He didn't like to lose control.

The leftover agitation from the dream was beginning to fade. He went into the bathroom and turned on the light, surveying his face closely. Nothing had changed. Somehow he kept expecting to look different.

Preoccupied, he urinated, then went into the kitchen to start water boiling for coffee. Then he kicked off his underpants and crawled into the shower. He'd been sweating in his sleep, and it felt as if he'd been doing hard labor outdoors in summer. Grimy. He scrubbed and scrubbed, but as he toweled off, he noticed that he was still sweating. Folding the towel neatly, he hung it over a rod.

The water was boiling. Spooning instant coffee into a mug, he added the hot water, then left it on the bar to cool while he shaved. Afterward he wiped off the cabinet top with the hand towel, rinsed out the sink, and hung the towel. The shaving gear went back into the kit beside the sink.

Between sips of coffee, he selected a clean shirt from the closet and opened the front door for the morning paper, carrying it back to the bedroom under his arm. Before he could open the paper, his heart began to pound so heavily that he sat on the edge of the bed.

Would there be anything about the other night?

For a few minutes he stared at his bare feet. Had he done the right thing? After all, she *had* seemed very nice. What if she was the wrong one?

Springing up from the bed, he began to pace, then stopped in front of the closet door. Opening it, he studied the bulletin board which hung on the other side, looking over each clipping. And he thought about *her,* and he knew that, no, he hadn't done the wrong thing. He *had* been right.

He'd be seeing her today. He couldn't wait to see the fear in her eyes.

When he was finished, everyone would know that he had been right.

After all, someone had to save the children.

Skye Meredith Portraits was located in a small, exclusive shopping center on Preston Road, along with various trendy specialty shops, a popular bar, and a cozy Italian restaurant. There were no discount stores or fast-food places. The buildings were Spanish-style stucco with red-tiled roofs and flagstone walkways. It was one of the new shopping areas that had sprung up in the city to cater to the droves of young, upwardly mobile urban professionals who had swarmed to the Sunbelt to make their fortunes and leave their imprints in the fresh concrete of a growing city. Most of those imprints faded fast.

Skye's first two clients were twin babies, about a year old. The session seemed jinxed. As soon as Tim had stopped crying, Kim would crank up, and their young mother seemed on the verge of tears herself.

"Why don't we take a little break?" Skye suggested finally. "You see if they need changing or bottles or something, and I'll be right back." The mother, whose glossy brown chignon was coming unraveled, gave her a grateful smile and began rummaging in a huge diaper bag.

Escaping into a small, adjoining dressing room, Skye groped in a cabinet for some aspirin. The pain in her legs competed with the headache for her attention. Downing the aspirin with a swig from a can of Coke she'd left when the twins arrived, she took her purse in one hand and cane in the other and limped out of the studio.

It was the kind of February day she hated, in which the whole city of Dallas looked gray: gray buildings, gray streets, gray sky, gray people. It seemed appropriate, somehow. The wind sliced through her clothes like a dagger, and she hurried into the toy store next door to her studio.

Playtime Toys made no effort to compete with large toy conglomerates. It offered a world of wonder and delight for any child whose parents could afford it. Skye marveled anew at the life-sized stuffed toy jungle animals that prowled the perimeters of the store behind plastic palm trees, dolls with hand-painted faces and human hair sitting at little tables having tea, and the miniature Sesame Street, complete with an eight-foot Big Bird.

She was tempted to head for Toddler's Corner, with its chintz-covered chairs for exhausted mothers (or more likely, their well-paid nannies). Big plastic shapes—triangle, square, and rectangle in red, blue, and yellow—

were filled with educational toys that children were encouraged to play with in the Toddler's Corner while their parents shopped. (Of course, all the toys were available for purchase in the store.) Skye could collapse on one of the soft chairs and entertain fantasies of never returning to the studio.

Instead, she wound her way through a miniature circus train that traveled in and around the store with cars big enough to hold small children. This cold weekday, it stood empty.

A man-sized robot wearing a cowboy hat approached Skye and bowed.

"Ro-Tex, I'm desperate this time. Twin babies, about a year old. They're scared of balloons. I've tried using some of the toys in my studio, but they're too busy crying and pulling on their mother to pay attention to them. We're all worn out." She sighed, shifting her weight to lean more heavily on the cane.

The robot gave another dignified bow and turned on its heel, heading for Toddler's Corner with a jerky gait. She followed, thinking with a smile that their strides weren't, after all, that different.

Reaching into a red plastic triangle, Ro-Tex withdrew a fuzzy, multicolored ball, about twelve inches in diameter. She took it from him, and the movement caused melodious chimes within the ball to ring. She shook it again, grinning in pleasure at the soft musical notes.

"Ro-Tex, you're perfect."

"What's this I hear about perfection?" Clyde Winslow, the store's manager, stepped from behind a nearby counter. He'd been hidden behind silver heart-shaped helium-filled balloons. Winslow was slight of build, balding, with little round glasses, the perfect stereotype for Caspar Milque-toast.

"These balls are perfect to entertain twin babies while I sneak a picture or two." She glanced at her watch. "What do I owe you, Clyde?"

"Nonsense. Borrow them until the session is over. Then send their mother over to return them. She'll be so tired and grateful she's bound to spend some money!"

Skye laughed, signaled her thanks, and limped out of the store, cradling two soft balls in the crook of her free arm.

Back in the studio, Skye placed a section of fluffy white carpet on the bare concrete floor in front of a large white screen. Affixing a soft-focus lens to the camera, she said to the mother, "Take their clothes off, please."

"What?"

"Their clothes. Take off all their clothes."

"But . . . I bought these outfits especially for the photo session." The woman's high forehead creased into a frown. Kim rubbed her eyes with her fist and whined, her face hot pink against the stiff white lace. Tim tugged irritably at the miniature tie at the collar of his shirt.

"Please, Mrs. Sanders. Trust me." Skye smiled.

Her body rigid with doubt, the mother obeyed while Skye readied herself with the cable release and delicate high-key lighting. She chose the Hasselblad with its auto winder for the main camera, and readied the Mimaya RB 67 with a close-up lens for backup. Most photographers preferred to use only one type of camera at a time, to prevent bumbling mistakes, but Skye enjoyed the variety of two.

Liberated from the hot, confining clothes, the babies romped onto the soft carpet in delight. Quickly Skye lowered the Hasselblad's tripod to floor level. Stretching her body out behind it on the floor, Skye rolled one of the balls toward them, its chimes sounding merrily all the way.

With a squeal and a gleeful grin, Tim flung his body over the gaily hued ball. His sister squatted in profile to the camera and reached out a finger toward him.

Skye snapped the shot.

Standing, Tim hugged the ball into his body and staggered toward his sister, who was sitting with her ball in her lap. They giggled.

Smiling behind the viewfinder, Skye snapped.

Within a few minutes, the twenty-four-exposure film was used up. Skye switched to the Mimaya and close-up. With a practiced hand, she adjusted the lighting and film exposure and crouched, ready. The children held their balls out to each other, each studying the other's face as if to detect a hint of mischief there. The balls touched in the middle.

Skye snapped.

Within twenty minutes, both cameras were empty of film and Skye said, "Okay, that's it. You can dress them now. Here, let me help you."

"But . . ." Mrs. Sanders began, catching Tim on the run to diaper him. "I never really thought about photographing them in the *nude*. I mean, for a formal portrait."

"Like I said," answered Skye, tickling Kim's tummy as she struggled to dress her in the crumpled lace dress, "trust me. I think you will be pleased with the results." She handed the baby to her mother. "The proofs will be ready in about two weeks."

As she strapped the children into a large double stroller, the woman gave her head a thoughtful tilt. "You know, the more I think about it, the more special I think those pictures are likely to be. I can't wait to see the proofs." She touched Kim's soft cheek with the back of her hand. "I took off work today for this. Silly, I know. The baby-sitter could have brought them." She kissed the top of Tim's head. "I just never get to *enjoy* them, what with rushing off to work and hurrying home to cook dinner. My husband helps, but . . ." A helpless look came into her eyes. "I still get so *impatient* with them, when all I want to do is love them."

"I think all mothers feel that way." Skye handed Tim his pacifier.

"Do you have children?"

Skye's cheeks burned. "No." *But how I wish I did. If I had Paul's baby now . . .*

"I'm sorry. I didn't mean to be personal." Mrs. Sanders pushed a long strand of hair behind her ear.

"Not at all," Skye assured her as she threaded a little arm

into a coat sleeve. "Would you do me a favor?" She handed each baby a ball. "Would you return these to the toy store next door? I just borrowed them for the session."

"Sure . . . and . . . thanks."

"My pleasure, believe me. Those are sweet babies." Skye resisted the urge to kiss one of the soft faces upturned to her, something she often had to do. They were not her children; they were clients and she was a professional. Their mother might not appreciate hugs and kisses from someone who was basically a stranger.

She helped the woman out the door and sank into a comfortable armchair she had placed in a small waiting area at the front of the studio near the counter.

Though her headache had eased somewhat, her legs were hurting as much as ever, in spite of the aspirin. Resting her chin on her hand, she gazed exhaustedly around the studio. She'd decorated it herself to be comfortable and inviting. She did not want her customers to feel as if their children were being run through a factory on an assembly line. It was one of the little "extras" that went along with the high prices.

A couch, covered in blue and violet chintz which matched her chair, sat catty-corner beside a round table which was covered in a color-coordinated fabric and topped with glass. A dainty silk flower arrangement in sky blue and violet graced the table. Thick pearl-gray carpeting covered the floor. Blue wainscoting divided the walls, soft blue below and white above. Carefully arranged children's portraits, in handsome frames, occupied the upper half.

Her head dropped back against the soft headrest. A hassock was needed, she decided, for propping up aching legs. Not that it mattered now. She still had work to do, appointments to keep.

After a while, Skye spotted Mrs. Sanders leaving the toy store and heading across the parking lot, pushing the stroller with one hand. In her other hand was a large red plastic sack from Playtime Toys. Skye laughed aloud. Clyde was never wrong about the parents who came into his store. It made her feel a little better. Maybe by the end of the day, the woman's face from the darkroom would fade from her mind altogether.

The man wandered around the toy store, stroking the plush animals, fingering the puppets, examining the games. He'd never had any games, but then, it wouldn't have made much difference, there wouldn't have been anyone to play them with him. There were so many things to choose from, and he would have been happy to have any one of the wonders available in this place.

So many shiny little Matchbox cars. He'd had one once, which he'd carried in his pocket until the wheels fell off. There was a collector's case with room for dozens. Imagine having more than one.

In the sporting goods section, he hefted a smooth cool bat in his hands. Mr. Peterson had given him one once, and a real ball—not one of the rubber toy ones he'd sold Coke bottles to buy, but a real official Spalding. They'd gone out to a vacant lot, and Mr. Peterson had shown him how to hit, and how to pitch, and how to catch.

"*Cradle it into your body, like this,*" he'd said. "*Don't hold your arms out so stiff. Do you want to catch the ball or have hand-to-hand combat with it?*" Smiling slightly, he dropped the bat back into the wire basket and wandered the aisles some more. Too bad the only team he'd ever played on consisted of him and Mr. Peterson.

"We just came from Ms. Meredith's portrait studio next door." A woman's voice drifted to him over the toy displays. With casual nonchalance, he moved in that direction.

"She asked me to return these balls." He could see her now, an attractive, well-dressed woman with long brown hair pulled back in a chignon at the base of a slender neck. The woman took a ball from the hands of one of the twin babies in her stroller and was rewarded with a loud shriek.

"Sugarplum, Mama has to give this back," she said in vain over the child's screams. The second child began to cry and clutched her ball closer.

"Oh, all right." She raised her hands in a helpless gesture. "I guess I'll buy these balls." He could hear her laugh clearly as the baby was handed his ball and stopped crying. He pretended to study a book by Dr. Seuss.

"That woman really has a gift with children. Would you believe she had me take off all their clothes?"

Murmured responses. More laughter.

"I have to admit they were the cutest little monkeys you ever saw, running around that studio buck naked with these balls. The proofs should be wonderful."

Cash register noises. Indistinguishable comments. "I guess I'll take one of these, too. Second thought, make it two!"

He stole a glance at her. She took a red plastic sack in her hand, struggling a little with the stroller, and headed for the door. Moving quickly, he beat her to it and held it open for her.

"Thank you," she said with a warm smile.

He stood at the door, watching, until she'd loaded the babies and the stroller and driven away. Then he smiled.

Chapter Three

WITH AN EXASPERATED sigh, Skye replaced the phone in its cradle and put her face in her hands. She'd been trying to reschedule some of the day's appointments and go home, but she hadn't been able to reach a man named Jared Martin, who was bringing in his daughter. Apparently he'd already left for the studio and there was nothing she could do but wait.

The little bell on her door jingled and she looked up to see the man from Metroplex Messenger Service.

"Oh, no, is it Friday already?"

" 'Fraid so. What's the matter, too much partying last night?"

"That bad, huh?"

"Nah, you could never look too bad."

She smiled at the man vaguely, rushing to gather up her undeveloped film for him to deliver to the professional film laboratory across town.

"Twice a week you come here, and twice a week I seem to be surprised," she said, signing for the portraits he was delivering.

"Don't worry about it. Did you write up your order for this film?"

"Oh, for heaven's sake, I don't know where my mind is today."

The phone rang, and Skye balanced it on her shoulder, trying not to lose her place on the order form.

"No, Mrs. Stubbs, your son's proofs aren't ready yet. I told you it would take two weeks . . . No, it's only been four days . . . Yes, four days. I have it here on my appointment book." She signaled her thanks to the messenger and pulled out some of the proofs he had delivered for a look. The doorbell jingled again. "Yes, Mrs. Stubbs, I promise I will call just as soon as they arrive . . . Okay. 'Bye."

A little girl stood in front of her. Thick mahogany hair with golden streaks tumbled to her waist. A smattering of freckles peppered her nose. She looked up at Skye with the most incredible pair of turquoise eyes she had ever seen and said, "Hi, I'm Chelsea Martin and I'm six years old. How old are you?" Deep dimples appeared.

Skye laughed in spite of herself.

"Aw, Chelsea, five seconds, and already you've humiliated me," came a laughing voice from the door, and Skye looked up to see a man who was unmistakably the child's father, a man unlike any of the other fathers she'd seen since opening the studio.

Most of the children were brought in by mothers, grandmothers, or nannies. Occasionally, if she made an after-six appointment, a father would show up, self-assured in his three-piece suit.

This man was wearing a slightly frayed, green army jungle fatigue shirt, with "Martin" stitched over one breast pocket, and the oak cluster and musket of the combat infantry badge, with the parachute and oak cluster of the paratrooper sewn over the other. The left sleeve had the Screaming Eagle patch of the 101st Airborne Division. This was worn with faded jeans and running shoes.

Judging from the lines running from his nose to the corners of his mouth, Skye guessed him to be about

thirty-five. He was tall, somewhat taller than Paul, who had
stood at six feet. He had his daughter's auburn-brown hair,
thick and somewhat shaggy, but his eyes, while the same
almond shape, were a warm brown with deep laugh crinkles
that fanned out from beneath gold wire-rimmed glasses in
aviator frames. His chin had a dimple in the middle.

There was a contained energy about him, a barely
suppressed vitality that made the room seem fussy and
small. He prowled around with a springy step, viewing each
framed portrait, his hands stuffed into his back pockets with
the thumbs hanging out. One of the pockets had a big hole
in it.

None of the portraits were "traditional" studio poses. In
one photograph, a blond-haired, blue-eyed child of about
four stood in a pale green dress in a field of daisies,
clutching a handful of flowers and holding them out toward
the invisible camera as if the viewer of the picture were the
recipient of the gift.

In another, a black boy of about eight, dressed in his
Sunday finest, sat on the porch steps of a white frame
house, cuddling a large white puppy in his arms.

Skye had had to argue with each set of parents before
getting the pose and setting she wanted. One critic had
called her work "corny commercial candids," but several of
her portraits had won photography awards, and her stub-
bornness had paid off as her reputation—and her clientele—
grew. By the time she was ready to open her own studio,
she'd had customers waiting.

"As soon as I heard Skye Meredith had opened a studio
in Dallas, I made an appointment for my daughter," he said.
"I've long admired your work."

"You have?" Skye scanned her memory, trying to place
his name or his face, and came up blank.

"Sure." He turned and grinned. "I took a photography
class once at SMU under your husband—one of those
six-week night things—and I was so impressed with him as
an instructor that I went out and bought your books." He

picked up a large flat volume from the glass-topped coffee table and read aloud, "*Cowboys: The Last American Heroes,* by Paul Schofield and Skye Meredith. This one was my favorite."

"Thank you. I feel sort of special toward that one myself. We took most of the pictures on my parents' ranch in West Texas."

"I know. Paul told us." He laid the book down and picked up another one. "I liked this one, too: *The Independents: Maine Lobstermen.*" He flipped through the pages.

Skye chuckled. "It was a nightmare to do. Half the time we were at sea I spent hanging over the rail."

He laughed. "Paul didn't tell us that. Where's the other one? Didn't you do one on the Louisiana bayou country?"

"Yes." She came around the corner of the counter and limped over to him with help from the cane. He cocked his head and studied her, as though surprised, but said nothing. "I didn't care for *From Bayou to Voodoo* as much. It was the publisher's idea, and although the people in Louisiana were wonderful to us . . . I don't know . . . it just didn't have the magic of the other two."

He nodded. "I have to say I agree." He put down the book. "Don't you do the photographic work together during the summers?"

"That's right. We did." She arranged the books neatly on the coffee table. "Paul taught at the university for nine months of the year. Summers we'd take our trip for the photography, then I'd do some of the darkroom work and most of the layouts and stuff with the publishers through the winter." She raised up to look him in the eye. "I'd free-lance some, too, mostly children's portraits. That's how I got started with this." She gestured around the room.

There was a furrow between his brows. "Did you say *did*? Aren't you going to do any more books?"

"Paul died about a year ago." There was no kinder way to put it. Skye had learned to say it out when someone clearly didn't know, in spite of the horror that inevitably crossed their faces. She felt sorry for him.

For a long moment he stared at her as if he hadn't heard, then a little voice they'd both forgotten piped up, "Dad, we've only been here five seconds, and already you've humiliated me."

They both looked over at Chelsea, whose wise, little-girl face smiled placidly back, then Skye threw back her head and laughed. Relieved, Jared laughed, too, reached down to tousle her hair, then wandered over to one of the portraits. Without turning around, he asked, "Would it be crass to ask how it happened? I mean, I only knew Paul in the classroom, but I had a lot of respect for him."

"I don't mind." She studied the framed photograph in front of them. "Our publisher had arranged for us to meet a man in Houston who could put us in touch with someone from the Amish community in Pennsylvania for our next book. Paul hated to fly, so we were driving. It was raining and we were running late." Her voice assumed the monotone of a story often told. "He was driving pretty fast—one of those winding, hilly, two-lane roads in East Texas with tall pines on either side. The other guy passed on a double yellow center stripe at the top of a hill. I never even saw him." She stopped and glanced down at Chelsea. "I think all I need to say is that I had my seat belt buckled. Paul didn't."

He turned to look at her. She read sorrow in his eyes, but no pity, for which she was grateful. He didn't say, "I'm sorry," and she was glad. Sometimes words *were* inadequate.

He moved over to another portrait and was silent for a moment. "I wanted you to photograph my daughter because you have a gift for making children look like children, not like stuffy miniature adults." He paused. "Do you have any of your own?"

"No."

"You should, someday," he said easily. "You'd make a great mother."

She went back behind the counter. "Someday" was something she never thought about anymore.

"Well." He wheeled and smacked his hands together, as though the subject were dismissed. "Shall we get started?"

"Started?" She rubbed her temples absently.

"You know . . . Chelsea?"

"Oh!" She'd forgotten all about the portrait session. "Actually, Mr. Martin, I was just getting to that. I tried to reach you . . . the truth is . . . I won't be able to do your daughter today."

"Why not?"

To her horror, Skye felt hot tears sting her eyelids and roll down her face. While her cheeks burned furiously, she fumbled behind the counter for a tissue.

"Hey, Pooh Bear," he said to Chelsea, "why don't you go back there into that big room and look at all the cameras and stuff. Don't touch anything," he added as she left the room.

In two strides he'd crossed to the counter, digging a large rumpled handkerchief out of the back pocket of his jeans.

"This is so dumb, really," she protested, as much to herself as to him. "It's just . . . a headache." She dabbed at her eyes and wiped her nose. "I just need to go home and lie down for a while."

"M-m-m-hm-hm." He watched her, chewing on the inside of his cheek. "Hey, Chels!" he cried. "We gotta take this lady here for The Treatment!"

"Oh, boy!" The child scampered into the room. Obviously she hadn't gone far.

"The treatment?" Skye stammered as he came behind the counter, took her elbow firmly in one hand and the cane in another, and propelled her toward the door. "What are you doing?"

"It's neat," said Chelsea. "You'll like it."

"But . . . what . . . I can't just . . ."

"Where are your keys?" he asked as they reached the door.

"My . . . what?"

"Don't you want to lock up? Ah, here they are." He fished them out of her purse.

"Wait, you can't . . . but . . . I . . ." Locking the door behind them and stashing the keys back into the purse, he continued to half drag, half push her toward a candy-apple-red '66 Mustang parked in front of the studio. "Mr. Martin, I don't even know you—"

"The name's Jared, and I'm harmless; just ask Chelsea." He opened the car door, and Chelsea catapulted inside. Skye resisted. Jared grinned at her. "Pretty ladies who cry simply must have a dose of The Treatment."

"C'mon, Miss Meredith," begged Chelsea from the rear recesses of the car. "I promise it'll be real neat. Honest. I get The Treatment all the time."

"It's true. The kid's a regular con artist."

"Well . . ."

"Then it's settled." He gave her a gentle push, and she sat down, a captive.

"Buckle up," said Chelsea, and they were off.

"I don't suppose it would do any good to ask where we are going," Skye ventured.

"Of course not!" cried Jared in mock harshness. "It's part of the rules—no questions." Chelsea giggled.

The car radio was tuned to a classic-rock station, music from the fifties, sixties, and early seventies, and Jared sang "Fun, Fun, Fun" with the Beach Boys at the top of his lungs. Chelsea joined in on the chorus. Skye wondered if she'd fallen into a time warp.

It was unseasonably warm, with bright, prespring sunshine. Jared leaned across her and rolled the window partially down. His closeness made her shy. Cool air lifted her hair off the back of her neck and she felt herself beginning to relax. Suddenly, she sat up straight and said, "Oh, no! I know who you are! You're Jared Martin!"

Catching his daughter's eye in the rearview mirror, he lifted his shoulders in an exaggerated shrug and said, "I thought I told her that. Didn't I tell her that?"

"But I read your column in the *Times Herald* all the time."

"Would you put that in writing so I can show my editor? I'm trying to convince her that somebody is actually reading it."

"But it's a syndicated column."

"That's what I've been trying to tell her."

He was teasing her. "I feel like an idiot," she said.

"Then we ought to get along fine."

They passed tall glass buildings in shades of copper and silver and futuristic buildings with round tops and curved corners.

"What other kind of writing do you do?"

"Whatever I can peddle. Magazine articles, columns, whatever . . . I even teach a class to aspiring writers." He lifted his eyebrows comically. "They give me their money and I tell them how impossible it is." Turning up the radio, he sang along with the Beatles, begging for *Help!*

Skye leaned back in her seat with a distinct feeling of being out of control, but in this case, it was not a bad feeling. It was more like being dunked against your will into a cold mountain stream and coming up refreshed. In some ways, the situation was so absurd, she didn't know how to react to it.

Once in a while she would sneak a quick peek at the man driving. He drove easily, one hand draped over the wheel, zipping in and out of traffic like a speedway racer. Singing along with the radio, he seemed to expect nothing from Skye, giving her the space she needed to compose herself.

Presently he pulled up in front of a gourmet ice cream store. "What kind of ice cream do you like?" he asked as he sprang from the car.

"Ice cream? But it's so close to lunchtime . . ."

"Right. I had you figured for a strawberries-and-cream type." He disappeared into the store.

Skye swiveled around to see Chelsea. "Is he always like this?"

"Most of the time," Chelsea answered matter-of-factly.

She looked into the child's contented face, then, "Aren't you supposed to be in school this morning?"

"Nope. It's in-service day. The teachers have to show up, but we don't. Neat, huh?"

Skye smiled. "How come your mother didn't bring you to the studio?"

Chelsea gave her a look of astonishment and said, "She's *working* today, of course. This is my dad's day to have me."

"Have you?"

"Sure. Some days my mom has me and some days my dad has me."

Skye was considering this six-year-old appraisal of divorce and custody arrangements when Jared came out of the store, balancing three ice cream cones like a circus clown.

"Let's see, now, chocolate fudge for the brat here, strawberries-and-cream for the pretty lady . . . and good ole macho Rocky Road for me." He climbed into the car and slid Skye a sideways, suspicious look. "Don't believe anything the kid tells you," he stage-whispered. "She's a pathological liar."

Chelsea giggled, and Skye decided their relationship was based on a foundation of total nonsense.

The shock of the icy treat melting on her tongue was sheer pleasure, and Skye gave in to it, blocking all unpleasant thoughts from her mind.

A woman walked past the car, her arm full of white cardboard posters of medium size. With some effort she balanced posters and transparent tape while she pressed a poster flat against the large glass window of the ice cream store and attached it with the tape.

Chelsea was chattering about school; Skye listened with half a mind as Jared scolded her to stop talking and eat the

ice cream before it melted all over her hand. She idly
watched the woman hang the poster, concentrating on her
own cone.

There was something about that poster. It was another of
the many Missing Persons posters that had become almost
commonplace in recent troubled years, advertising lost
children begging to be found before they grew up.

Only this wasn't a child. It was a young woman.

"Whatd'ya think, Chels, should we give her the whole
Treatment, or just a taste of it?"

"Let's do it all!"

She had long dark hair.

"Should we give her a hint?"

"No! Let's keep it a surprise!"

She was smiling. Her face was not swollen.

"Hey, where are you going?"

How had she come to be standing in front of the poster?

"What's the matter, Skye?"

Her name was Sharon Smith. A simple name. She was
nineteen. She'd only been missing a few days.

The ice cream fell with a sticky *plat* to the sidewalk. A
strong arm slipped around her waist just as her knees went
weak.

"For God's sake, what is it? Skye? Do you know this
girl?"

"Please, Jared, take me back to the studio. I've got to get
my car."

What she wanted to say, what she couldn't say, was, *I've
got to get help. I can't wait for another roll of film to arrive
in the mail.*

Chapter Four

THE DALLAS POLICE Department looked more like an old-time Texas county courthouse than the police station of an image-conscious city. Solidly constructed of gray stone with Victorian curlicues, it crouched among sleek new buildings in downtown Dallas. So many sections of the building had been added onto through the years that it could be entered from three separate streets, Main, Commerce, or Harwood. Parking, while not hard to find, was expensive. After wandering around the building from Main to Harwood, Skye chose what looked like the main entrance and hesitantly climbed the steps.

She'd never been in a police department before and wasn't sure what to expect. Lots of uniforms, maybe. Bustle and activity. People being arrested.

Instead, she walked into a semideserted area gaily painted with large blue and red stripes surrounding the wall at head-height. A modern counter faced the door with a sign that read "Information Desk."

Skye approached the desk. Like a TV set between takes, the desk was empty. No people, no phones, no information. Bewildered, Skye stood for a moment and looked around. There was a pair of elevators down the hall and a set of stairs beside the information desk leading up. There was no one around.

Maybe she should just go home. What did she have to report, anyway? Leaning against her cane, Skye had just about talked herself into leaving when the elevator doors opened and two young women in uniform came out.

"Excuse me," she mumbled as they brushed past her, half hoping they wouldn't hear.

They stopped. They seemed so young. Younger than she was, even. One had black hair and sharp green eyes. The other had flaming red hair and freckles.

"I, uh, I need to report, um, a murder, I think."

The officers exchanged glances. "You *think*?" said the one with black hair.

Her mouth was dry. "Well, I'm not sure, uh, you see . . ."

"That'll be downstairs, in the basement," said the red-head with a bored look.

"Ignore the rookie," said the other. "Upstairs, 'Capers,'" she said to Skye with a jerk of her thumb toward the stairs.

Skye glanced at her nervously. What must they think of her? The dark-headed woman was smiling at her, as if to soften her words. Apparently she'd seen most everything on the job and found nothing unusual about Skye.

The stairs were not steep. With relief, she headed upward, hurrying as much as she could, wanting to get it over with, wanting to go home. Wondering what the hell "Capers" was.

There was one door at the top of the stairs, opened wide against the wall and held back with a doorstop. Skye read, backward, the words painted in black on frosted glass, "Crimes Against Persons."

She entered a tunnel-like area with glass walls on the left, behind which were numerous desks with computer termi-nals, like a newspaper office. Most of the desks were empty. To the right was a desk behind a glass window with a little hole cut out, like the ticket booth at the theater. A man with a paunch and thinning gray hair sat behind the desk, busy with paperwork. He was not wearing a uniform.

"Excuse me," she ventured, her courage failing her again.

He glanced at her in a distracted way.

"I need to see someone about a murder."

"You a witness?"

"No . . . not exactly."

"What do you mean, not exactly?" His attention sharpened. She felt her cheeks burn.

"I saw pictures of the victim."

He laid down his pencil. "Wait a minute. Tell me who this person is."

The girl's smiling face, frozen on a poster, flashed in her mind. "Sharon Smith."

Picking up the phone, he spoke into it a moment, then went back to his paperwork as if Skye weren't there. She shifted uneasily on her cane. Her legs were hurting. In a moment the phone buzzed, causing Skye to jump. The look he gave her was carefully bored.

"May I have your name, please?" Frowning slightly, he picked up the pencil.

She told him, and he wrote it on a form, along with her address, place of employment, and phone number.

"Miss, uh, Meredith, we have no homicide of a Sharon Smith reported."

She felt her cheeks grow hot, and cursed the telltale trait. "I saw her name on a Missing Persons poster."

He laid down the pencil again, regarding her through the window. "I thought you said you saw pictures of the body."

"I did. And then I saw her face on a Missing Persons poster, and that's where I got her name."

"Uh-huh." He crossed his arms on the desk and leaned forward. "Can I see the pictures, please?"

Skye's whole face felt hot. She knew she was flushing a

deep, rosy pink. "I don't have them anymore. I burned them."

A tall, slender dark woman in a white turtleneck sweater and slacks walked past and started to enter the glass-walled office area with the computer terminals. Her long black hair was pulled back in a severe knot at the top of her head, giving her an exotic look. Her eyes were large and brown and hard.

"Hey, Ruis," the man called. "Why don't you talk to this girl here. She's got some story about dead bodies and pictures or something, I don't know." He went back to his paperwork with a sigh.

The woman spoke around a cigarette. "I'm Investigator Ruis. What can I do for you?"

Skye looked around her. Some of the people had looked up from their work to stare, as if she were a fish behind the glass walls of an aquarium. "Can we go somewhere private?"

"Sure."

Investigator Ruis led the way into the large office area, through some of the desks, and into a tiny room with high white walls, a scarred wooden table, two chairs, and an ashtray. A video camera was mounted in an upper corner of the room. There were no windows. Make a good darkroom, Skye mused.

Collapsing gratefully into one of the chairs, Skye gripped the cane with both hands as if it could give her support. Her heart was pounding and her mouth cottony. Ruis perched on top of the table, one leg swinging. Skye felt like a child, looking up at a disapproving parent, even though Ruis's face was devoid of expression.

"Let's take it from the top, okay?" she said with a trace of a Spanish accent, flicking ash into the ashtray.

"I'm a studio photographer," Skye began, but her tongue seemed to stick to the roof of her mouth. "Could I have a drink of water, please?"

With a slight lift of the eyebrows, Ruis said, "Coffee do?"

Skye nodded, and stared at her hands until the investigator returned with the coffee, which was hot and black. She took a grateful sip. "I'm a studio photographer . . . I already said that, didn't I? Anyway, yesterday I got an envelope in the mail that had a roll of film in it. Undeveloped."

"How did you know it was undeveloped?"

"You can tell by the end piece that sticks out of the canister."

"Go on."

"I have a darkroom at home, so I developed it . . . I thought somebody had sent me something silly, or something. As a joke. It wasn't silly." She shuddered a little. "It looked like a woman had been strangled to death."

She took another sip of the coffee and looked up at Ruis. The officer's face was expressionless. "I thought it was a sick joke, so I burned the prints."

"What about the negatives?"

"Them, too. All of it. Then today . . . I saw this poster of a missing woman, and I'm sure it was the same one. This Sharon Smith. I think someone murdered her, took pictures of the body, and sent the film to me."

A faint shadow crossed the investigator's face, not even an expression, really, just a flicker of the eyes. Skye, watching her closely for any reaction, read the change. It was disbelief.

It had never occurred to her that she wouldn't be believed.

Investigator Ruis picked up a cream-colored telephone that Skye hadn't noticed at the end of the table, pressed four numbers, and waited.

"Sergeant Townsend, this is Ruis in Capers." She trilled the *r* in Ruis and accented the second syllable. "What can you tell me about a missing person by the name of Sharon

Smith? Yes, I'll hold. Thanks." They waited. Skye stared at her hands. Surely this would straighten everything out.

"Okay . . . Yeah . . . I see. 'Preciate it, Sergeant." Ruis hung up the phone. "The parents of Sharon Smith reported her missing a few days ago. They claim she disappeared from work, but when the officers questioned them, they got the impression that she'd been fighting with her folks for some time. She had a boyfriend in the Army, stationed in North Carolina. He says he hasn't seen her, but it's possible that he's lying." Ruis examined the end of her cigarette.

"The Missing Persons people didn't think it necessary to put out an all-points on her under the circumstances, at least not for a while—she's nineteen, after all, not a child, and there was no sign of foul play. The parents got all in a huff and had the posters made up." She stabbed out the cigarette in short jabs. "These posters bring in all kinds of crazies . . ." She glanced at Skye. "Sorry. What I'm trying to say is that there is nothing we can do. So far no bodies have turned up that match her description."

"But the poster said that the police suspected foul play."

"No," said Ruis gently, "the *parents* did." She stood, and so did Skye. "We'll let you know if anything turns up."

She was being dismissed. With a helpless feeling, Skye thanked the investigator, and as she walked out, heard laughter at her back.

It was a long walk to the door.

The child was crying. He could hear it. Frantically he beat on the door, trying to get to the child. The darkness was a thing he could feel, the closeness of the walls alive. The crying was getting worse.

"*Let me out!*" he screamed, pounding on the door. He could smell the stench of his own sweat and excrement in the close, airless room. He tried to wipe his hands on his jeans, but forgot that he was nude. His thighs were sticky and clammy.

"*Please,*" he cried. "I won't do it anymore if you'll just let me out."

The child's voice grew louder, more urgent.

He had to get to the child. Pulling and yanking on the doorknob, he cursed and screamed in frustration. There was nothing that would help him get the door open; he'd already felt around in the darkness.

He was suffocating. He lay down on the floor and put his face next to the crack under the door for some air. The cries sounded louder, nearer, as though the child were just on the other side of the door.

Weak from hunger and thirst, he lay a moment, listening in impotent rage. How long had he been in here? How much longer would it be? Time had melted into the darkness.

"I'm sorry," he wept. "I didn't know it was bad. I didn't mean to be bad." His cries grew louder, drowning out the voice of the child, *becoming* the voice of the child.

He *was* the child.

Sitting bolt upright in bed, he struggled to get his breath. The sheets were drenched, his heart pounding in his ears with throbbing force. The dull glow of the clockface read 3:00 A.M. The room was black-dark. Somehow he'd forgotten to leave on a light. He reached over and turned on a bedside lamp.

Lying back, he covered his face with his hands, breathing deeply, trying to slow the pacing of his heart.

He'd read someplace that people didn't dream about real-life experiences. It wasn't true. Every time he tried to put those days out of his mind, they came back to haunt him in his dreams.

Always, the same dream.

The sheets were wet and cold. Just like when he used to wet the bed. He'd wake up cold and wet and stinking. Have to get up in the middle of the night, strip the bed, wash the sheets in the bathtub, put them on wet, and lie there, miserable, the rest of the night. By the time he got home from school, they were dry. That way, he wouldn't have to worry about getting caught.

He'd learned to sleep sitting up, at his desk in school.

He got up and went to the bathroom, where he splashed cold water on his face. There would be no sleeping tonight, either.

It was *her*. He'd seen her. Seeing her always brought on the dream. He shivered. Wrapping a towel around his shoulders like a shawl for warmth, he sat back on the edge of the bed.

There was something about her that got to him, deep in his gut. A vulnerability. A childlikeness. Maybe it was because she didn't wear any makeup. And she had seemed upset when he saw her.

Maybe he was getting to her.

And then it came to him. A solution so bold, so incredible, *of course*!

He wouldn't *have* to kill her to get the evil out of her.

He would *love* it out of her!

When he showed her the error of her ways, he would *save* her! And *she* would love *him*, too! Together, they would be able to save all the children.

Bouncing off the edge of the bed, he paced the floor with the restless energy of a caged cat. It was the perfect solution.

In fact, the more he thought about it, the more convinced he became that she already loved him a little bit. Yes . . . now that he thought about it . . . the way she acted toward him was just a front, to cover up her true feelings.

Once she knew the truth, once she knew how she really felt, she would abandon the evil she was doing . . . yes, they would destroy the studio together, in a symbolic act. It excited him to think of them taking an axe to all those expensive cameras.

Then they would mount a crusade to abolish all evil

against children everywhere. How much stronger he would be with her at his side!

A sharp pain clutched at his testicles, doubling him over. Oh, no. Not now.

Another stab of pain. Groaning, he looked down. Yes, he was getting an erection.

The pain was getting worse. Why did this always have to happen?

Hobbling into the bathroom, he turned on the cold water in the shower full blast and crawled in, gasping.

It was God's punishment.

Quaking all over and catching his breath in great gulps, he stood in the shower until the pain subsided. Then he turned off the water and stood there dripping.

One thing was for sure. Their relationship would always be pure . . . even holy.

Maybe that was why she never dated any men. Deep down inside, she *wanted* to be pure and holy. Yes, that was it. Rubbing himself briskly with a towel, he smiled.

She must have been waiting for him, saving herself for him, all along.

Chapter Five

THE FRIDAY FIASCO at the police department had almost faded from Skye's mind by the time she slowly mounted the stairs to her apartment Tuesday evening. She had endured the weekend's long, unstructured hours and had even managed to convince herself that it did not matter whatsoever that Jared Martin had not called. She wasn't ready for a new man in her life, she told herself. Besides, those streamroller tactics of his could get old.

Her legs ached and the sight of the old house was a welcome one. Only a few blocks from the shopping center where her studio was located, the house had been scheduled for demolition when its owner, Opal Thomas, persuaded the city Historical Society to preserve it. Under stipulation from the society, extensive remodeling was necessary to justify the preservation, so the ingenious and stubborn woman made the upper half of the house into an apartment, which Skye now rented.

Tommy Thomas, who had lived at home all his life, moved out during the renovations; angry, it was said, because his mother hired a contractor instead of him to do the work. Skye never got over the feeling that Tommy blamed her for the split. Still, he managed to spend much of his time at his old home, mostly enjoying his mother's cooking, free laundry service, and whatever other handouts he could get.

She reached the top of the stairs and took the door into her bedroom. Her apartment was shaped like the bottom half of the letter "H"; each end of the apartment contained one long room which culminated at the front in bay windows. The rooms were separated by a short, narrow hallway with two separate entrance doors. The rear of the living area gave into a tiny kitchen, which then opened into a small laundry room, which Skye had converted into the darkroom. Another door led out of the darkroom into the rear portion of her bedroom, which she used as an office area. The bathroom flanked the darkroom and was accessible only through her bedroom.

"God Almighty!" Tony Venatucci had grumbled the day he helped her move. "Guy wants to take a leak, he's gotta wander halfway to Oz for the privilege."

But Skye had fallen in love with the fireplaces—one in the living area and one in the bedroom—with the high ceilings and window seats and hardwood floors, and with the stained glass on the stair landing. She'd filled the apartment with plants and flowers, black-and-white chrome-framed photograph prints, floor cushions, and books.

"*Must* you live on the second floor?" her mother had fretted once during a visit. "You'd be so much better off with a little ground-floor efficiency somewhere. And these floors will be so hard to keep up. I simply do not understand why you persist in making life so much harder on yourself than it needs to be."

But Skye, lost and adrift without Paul, knew she had come home.

She stretched out on the bed. How she longed to talk to him, not just about the serious matters, like the missing girl, but about the small things, life's trivia. Difficult clients, charge account snafus, something she'd seen on the news. Losing him had left a gaping loneliness that no amount of well-meaning friends could fill.

He would have known what to do about the film. He wouldn't flounder about, as she did, changing her mind each day. He would make a decision, act on it, and put it out of his mind. In six years of marriage, Skye couldn't remember one night that Paul had been unable to sleep. Now she couldn't remember one night when she *had*.

A pounding on her other door snapped Skye out of her reverie. She struggled up from the bed and opened the bedroom door. Tommy Thomas turned from the living room door. If he was trying to emulate Don Johnson's sexiness with that greasy hair and three-day beard, he had failed miserably. As he approached her, Skye stepped back instinctively. She'd never been able to look into those hard black eyes for long. There was something about the expression in them that gave her the creeps.

"Rent's due today," he said, and she stifled the urge to make a quick, angry reply. She'd never been late on her rent, and suspected that those days when he came by to collect it, rather than wait for her to pay his mother in person, he intended to sponge a few bucks for himself when her check was cashed.

"I'll write you a check," she said stiffly, and made her way over to her desk at the rear of the long room. To her dismay, he followed her.

"Never seen your bedroom."

She fished out her checkbook.

"Pretty."

She dug out a pen.

"You know, you and me could get along a lot better if you'd just try."

Grinding her teeth, she made out the check.

"Whatsamatter, cat got your tongue?" He reached out to stroke Bartholomew, who leaped out of his way and hid under the bed. "I hate cats."

She tore off the check and gave it to him. He sat on the edge of the bed. "What do you want, Tommy?" she asked wearily.

"Like I said, I just thought maybe you and me could be friends." He smiled, showing yellow teeth. His black eyes glittered.

She sighed.

He stood and began wandering around the room, stopping beside the bedside table, where he picked up the snapshot of her and Paul. "This your old man?"

"Put that down." She took it from him and put it back.

"What's your problem? I's just lookin' at it. The guy was a lot older'n you. What was he, your sugar daddy?"

"Get out."

"Kinda touchy, aren't you? Must be that time of the month."

"If you don't get out of here . . ."

"You'll what? Huh? I can get in here anytime I want, you know. This is my house. You'll figure that out soon enough."

Trying not to show fear in her eyes, she yanked the door open wide and stood as tall as her five feet five would allow. "I said get out."

Sauntering past, he stopped for a moment to grin down at her, then left. She slammed the door and locked it.

What did he mean, he could get in anytime he wanted? New locks had been installed when the remodeling was done. Had he somehow gotten hold of his mother's key, made a copy of it? A shudder seized her and she sat down on the bed.

What could she do about it? Even if she had new locks installed, Opal had to have a key. It would be a simple matter for him to get hold of any of his mother's keys.

A new thought, even more insidious and frightening, intruded. *Could Tommy have sent the film?*

It was just the kind of sick idea he would get. Maybe that was the reason he had collected the rent. He wanted to watch her, see if she reacted differently to him. But why all that talk about being friends?

Her bedroom still shouted with his presence. Moving into

the kitchen, she put a frozen dinner in the microwave and turned on the television for a little mindless company. Every move she made had taken on a new quality, a vulnerability that she hadn't felt before. Worse, even, than after the film. The film had come in the mail. Tommy's threat had been delivered in her bedroom.

And what if he *had* sent the film? Was it a coincidence that the woman resembled the woman in the poster? The police seemed to think so.

Yet a little corner of her mind, that corner where all her secret fears lurked, couldn't resist sending out a little *what if* signal . . . what if it *was* the same woman?

It couldn't be.

She didn't want to think about it anymore.

A loud buzz from the microwave jarred her back into the real world, the world of empty stomachs and evening chores. She ate her "lite" frozen dinner straight out of the container, at the bar, trying to forget herself in a few sitcoms. Roseanne Barr had just made a crack that made her laugh when she heard a loud knock at her bedroom door.

Curious. Her friends all knew which door led to her living room and always called for her there. She opened the living room door just in time to see Tommy Thomas straighten up from her bedroom doorknob and quickly pocket something.

"Aw, gee, what a disappointment. I's hopin' you'd still be in your bedroom, if you know what I mean."

"What are you doing?"

"Nothin'. Just payin' a little social call, that's all."

"What do you want?"

"You know, sometimes I think you're just like a little robot that's been programmed to say certain things in certain situations. Seems like all you ever say to me is, 'What do you want?' Maybe I just want to be friends, didja ever think of that?"

He was standing in her doorway. He smelled of onions. She pushed the door a little and sighed. "You've got to want something, Tommy, so let's just get on with it, shall we?"

"Ooh, so nicey-nicey. I like that 'shall we' stuff. Okay, since you wanna be that way about it. Mama thinks it's time you started payin' for the privilege of usin' her washin' machine. You coulda had your own laundry room, but no, you had to tear it up for all that fancy darkroom equipment."

"I paid for permission, and I paid for the remodeling. You know that. And as for using your mother's washer and dryer, she never minds in the least. We always have a good visit."

"Yeah, you have a good visit, all right, while you sponge off her good nature."

Her cheeks flamed. "You ought to know about sponging, Tommy, you wrote the book on it. God knows how much more comfortable your mother would be if she didn't have to support you as well as herself."

His homely face grew ugly. "I'll make you sorry you ever said that, you bitch. I tried to be nice, but no, you's too good for that. Have it your way."

He turned and started toward the stairs. "You'll pay," he called over his shoulder. "And I don't mean just for the laundry service."

After a hearty slam of the door, Skye picked up a glass she'd been drinking iced tea out of and hurled it across the room. Glass and ice cubes shattered over the fireplace. When an answering knock resounded from the door, Skye covered the distance from the couch in record time, shouting, *"Why don't you go straight to hell, you son of a—"* and yanked open the door to a blinking Jared Martin.

"Something I said?"

She whirled and moved back to the couch, where she collapsed and put her face in her hands.

"I have to tell you," he said as he shrugged out of a worn brown leather jacket, "that I often have that effect on people."

She stared at him. He was wearing a white sweatshirt

with the words "Stop Apartheid" on it. The crimson letters were designed to look like blood smears.

"Disgusting, but effective, don't you think?" He grinned and sat down beside her. "You weren't aiming those remarks, by any chance, at the charming fellow who passed me in the hall, were you?"

"My landlady's son. A real . . ."

"Yeah, I heard."

Skye laid her head back against the couch. "I don't know what gets into me with that guy."

"Chemistry, no doubt." He gestured toward the fireplace. "Bad day?"

"As a matter of fact, yes."

She raised her head. "How did you know where I live?"

He grinned. "A combination of talent, bravado, and a telephone book."

"So, why didn't you call first?"

"What, and ruin this great surprise?" Jared rose and crossed to the fireplace, where he began picking up shards of glass.

"You don't have to do that," she protested weakly.

He ignored the comment. "I came over to tell you how much me and Chelsea enjoyed Friday. I had to fly to Denver that night for a writer's conference—they wanted me to speak on column writing and it's so dumb; there's no easier form of writing in the world—anyway, I just got back this afternoon." Wandering into the kitchen with hands full of glass, he called, "Where's the trash?"

"Under the sink. Do you ski?"

"I like what John Denver calls the downhill stuff." He grinned around the corner of the bar at her. "Funny thing, there I was, right in the middle of these great big mountains, and all I wanted to do was get back here. Broom?"

"Corner pantry." She watched with weary relief as he swept up the glass, trying not to think too much about that last comment.

"Now, if you've got some more of whatever this was, it might go good right now."

"Iced tea."

"In winter?"

"It's one of my few vices."

He lifted the broom. "Do I have to throw the glass across the room when I'm through?"

"Only if you lose your temper," she said with a smile, struggling to her feet. "I think I can offer you some wine, or maybe even a beer, if you'd like. I don't keep liquor around."

"That's okay, neither do I."

"You don't?" she asked in mock surprise. "I thought all writers were alcoholics."

Rummaging in the cupboards for glasses, he didn't answer. As she made her slow way into the kitchen to stand beside him by the sink, the lights flickered and went out.

"What the—"

"It's this old house," she explained, reaching in a drawer for candles. "If it's not the plumbing, it's the electricity."

"Want me to check it out?"

"Don't bother. It's one of the few things that make Norman bearable. He's handy with stuff like this."

"Norman?" Jared's voice seemed very close.

She rooted around for matches. "His name is Tommy, but I like to call him Norman sometimes, like Norman Bates in—"

"*Psycho!*" Jared laughed.

"Right." Skye was beginning to feel nervous. She couldn't find the matches, and Jared's masculine presence in the dark was very near. He smelled of soap and the outdoors.

"Here. Let me help you." He reached into the drawer and their hands touched warmly. She jerked hers away.

A scratching noise, pungent smell, and glow of a match. "There." Jared lit the candle she held out. Their faces were struck by its small golden light. She looked into his eyes and felt a disturbing pull, a magnetism she hadn't felt for a long time, and she couldn't look away. He covered her hand with his . . . and the phone rang.

The loud jangle caused them both to jump, and Skye fairly dived for the phone over the bar.

"Hello?"

"Ms. Meredith, this is Investigator Ruis from the Dallas police."

The lights came on. Skye blinked and sank onto a barstool.

"Are you there?"

Jared blew out the candle and turned away.

"Yes." Her hand was beginning to sweat against the receiver.

"There has been a new development on the Sharon Smith case, and I need to speak to you right away, if you don't mind. It's urgent."

"Of course." Trembling set in.

"I'm just getting off duty, so why don't I stop by your place and we can talk there?"

"Um, sure. It-it's the upstairs apartment. The address—"

"I have it. See you soon." The line went dead.

Staring at the opposite wall, Skye sat for a moment, still holding the phone.

"Hey, are you all right?" Jared pried the phone gently from her hand and hung it up.

"Jared, you're going to have to leave now," she said in a prim little voice. "Someone is coming to see me and it's very important."

"Sure." He stood for a moment, studying her, as if trying to decide something. "Are you sure you're all right?"

"Fine. Can you show yourself out?" She took a deep breath, clutching her hands together in her lap.

He sat on the barstool next to her and took one of her cold hands in his. "Listen, I don't know what you're going through right now," he said, "but if you need any-thing . . . if you need to talk . . ."

"It's all right, really. I can't . . . it's not something I can talk about." There was a hard pit in her stomach.

He gave her hand a slight squeeze and stood. "I'll take your word for it . . . now. Call me anytime; I'm in the book."

She nodded without looking up at him, and she still hadn't moved when she heard the front door softly close behind him.

Chapter Six

THE "THIRTYSOMETHING" THEME song was playing when Investigator Ruis knocked on the door. Skye had gone around nervously straightening the apartment, trying to fill her hands with busyness and keep her mind empty. She didn't want to think, not at all.

Ruis looked stunning in a ruby-red turtleneck sweater, gray wool slacks and jacket, and a matching red woolen scarf layered under the jacket lapels. Stepping in the door with only the briefest of courteous smiles, she looked around her with open curiosity.

"Nice place."

"Thank you. I was lucky to find it."

Ruis sat on the couch and began rubbing her temples. "Mind if I take my hair down?"

"Er, no, not at all." Skye perched on the edge of a chair.

Ruis began pulling long pins out of the tight knot at the top of her head. "This may not be very dignified or professional or whatever," she said through the pins in her teeth, "but I've got a splitting headache." A thick black gloss of hair fell to her shoulders.

My God, thought Skye, *if I were a man, I'd be in love*.

Ruis stuck the pins into her purse and rubbed her fingers briskly over her head. "Good thing I've got a liberal sergeant or I'd never get to keep it this long. He says as long as I can put it up, it's okay. Couldn't have got away with it when I was still in uniform, though." She gave an apologetic smile, surprising Skye with the softening of the shrewd lines of her face. "After a while, these pins can be killers."

"Why don't you cut it?"

She gave Skye a level look and said, "Because I like it long."

Skye stood. "I've got plenty of aspirin, if, um, you think it would help."

"As a matter of fact, I could stand a couple." Ruis settled back on the couch and Skye had a hard time remembering who the woman was and why she was here.

Skye kept aspirin in the kitchen as well as in the bathroom medicine chest, to save steps. Two ice-filled glasses remained where Jared had left them. She filled them both with tea and carried them into the living room. It was slow going, without the cane, but Skye was glad that Ruis didn't jump to her feet and fuss over her . . . much the way a stutterer feels when someone completes a sentence for him.

"What's this?" Ruis took the glass from her hand and swallowed both aspirin at once.

"Tea."

"Iced tea in winter?"

"Would you rather have hot?"

Ruis took a big gulp. "No, this is refreshing, thank you."

For a moment, no one spoke, then they both spoke at once, "Sugar or sweetener—Would you mind—" and laughed.

Ruis took the initiative. "No sweetener, thanks, and would you mind turning off the TV? I'm afraid I might get involved in the story and forget what I'm doing." She moved toward the set.

"Sure." Skye's heart began to pound. Now for the business.

Ruis sat on the couch and leaned forward, her elbows on her knees, the tea glass in both hands. "They found Sharon Smith's body," she said simply. "Strangled."

A fist in her solar plexus would not have had a stronger effect on Skye. Of course, she *knew* it, she'd known it all along. She just hadn't let herself believe it.

Ever since the night she burned the photographs and negatives, she'd tried hard to convince herself that the whole thing wasn't real. She'd kept busy, kept her mind occupied. When no one at the police department had taken her seriously, she'd convinced herself that they were right, it was all in her mind, too ludicrous to believe.

At least she'd tried to. The nightmares, though, there wasn't much she could do about them. And tonight, with Tommy . . .

It wasn't him. It was that girl, her face. Now she'd never be able to get it out of her mind.

"Ms. Meredith? Are you all right?"

"Please, call me Skye." She got to her feet and wandered over to the fireplace, staring into the dying flames. "I can't believe that poor girl is dead."

"Believe it." Ruis pulled a cigarette from her purse. "You mind?"

Skye shook her head, picked up a never-used ashtray off the mantel, and took it to the investigator. Her legs felt leaden, and she collapsed into a chair. "Why me?" she asked softly.

"Why you what?" Ruis narrowed her eyes behind a cloud of exhaled cigarette smoke.

"Why did he send me the pictures?"

"Who? Who sent you the pictures?"

"I don't know. I don't know." Skye put her face in her hands.

"Skye." Ruis tapped ash into the ashtray. "I want you to tell me exactly what happened, from the beginning."

"I already told you." She felt so very tired.

"Refresh my memory."

It seemed years since she'd taken her good feelings and the film into the darkroom. Years. Her life, while not particularly easy, had been so cut-and-dried. In a flash of *déjà vu,* she thought of the nurse who'd come into her hospital room and told her Paul was dead. She'd known then that her life would never be the same again, and now she had that same feeling.

"Skye?" Ruis was gentle but insistent.

With a shaky sigh, Skye started from the beginning, and as she talked, Investigator Ruis listened and smoked. She never interrupted, never asked any questions. She sat with her arms crossed, her eyes on Skye's face, but there was no readable expression in them.

When she got to the part about the police department, Ruis looked away and stabbed out her cigarette. Skye's voice petered out. There was no point in going on. Ruis took another drink of tea, and so did Skye. Her mouth was parchment.

"I'm sorry about that," Ruis said finally. "We should have taken you more seriously. But . . . it's not the first time an officer has thought, 'I should have.'" She reached into her purse then and pulled out a small notebook, about five by seven inches long, with removable pages, and a felt-tip pen. The notebook was full of scribblings, and she flipped to a clean page, made a brief notation at the top, and said, "Now I'm going to have to ask you a few questions. Just to clarify things, make sure I have it straight."

Skye nodded and took another drink. She was beginning to feel a little better about things, now that someone was taking her seriously. Maybe now she would be able to get some help. The police would find whoever had done this terrible thing and she could go back to at least a semblance of normal life.

"First of all, Skye, what kind of envelope did the film arrive in? Was it a regular business envelope?"

What a strange question. "No, it was a little larger, brown, and flat."

Ruis made a note. "How large? Say, eight by ten inches? Or smaller, like about this size?" She held up the notebook.

What difference does that make? "Er, about that size, I guess."

"Five by seven inches?"

"That's right." She watched Ruis write it down.

"Would you say the envelope could be bought at any variety store, or was it specialized, something you'd find only at a stationer's?"

"I don't see what all this has to do with—"

"Please, Skye."

"You could get them most anywhere, I imagine. I see them in variety stores, right next to the notebook paper." She couldn't help letting a little barb of sarcasm creep into her tone.

"Okay." If Ruis noticed the hook, she wasn't biting. "Now, what was the handwriting like? Was it scrawled, or printed carefully? Was it easy to read?"

"Block printing. All capitals. Very clear." This was more like it.

"What kind of pen was used?" Ruis kept writing.

"Well . . . it was a lot like the one you are using now." Ruis looked up, pursed her lips, and went on.

"What kind of film was it?"

"Just a standard black-and-white-print film."

"C'mon now, Skye," said Ruis, "you can do better than that. You're a photographer, aren't you?"

Skye's cheeks burned. She had to think a moment. "Kodak ASA Tri-X 400. Thirty-five millimeter. Twenty-four exposures."

"That's better. Is this film easy to find, or would you need to get it at a photography supply store?"

"Not all that hard, but most people who do candid photography at home of the kids, or whatever, prefer color film, which can be found most anywhere." She lifted her aching legs onto the nearby hassock. "Sometimes you have to go to a photography supply store to get black-and-white film, but it's not rare or anything like that."

Ruis nodded, writing rapidly. "Now, about the pictures themselves. Where were they taken . . . on a bed, for instance, or a couch? Outdoors?"

"I couldn't tell for sure." Skye drained her tea.

"Why not?"

"I could only see her in close-ups, from the waist up. I told you that." She was getting tired, irritable.

"Surely you could tell what the woman was lying on, Skye. Was it a bed, or grass, what?" Ruis watched Skye closely.

"*I couldn't tell!*" She got up and crossed to the fireplace to stare at the embers. The room was getting cold. Clasping her hands on her arms, she could hear Ruis lighting another cigarette. "Wait a minute."

"What?"

"It looked as if she was lying on carpeting of some kind."

"What kind? Plush, or . . ."

"The flat, indoor-outdoor kind people put in their kids' rooms."

The investigator moved her glass in a tiny circle. The melting ice swirled around. "How could you tell that, Skye, from a small black-and-white enlargement, when you said you could only see her from the waist up?"

"I don't know." Skye leaned against the back of the chair. Somehow this wasn't what she had expected. "I just have a picture of it in my mind. I don't know why."

"About the girl." Ruis changed the subject easily. Skye was unutterably weary of the whole interview. Never had she expected to be grilled on such *detail*. She'd looked at the photographs for such a short time. Didn't this woman know that?

"Excuse me, do you want me to repeat the question?" Ruis turned to a new page in the notebook.

"I'm sorry. Yes." Skye returned to the chair and reached

for her tea glass. It was empty, but the ice was melting. She drank some of the cold water. It helped.

"I said, didn't you say the woman was wearing a coat with a fur collar?"

Skye pressed the cold glass against her forehead. "No. It was a simple cloth coat or jacket—like yours, I guess. It wasn't buttoned."

"And she was wearing a low-neck blouse underneath."

With an impatient shake of her head, Skye said, "I told you. A sweater, or tee-shirt, something with a kind of scoop neck, I guess. I didn't exactly study it, you know." She frowned. Something was bothering her. Something on the perimeters of her mind. Something she was forgetting. What was it?

"Skye?"

"Yes?"

"Is there something else?"

She shook her head. "No."

Ruis put out the cigarette and tucked one long leg underneath her. "How was it that you were able to tell that the woman had been strangled?"

Skye shuddered. "Marks on her neck. And her face . . . kind of . . . bloated, I guess. And bruised . . . Do I have to go on?"

Ruis shook her head. "Tired?"

The question surprised her. "Yes, I am, very. I often am, this time of night." She glanced at the clock and was astonished to see it was ten-thirty.

"I only have one more question for now, and I want you to think very carefully." Ruis leaned forward, holding Skye in her gaze. "Can you think of anyone, anyone at all, who would do this—send you these pictures, I mean . . . An old rival, someone you've quarreled with, an enemy . . ."

Tommy Thomas's face crossed her mind. "No," she said finally. "Not anyone who would murder somebody."

"All right." Ruis got to her feet. "If you think of anyone,

or if you think of anything else you want to tell me, call me here." She handed her card to Skye.

"Is it over?" Skye asked in relief.

"Well, not exactly, I'm afraid." Ruis busied herself putting the notebook back in her purse. Skye noticed a heavy handgun before Ruis flipped back the lid of the purse.

"What do you mean, not exactly?" A sense of foreboding crept over her.

Ruis put her hands in her pockets. "I'm going to have to ask you to do us a favor. It's very important."

"What is it?" Skye put her hands on her knees. Ruis looked very tall from where she was sitting, giving Skye that childlike feeling again.

"We know that the woman who was found was Sharon Smith. Her folks have already identified her."

"Yes . . . and?" A sick feeling settled in the pit of her stomach.

"So . . . we're going to have to ask you to come with us in the morning and identify positively the body as the one you saw in the photographs."

Skye tried to swallow, but her throat was too dry. "You mean . . ."

Ruis's eyes were kind. "I'll come by in the morning and pick you up around eight-thirty. Then we'll run out by the forensics institute and take a quick look, so that you can give us a positive ID."

"You want me to look at that woman's body?"

Ruis slung her purse over her shoulder and smiled. "It won't be as bad as you think."

Skye felt trapped, a moth inside a glass jar.

"The truth is," said Ruis as she headed for the door, "you are the closest thing to a witness we have."

She opened the door and turned back to Skye. "Be sure and lock your door." Then she was gone.

For a long time, Skye sat in the cold, empty room, listening to the ticking of the clock.

Chapter Seven

THE SOUTHWEST INSTITUTE of Forensic Sciences was a white, unassuming five-story building (counting the basement), located adjacent to the emergency room entrance of Parkland Hospital, made famous that sunny November day that turned so black for the city of Dallas many long years before. Ruis explained to Skye on the way that the institute had been built, in part, because of the cataclysmic events that characterized that whole weekend. Dallas wanted a forensic lab that would be able to compete with any in the country. Dallas didn't want to be humiliated again.

They entered a simple lobby with an off-white stone floor and cream walls. Plastic-covered chairs in olive green and orange with wrought-iron armrests lined one wall. It looked like the waiting room of a public health clinic. Ruis went up to a sliding glass window and spoke briefly to a receptionist, then motioned Skye to one of the chairs. She sat and chewed on a hangnail.

After a few moments, a uniformed officer and two weeping Hispanic women came through the front door, spoke to the receptionist, and took three other chairs. The women spoke in Spanish to one another while they held hands and wiped their eyes.

"They're here to identify someone," said Ruis softly to Skye. "A brother, I think. Bar fight."

Skye's heart pounded so hard she was afraid she might faint, and she took a few deep breaths. *What were they waiting for?*

In a few minutes, a short, wiry man wearing black horn-rimmed glasses and a white coat emerged from elevator doors down the hall and approached Ruis and Skye.

"That's a field agent," murmured Ruis. "Special investigators from forensics who go to the scenes of the crimes and deal with the public. They are different from the ones who help with the examinations, the autopsy technicians." Skye gripped her cane. She'd hardly been listening and wondered why Ruis felt it necessary to tell her.

"Investigator Ruis?"

"Yes."

"Is this the witness?"

"Yes."

The young man turned to Skye and handed her a black-and-white glossy photograph. She glanced at the photograph, back to him, then back to the photograph for a longer look.

Sharon Smith.

"My God."

"Skye, is this the woman whose photograph you saw?"

"Yes, only . . . her face doesn't seem as swollen." *Is this really happening?*

"That's natural," said the agent. "The body was dumped faceup, so the blood tended to shift toward the back of the head."

"Not too much decomposition," remarked Ruis.

"Cold weather."

The photograph blurred.

"You okay?" Ruis touched her arm.

She couldn't tear her eyes away from the photo. God, how she'd hoped never to see that face again. Ruis took the photograph from her and handed it back to the field agent.

"Thanks."

Another agent approached the two Hispanic women. Skye and Ruis got to their feet. The agent spoke; the officer answered, and Skye and Ruis headed for the door.

Shrieks and howls behind them. The closing door blotted out the sound.

A razor wind pushed foaming clouds as Skye climbed into Ruis's plain beige sedan and pulled on her gloves. When she spoke, her voice was dull and without life.

"I thought I was going to have to look at . . . Why didn't I have to look at the b—the woman?"

"You mean like on TV?" Ruis started the car. "All that drawer stuff is outdated. At least that's how one of the medical examiners explained it to me once. She said that the more a body is handled, the greater the chance of valuable evidence being disturbed or lost." She maneuvered the car out of the parking space. "Dragging it off the stretcher, putting it in a drawer, back onto the stretcher . . . and then if you have hysterical relatives like we just saw, it's just too impractical, especially if the body has deteriorated very much. The skin gets mushy, you see . . ." She glanced over at Skye. "Sorry. I think it's fascinating, that's all. I forgot myself, there." They headed out of the parking lot. "This way, they keep the body on a mobile, wheeled stretcher in a cold room till time for examination, then they just roll it into a little room with a stepladder. They climb up on the stepladder and take the picture. Nine times out of ten they can get an ID without having to show the body to the kinfolk. Simple."

So young. Only nineteen.

Ruis began concentrating on the traffic and left Skye to herself.

Never had she had a nightmare as bad as this, yet every move she made had a dreamlike quality to it. In the picture on the poster, Sharon Smith had been pretty, smiling. But that wasn't the face that burned into her mind. All Skye could see were hideous marks around the young woman's neck, a scraped cheek, long hair plastered against her face . . . All she could hear were the cries of grief.

She put her face in her hands and wept.

Sitting behind the wheel of his car, he held the cat's-head pins in the palm of his hand and sifted them into the other hand.

"Here, kitty, kitty, kitty," he said softly, and laughed to himself.

What to do? It was a fine balance, trying to decide what to do. On the one hand—he sifted the pins into the other hand—he wanted to love her, was *trying* to love her. On the other—sifting the pins back—she had betrayed him. He'd seen another man at her apartment.

And that wasn't all. She still wasn't treating him the way a man of his qualities deserved to be treated. Surely she knew that.

And then—he hefted all the pins in one hand—she was still at it. Still doing the evil. He had proof, this time.

What to do?

She needed some more discipline. After all, she had to pay the price. If the bad girl were *punished* for what she was doing, if he made her *realize* the consequences of her actions, but let her know that he still loved her in spite of it, well, she would have to stop, wouldn't she?

But how best to handle it?

Maybe it wasn't all her fault. Maybe she was under the influence of wicked friends. Yes, that would explain it. In fact . . . he straightened up in the seat. *Of course!* That was it!

If he took away this evil influence, then she would be *grateful* to him. He would be her rescuer.

Probably she didn't mean to hurt the children at all. She was probably gentle to them, the way Mr. Peterson had been with hi—never mind. He wouldn't think about that.

This way, he could save the children, and he could save

her, too! And she would be *doubly* grateful to him, because of saving the children, and all.

Then they would be together. He hoped she was saving the negatives. When they wrote their book together, and explained to the world about how they saved the children, those photographs would come in handy. More proof that he was the savior of the children. He wouldn't want some sicko to come in and claim credit for the killings.

Folding his fingers over the cat's-head pins, he worried about that for a moment, but the solution was simple. Next time he would simply take *two* rolls of film. She would admire him for his intelligence and cunning. Everyone would, in time.

Meanwhile, he had some planning to do.

Before starting the car, he scrawled a note to himself on the pad beside him on the seat: *Buy more film.*

"Would you mind running back by my office before I take you home?" asked Ruis.

Skye looked sharply over at the investigator. "Why?"

"My sergeant would like to ask you a few more questions, that's all."

"But I've told you all I know." Skye was beginning to feel uneasy.

"Well, see, this is a difficult case, and it sometimes helps to have a second perspective on it." Ruis's face was inscrutable.

"I need to get back to the studio. I had to put off several clients this morning as it was." For some reason she was feeling stubborn.

"This won't take very long, I promise."

Skye could see that the car was already headed downtown, in the direction of the police department, and realized that nothing she said would make much difference, anyway. While somewhat embarrassing, the tears had been a sort of release, and she had to admit that Ruis had handled it well, digging in her purse for a tissue without taking her eyes off the road, and handing it to Skye without comment. She'd gotten herself under control quickly enough, but she was ready to go home now. She was tired of the whole thing.

Skye wasn't sure how to take Investigator Ruis. All her life people had warmed to her easily and she never had any trouble making friends or getting along with her clients. But Ruis had a touch-me-not way about her, a certain detachment. She was kind enough with Skye's emotionalism, and patient with Skye's impatience, but beyond that, she seemed removed from it all. Skye wondered if all police officers had that quality. Perhaps they had to, to survive.

Maybe she would have to learn to be that way, herself, before this was all over.

She shifted her weight in the seat of the car, trying to stretch her legs. Cold weather had a way of seeping into her bones, driving the pain down deep. It made her want to crawl in a hole somewhere and hibernate until it was warm again.

Ruis, sensing her discomfort, began making small talk about Skye's family and the ranch in West Texas where she'd grown up. By the time they arrived at the police department, Skye had almost managed to forget where they were going.

There were more people behind the computer terminals this time, and two men leaning against a table at the back of the room, talking and laughing together. When Ruis and Skye entered the room, one of them disengaged himself and came toward them. He was a tall, barrel-chested black man with very dark skin, short gray hair the consistency of steel wool, and a large smile. There was a gap between his two front teeth.

"Skye, this is Sergeant Moses Malone, but I call him 'Doc.'"

Malone's hand was large and warm, his handshake firm, and he looked her in the eye as he shook her hand, something many men did not do. Most men took a woman's hand as if it were spun glass and looked anywhere but in her eyes. Skye had learned to judge a man's character and attitude toward women by his handshake. She liked Sergeant Moses Malone.

"Why 'Doc'?" she asked him.

" 'Cause he saved my life one time, and I've called him Doc ever since," answered Ruis.

"What happened?"

"Aw, it's a boring story. You two get acquainted in the interro—in that little room where we talked before, and I'll fetch us some coffee."

"Carmen knows her place," said Malone, and she gave him an affectionate punch on the arm as she left.

Malone's presence seemed to fill the tiny room as they took their seats.

"What happened, really?" she persisted. She was curious, but it was more than that. She much preferred talking about anything other than the purpose for which she had come.

"Carmen was working undercover as a hooker, trying to help us catch a slasher who'd been cutting the girls' throats. She was wired and everything, but the guy acted too fast, just grabbed her off the street and into an alley. We got there quick enough to interrupt him—that's what saved her life—but he'd already cut her by then." He shook his head and looked down at his clasped hands on the table.

"You mean . . . he cut her throat?"

He nodded. "We got to her before he was finished, see. He didn't get the jugular or tear up the windpipe too bad, but that poor kid . . . She's a tough little bugger, though. Came right back on duty as soon as she was healed."

The door opened then and Ruis came in, balancing three cups of coffee. Skye couldn't help but stare at the royal-blue turtleneck sweater Ruis was wearing. Turtlenecks. She hadn't seen her wear anything else.

"I brought everybody black," Ruis said. "And I don't want any lip about it," she added, giving Malone a pseudo-hostile look.

"This is the gratitude I get," he said with a shrug and a roll of the eyes.

When everyone was situated, Malone asked Skye to run through the whole story again, for his sake. "I'm an old man," he said. "I can't remember much of what Carmen told me."

When she was finished, she stared at her hands and sighed. She was already numb with fatigue and it wasn't even time for lunch yet.

"When did you receive the film?" Malone asked.

"Let's see . . ." She did a little backward counting. "This is Wednesday . . . Last Thursday."

He nodded. "We don't have the autopsy report yet, but the field agent from the forensic lab said he thought she'd been dead since Monday or Tuesday. If the guy killed her and took pictures, you'd have to allow a day or two for mail delivery. Did you receive the film at home or work?"

"At work. Does that make a difference?"

"It might."

"Could I ask a question?"

"Sure."

"Where . . . did they find her?"

"Lake Ray Hubbard. It'll be in the papers today, I imagine." He took a careful sip of the hot coffee. "Ugh. Needs sugar." He looked over at Carmen, who smiled but said nothing. "Now, is there any chance that you knew, or had any business dealings with, Sharon Smith?"

"None. I never saw her before in my life before I got the film."

"Have you ever had a disgruntled client, someone who wasn't pleased with the job you did on them or something? Someone who didn't pay their bill, or whatever?"

"Well, I haven't had the studio open that long, although I've done portraits before. I have to say no, I never have. I specialize in children's portraits and the parents are all pleased with the results."

"Mind if we take a look at your appointment book?"

"Please do . . . Sergeant Malone—I feel sick about this whole thing. I'm willing to do whatever is necessary, cooperate in any way possible to find who did this. I hope to God it's not my fault."

"What do you mean?" Ruis's voice was sharper than usual.

"Whoever did this sent the film to me, didn't he? He must hate me for some reason. At least, that's all I can figure out. What if he killed this girl to get back at me for some reason?"

"But you said you don't know the girl."

"I don't. I don't know anything." Skye put her face in her hands and rubbed her eyes.

"I just need to know one more thing for now," said Malone in a gentle tone. "Then you can go. Carmen will take you back home."

"Okay." Skye straightened in her seat.

"What were you doing last Tuesday night? Were you home?"

"Yes, of course I was home."

"Do you have anyone who can verify this?"

"What do you mean? Don't you believe me?" The fear was back.

"I didn't say I didn't believe you, Miss Meredith. I just need to know if anyone can verify it."

"My landlady—Opal Thomas—could. No, wait. She was out Tuesday evening."

"Is there anyone else, a boyfriend, anyone?"

The room was getting hot. Why was that? Her cheeks were flaming. Why were they asking these questions? What difference did it make what *she* was doing Tuesday night? Her palms were sweating. They were staring at her.

"Miss Meredith?"

"No," she said. "There is no one."

Chapter Eight

"SHE'S THE CLOSEST thing to a suspect we have," said Carmen Ruis to Moses Malone as Skye disappeared down the hall in search of the bathroom.

"Aw, now, Carmen, we're a long way from naming suspects in this case and you know it."

"I don't know, Doc. I've got this creepy feeling."

"Oh, please. Do I have to hear about women's intuition again?"

Carmen smiled. None of the other female officers liked Doc. They misinterpreted his so-called sexist remarks, took them seriously and got all defensive about it. The word was that he was a flaming male chauvinist, and he loved it. He took every chance he could find to get in a barb and see a female officer's hackles rise. Only Carmen knew better, knew that it was all a big joke.

She was convinced that if it hadn't been for Doc, she'd have died that night. It wasn't that the other officers weren't as well trained; it was that special ability Doc had of inspiring her trust. He was the closest thing to a father she had, and she would gladly put her life on the line for him if it was called for.

"Still," she answered him. "My instincts have been right before."

"You're doing it again, you know."

"Doing what?"

"Looking for Maria's killer."

She turned away from him and walked over to her desk to hunt for a cigarette. He followed.

"Every time we get a similar case, you do the same thing."

"This is not a similar case, Doc. The MO is different."

"That's not what I'm talking about and you know it." He pulled open her top drawer and handed her a cigarette which was lying loose with the pencils. "Death weed."

She yanked it from him and dug her lighter out of her purse.

"Ever since your little sister was murdered on the side of the highway when her car broke down, you've seen her killer in every case that resembles it."

"We never found the guy."

"That's what I mean."

"You're making a big deal out of this. All I said was that I had a feeling." She made a show of shifting through some papers on her desk.

"We're not in the feelings business, Carmen. And we're not out to get anybody." He sat on the edge of her desk. "We are truth-seekers. That's all. We just want to find out the truth about what happened."

She took a long drag on the cigarette. Doc was the only person in the world who could get away with talking to her like this.

"You're one of the best detectives I've got—"

"Why do you insist on using that word? We're all investigators now."

"Newfangled, pretentious word. As I was saying, you are one of my best detectives, but when we get into these cases—young women murdered for no apparent reason with no suspects—you begin to lose your objectivity. You can't do that. I'll pull you off the case if you do."

She stabbed out the cigarette. "I won't lose my objectivity. I'll do it by the book—start with the crime and work my way backward: criminal evidence, autopsy report, interviews with family and friends."

"See that you do. And leave your feelings out of it." He squeezed her shoulder to take the sting out of his words and left.

"Doc—"

He turned back.

"It's just . . . I just have this creepy feeling that it's going to happen again, and I feel helpless. I hate that feeling."

He regarded her for a moment. "Don't borrow trouble, kid. Just take it a step at a time. That's all you can do. That's all any of us can do." He turned away.

She rubbed her temples absently. There were other cases on her desk to be investigated, and there would be more tomorrow. Maybe she was getting a little paranoid, herself.

Skye appeared in the doorway then, looking around for her in that bruised, bewildered way of hers. Perhaps she was as much a victim as the dead girl.

Truth-seekers, huh? Doc was waxing poetic. He was right, though, as usual. She would do what she could to find the truth.

Gathering her things together, she got to her feet. Time to take the photographer home and get to work.

The Metroplex Messenger truck was parked in front of the studio when Skye arrived, determined to salvage what she could out of the day in spite of her exhaustion. The man, who had been peering inside the glass door, stepped aside as she unlocked it and followed her in.

"It's that day again," he said as she plunked her things down on the counter.

"Well, I'm not ready," she said irritably. "Can't you come back later?"

"I don't mind waiting."

With a heavy sigh, she took the package he held out and

flipped through its contents. "Great, just great." She slammed the package down. "Mrs. Stubbs's proofs aren't in yet and that woman has been calling me every day. Are you sure you got everything?"

"That's it."

She turned away, unreasonably angry. It was the pain. One of the benefits of living alone was that she didn't bite anybody's head off on bad days. That trip to the forensics lab and the police department didn't do much, either, for her legs or her disposition.

Perching on the edge of the stool behind the counter, she tried to collect her thoughts. There were several rolls of portrait film ready to be sent to the lab, but she hadn't filled out the orders yet. Restlessly she limped into the back room and rummaged around in one of the drawers for the necessary forms, then caught herself staring at them as if she'd never seen them before. The front bell jingled. Panic stabbed at her. A client? Had she forgotten about an appointment? She wasn't ready.

Cramming the forms back into the drawer, she hurried into the front door to find Jared Martin thumbing through her appointment book. The messenger was still waiting patiently by the counter.

"Where ya been?" Jared asked with a warm smile. "I came by earlier."

She felt foolishly glad to see him. "I had some business to attend to."

"Thought I'd come by and make another appointment for Chelsea. Besides, I was a little worried about you after last night." He tilted his head to the side. "You look like you could use a pizza."

"Come to think of it, I don't seem to remember eating today."

"You notice I conveniently came by at lunchtime. I've learned that women will go out with me only if I feed them."

"Ma'am?"

They both looked at the man from the messenger service.

"Oh . . . I won't be sending any film out today. I'll have it ready the next time you come by."

"Whatever you say. Sign this, please."

They decided to eat at Chili's, rather than have pizza, and got acquainted over huge taco-flavored burgers and boats of french fries. Chili's had a party atmosphere and was popular with college students and young families. It was noisy and full of laughter. Over a beer, Skye felt herself beginning to relax. Jared drank Coke.

". . . So then I figured that if I was going to do a story on hang gliding, I had to experience it firsthand. Everything was going great until I noticed that I hadn't buckled on the safety harness. Took me three weeks to get my fingers uncurled."

Skye laughed. It seemed that she had laughed nonstop since they took their seats. She'd thought, once, that she would never laugh again. "You seem to get yourself into a lot of trouble."

"Expect the unexpected. That's my motto."

"My life seems so dull in comparison."

"Are you kidding? Three theme books on photography in three fascinating parts of the country? Sounds like a blast to me."

"That was all Paul's doing, I'm afraid."

"I don't buy that, Skye."

He was looking at her with that intense, consuming gaze of his, and she felt suddenly uncomfortable.

"You ought to do another book. One on children."

"Oh, I could never do one without Paul."

"Why not?"

"Well, it just . . . he . . . I just . . . We did them together, that's all."

"I thought you said you did the layouts and so forth yourself."

"I did, but—"

"And your gifts with children are unmistakable. You should consider it."

"I don't want to consider it." Her face was hot. She was angry with him, and she wasn't sure why.

He leaned forward. "Why do you insist on selling yourself short?"

"I don't sell myself short. And I don't want to talk about it anymore, Jared." She pushed her plate away.

"Okay, fine. But just consider this. Did Paul ever do a book before y'all were married?"

"No, he didn't. But that doesn't make any difference. We were a team. I need to get back now, if you don't mind." She got to her feet stiffly and turned her back to him while he dealt with the check. Everything was ruined between them and she was angry at him for ruining it.

As he started the car, he said, "You wouldn't be so mad if you didn't realize that there is some truth to what I'm saying. I just think you should think about it."

She had expected him to apologize, to ask her not to be mad, to make things better. Her cheeks flamed. "This is none of your business."

He regarded her seriously for a moment before shifting gears. "This may sound like a cliché," he said without smiling, "but you are beautiful when you're angry." Then he grinned.

Never had she been so tempted to hit another person. She gave him the cold shoulder on the way back to the studio, determined never to speak to Jared Martin again.

Anger can be a great adrenaline-pumper, and Skye completed her day with renewed energy, but by the time she let herself in at home, the exhaustion hit with all the force of stepping from an air-conditioned building into a hundred-degree summer afternoon. No sooner had she closed the door than she had an immediate feeling of something wrong. The first sign was Bartholomew, cowering under the coffee table. He would not come out.

Moving over to the bar, she held her breath and listened . . . for what?

Someone was in the apartment.

Kicking off her shoes, she crossed to the darkroom on stocking feet and peeked in. Empty. Quietly she made her way to the edge of her bedroom.

From the bedroom came the sound of a floorboard creaking. Heart pounding, she waited. Footsteps, moving away. The bedroom door opening into the hall.

Without thinking, she bolted into the bedroom. The door was closing. Slipping on the hardwood floor, she flung herself to the door and yanked it open.

Tommy Thomas's head was disappearing down the stairway.

"Tommy!"

He stopped, turned, and came slowly back up.

The day's accumulated frustrations swept over her. "How *dare* you come into my apartment when I'm not here! You have no right sneaking around!"

"Sneaking, huh? In my own house?"

"From this point on it's not your house. It's mine, and if I ever catch you here again when I get home, I'll call the police!"

"Oh, I'd like that," he said with a malicious grin. "Then I would explain all about how the sewer backed up downstairs, and how the landlady called the handyman—that's me, you know—to come fix it, and how I came up here to check out the plumbing at your place." He dangled a toolbox in her face. "You don't want anything fixed around here, that suits me fine." With that, he turned his back to her and left.

Slamming the door behind her, she collapsed onto the bed, her heart pounding.

Had the sewer really backed up?

She went into the bathroom to check. The tub and toilet were clean. If he had been in here, there was no evidence of it.

Moving over to her desk, she opened a drawer. Was it messier than when she'd left it? Nothing seemed to be missing.

Must be getting paranoid again.

Bartholomew came and jumped onto the bed. She sat next to him and pulled him into her lap. "You have good instincts," she told him.

He'd said he would make her pay. He'd also said he hated cats. With a little shiver, she checked Bartholomew over. He seemed fine. She hugged him.

I can get in here anytime I want.

He'd done it, too. When would he do it again?

The young woman's battered face crept, unbidden, into her mind.

"*What is going on?*" she cried aloud.

There was no answer, and she was afraid.

Chapter Nine

SHARON SMITH'S PARENTS had been less than cooperative, reflected Investigator Ruis as she wound her car over and under a cloverleaf and threaded the needle across four lanes. In fact, they had been downright hostile.

"If you people had been doing your job," cried the mother, tears smearing her mascara, "you wouldn't be looking for my baby's murderer now."

"We tried to tell you she was in trouble, but no, you had to have your goddamn procedure," joined the father.

Ruis was tempted to tell him that the girl was probably dead before they reported her missing, but kept her tongue, as usual. Threats of lawsuits flew through the air, but not before Ruis was able to observe that their carpet was orange shag. Judging from the cheap seascape "sofa painting" print over the couch, and the oil bull on black velvet in one corner, they didn't appear to be photography buffs, either.

Sharon's supervisor had been somewhat more helpful. Sharon had worked in one of the children's day-care chains, located in a shopping center. According to the supervisor, she rode in to work with a neighbor and called her mother to pick her up at the end of each day, in case she had to stay late waiting on a parent. When Sharon failed to call, her mother had called the supervisor, who had gone out to check. Sharon was gone. She'd taken her coat and purse. There was a linoleum floor.

Standing in the midst of four screaming children, Ruis had looked through the center's client list. The supervisor gave her a copy. Later, she checked the parking lot. Nothing.

"Sharon hated her parents," said the supervisor to her as she left. "All she wanted to do was save enough money to join Bobby in North Carolina."

"Bobby?"

"Her boyfriend. It didn't shake me up too bad when she disappeared. I just figured she'd finally got free."

She did.

Slamming on the brakes to avoid hitting the car which had just swerved in front of her, Ruis let out a stream of Spanish and gunned the motor to get around the car. She'd once read an article in the *Morning News* about how to avoid getting your head blown off on Dallas freeways. The reader was cautioned not to curse out the window or shoot the finger at unpleasant motorists, who might leap out of their cars and attack you with a crowbar or a .357 Magnum.

Screw the Sunbelt, she thought. *Yankee, go home.*

She survived the trip to the department well enough, however, and was pleased to find the autopsy report on her desk when she got back.

Cause of death: ligature strangulation
Mechanism of death: asphyxia
Manner of death: homicide

Ligature strangulation meant the use of a rope or cord of some kind. The report stated that markings indicated that the cord had been passed around the victim's neck from behind. Scratches on the neck were most likely caused by the fingernails of the victim as she fought to remove the encircling object. Facial abrasions were probably caused by a fall as the victim struggled. Presence of fine dirt and gravel in the abrasions suggested a street or alleyway.

Or parking lot, maybe?

The rest of the report had to do with blood analysis and so on. No drugs or alcohol were detected in Sharon Smith's system, and there was no evidence of sexual assault at the time of examination.

The crime lab report wasn't ready yet.

Leaning back in her chair with a cigarette, Ruis tried to set up a picture in her mind. Someone induced Sharon Smith to willingly leave her workplace after her boss and all the children had left. How could that someone know she was alone? Watching, perhaps.

It had to be dark by then. They went to the parking lot—maybe the killer had offered her a ride home? Plausible. So, perhaps she knew the person. It was unlikely that she would accept a ride home with a stranger.

Once in the parking lot, the killer had surprised her from behind with a cord of some kind.

Like, maybe a time-delay cord on a camera?

You wouldn't have to be particularly strong to kill someone in that manner, either. Just determined.

Seized with a sudden hunch, Ruis stubbed out her cigarette, grabbed her coat, and headed for the car. A connection. She was looking for a connection.

Taking the Stemmons Freeway to the Dallas North Tollway, she got off at the LBJ Freeway and took the Preston Road exit. From there, it was straight enough to Skye Meredith Studios.

Skye was busy with a client in the back room. Good. Ruis turned the appointment book around to face her and began scanning through the pages.

Nothing.

Hurriedly she took the list from the day-care center out of her pocket, referring to it as she looked through the appointment book, each entry made in neat, careful handwriting.

Wait.

Three weeks ago, Skye had done a portrait of a little girl with the lyrical name of Amber Dawn Salerno. That name had stuck in Ruis's mind once before.

Spreading out the day-care center's client list on top of Skye's appointment book, Carmen ran her finger down the names.

Amber Dawn Salerno.

Bingo.

Skye was aware that the front-door bell had jingled twice, which meant that someone had come into the studio and left before she had a chance to talk to them. Sometimes it happened, and it was always frustrating because she never knew if she'd lost a potential client that way. Someday she would hire an assistant to take over the front desk and bookkeeping. *Someday.* There was that word again. Maybe it was a good sign that she was starting to think in terms of someday again.

It had been a good session. She'd borrowed a kitten from the pet store around the corner to draw a sweet, shy little boy out of his shell. He had blossomed for the camera. As the child and his mother left, Skye checked her appointment book.

Oh, no. On the slot beside four o'clock Friday afternoon a scrawling but legible note said, "Save this dance for me."

Jared. This must be his way of making an appointment for Chelsea, which meant she was going to have to see him again, which meant she was going to have to speak to him. Nicely, no less.

Closing the book with a smack, she got her purse and retrieved the kitten from under the counter. Obnoxious man. Still, there was Chelsea to consider. Stroking the kitten's soft throat, Skye found herself thinking about the session professionally. What would be the best background for that beautiful child?

The picture came to her as clearly as if she could see it

framed in front of her. It often did when she opened her imagination to impulse. Outdoors. Blue water, blue sky, Chelsea's blue eyes. The lake . . . maybe White Rock Lake; it was picturesque . . .

No, no. Not in February.

The kitten began to squirm. She'd have to think about it later. Heading down the street toward the pet shop, Skye suddenly remembered that Clyde Winslow wanted her to drop in and discuss a business promotion involving a drawing for a free Skye Meredith portrait. "With each purchase of a toy, the customer could enter the contest," he'd said. "It would help us both out." Skye knew as well as he did that most people could never settle for one eight-by-ten, but would want extras for grandparents, wallets, and so on. She entered the toy store.

Clyde waved at her from a corner display which he was in the process of dismantling.

"Miserable time of year for toy stores," he said as she approached him. "Christmas is over, after-Christmas sales are over. Nobody wants to buy any toys." He spied the kitten. "Whatcha got there?"

"Isn't he sweet?" Skye held the kitten out.

Clyde backed away, his arms outstretched. "Keep your distance," he said. "I'm allergic to cats." He sneezed for emphasis.

"Oh, I didn't know. Sorry." She backed away a few steps. "About that promotion . . ."

They worked out the details, and as Skye was getting ready to leave, the news came on over the Muzak station Clyde piped into the store "to tame the savage beast and hypnotize his mother into spending more money." The headline story concerned the indictment of a public official for sexual assault on a child.

"Bastard," said Clyde grimly. "They ought to hang that sleaze up by his balls, cut off his dick, and stuff it up his—"

"*Clyde!*"

"Man's an animal, Skye, an insect. There is no worse

crime on the face of this earth, if you ask me." There were two spots of color high in his cheeks.

"I didn't know you felt that strongly about it." She hadn't known Clyde Winslow felt that strongly about anything.

"A child is the embodiment of pure innocence, honesty, and love. All a child asks in this world is to be loved. Take a man like that, who betrays a child's trust and destroys his innocence, who twists the very concept of love into something sick and degrading . . . the child is ruined then; for the rest of his life he doesn't know what real love is. Somebody ought to strap that man to a chair and work him over with a cattle prod."

She stared at the little man. As he talked, he ran his fingers through the few remaining wisps of hair atop his head, and they stuck out like spikes. Two red spots under his eyes gave him a clown look. His mouth had hardened into a flat line. She had watched him transform from a Caspar Milquetoast into a Rambo.

Obviously he had a personal interest in the issue and she wondered what it was. Most people were disgusted by child molesters, but few got as suffused with rage over it as Clyde had.

She was beginning to feel uncomfortable. She made as if to leave, but Clyde grabbed her arm. "The judicial system lets these worms slip right through the cracks. A smart-talking lawyer can send them right back onto the streets. And what do you think they do when they get out there, huh? Yeah, they go find another little child to destroy. Animals, I tell you, they're animals."

"Clyde, you're hurting me . . ."

"There was a time when a creep like that would be strung up in the streets by the crowd. He wouldn't get another chance. This is what civilization has brought us."

She extricated her arm from his grip. "I've got to go now, Clyde."

"But don't you agree with me?" A deep line had appeared between his brows.

"Well . . . we are supposed to be innocent until *proven* guilty . . . aren't we?"

He stepped back and crossed his arms. "Are you saying, then, that the child who accuses this molester is a liar?"

"Of course not."

"Then what are you saying?"

What was going on here? She didn't want to get into a debate with Clyde over child molesters. Why was he so upset? The kitten mewed and struggled against her. Clyde's intense gaze dropped to the kitten and immediately he started to sneeze.

"I'd better return him to the pet store, Clyde."

Nodding, he backed up and sneezed again.

Skye turned to leave and almost fell over Ro-Tex, who must have been standing there all along. This place was beginning to give her the creeps.

The brisk February wind cleared her head. It was cold out, but not unbearable, with temperatures in the forties. Bundling the kitten under her coat, Skye limped down the street with her cane toward the pet shop.

She had this feeling that everything in her life was completely out of kilter, like a photograph in which the camera has been tilted slightly. Somehow she knew that, even if the camera were straightened, the picture would never again be quite the same.

The decision was made, and it gave him a tremendous feeling of relief, especially now that he knew what to do and how to do it. So excited was he to get started that he had to remind himself not to lose his cool. He had to be smart. He wasn't ready to show the world his genius yet.

There was no doubt about it. She needed discipline. In fact, she was sort of like a child herself; he suspected that, deep inside, she *wanted* discipline.

Only one thing bothered him. Taking a cat's-head pin out of his pocket, he fingered it. He was beginning to get the impression that she didn't love him, after all.

He'd given her another chance, hadn't he? He'd tried to be nice to her, but she still resisted him. Obviously she was unaware of the gravity of the situation, of her *duty* to save the children.

It was up to him to show her. He didn't want to have to hurt her, but, as when a father disciplines his child, it was sometimes necessary for the greater good. Surely she would understand that, in time. And when she did, he would be there for her.

She would recognize their destiny.

He'd been thinking a lot about his book, the one he was going to write when it was all over. He was tempted to start on it now. What really excited him, though, was the thought that maybe he would be able to convince her to do the book *with* him. That's the way it should be, he reflected.

An ugly little thought intruded on his dreams. What if she didn't love him at all? What if she wouldn't learn her lesson?

He shuddered. He didn't want to think about that. If he couldn't make her love him, if he couldn't get her to share his vision . . .

He shoved the pin deep in his pocket. No matter what happened, his mission was clear: to save the children. He would make any sacrifice necessary to that end. It would be the noble thing to do.

Chapter Ten

RADIO ANNOUNCERS WERE ecstatic in their weather predictions as Skye dressed for work Friday morning. "Unseasonably warm . . . great golfing weather . . . perfect for sailing . . ." So far February had been even drearier than usual, drizzly, blustery, and cold. Now Dallas was earning her Sunbelt reputation.

Skye dragged out the huge Metroplex telephone directory. Sure enough, Jared Martin was listed. She dialed the number before she could lose her nerve.

"Hello?" The voice was sleepy.

"Jared . . . this is Skye Meredith."

"What a sweet dream I must be having!" he cried. "I thought you had decided never to speak to me again."

She ground her teeth and rolled her eyes. "I'm calling about Chelsea."

"That's right . . . this is Friday, isn't it? You're not going to cancel the appointment, are you?"

"No, no, nothing like that. I wanted to tell you to dress her in a pair of bibbed overalls, if she has them, and a blue sweater—turquoise, if possible."

"Let me get this straight. You want my little girl dressed in bibbed overalls for a formal studio portrait."

"That's right." She smiled into the phone.

"Now, a regular ignorant jerk would protest such an order, but, although I can be a jerk at times, I am most certainly not ignorant. I'm wise to your style."

"I'm glad you are also wise to the fact that you can be a jerk." Dammit, she was warming to him again.

"See, I admitted it. That makes me a humble jerk. You going to be nice to me now?"

She laughed in spite of herself. "Just bring Chelsea at four, dressed like I said."

"We'll be there, smiling faces and all."

Jared proved true to his word. Chelsea was adorable in turquoise-and-white-striped OshKosh bibbed overalls and a soft turquoise sweater, making her eyes so blue as to be almost unnatural. White barrettes held the thick auburn hair back from her face while allowing it to fall free.

But it was Jared who captured Skye's attention, dressed in cowboy boots and hat, Levi's, and a western denim shirt with pearl fasteners. Skye, who had grown up with "real" cowboys (as opposed to the dime-store variety), noted that the shirt was sun-bleached, the Levi's faded, the hat stained, and the boots comfortably worn. To her, he looked terribly sexy. Something flip-flopped deep within her.

With somewhat flustered movements, she gathered the camera case packed with her trusty Nikon, zoom lenses, and special filters. Shouldering the heavy case, she handed Jared her tripod. "Let's hit the trail, Roy."

"Where are we going?"

"Ah, now it's my turn for surprises."

"Oh, boy!" shouted Chelsea, clapping her hands.

Loading them into her own car, Skye took the LBJ Freeway to Central Expressway south, exiting at Northwest Highway.

Jared was too tall to wear his hat in the car and balanced it on his knee. "Is this the scenic tour of Dallas traffic?" he asked once, but Skye only gave him a mysterious smile.

He fiddled with the car radio, turning it off the easy-listening station and tuning it in to his favorite classic-rock station, bellowing along with B.J. Thomas that he was hooked on a feeling.

Skye turned up the volume, trying to drown him out with B.J. Thomas, but gave up when Chelsea joined in.

"I know where we're going," cried the child suddenly, in the middle of a verse. "We're going to the lake. *Neat!*"

"Expect the unexpected," said Skye.

White Rock Lake was one of the prettier lakes in the Dallas area. Skye chose a scenic spot to park, beside a meadow that sloped softly down to the water. There were no crowds this February Friday, but a few hardy sailboats graced the blue waters in the distance. Spangles of sunlight skittered over the surface of the water. Across the lake rose gentle hazy hills scattered with large stately homes. Sweet shoots of shy new grass tainted the meadow with shades of pale green beneath the brown of winter grass. Skye's hair tumbled around her face in the breeze and she took a deep, cleansing breath.

"This is where we'll set up."

Jared stood aside with a look of amused tolerance as she unloaded her gear and headed for the trunk, from which she retrieved a bright red diamond-shaped kite.

"Oh, Skye, that's so neat!" shouted Chelsea, jumping up and down. "Can we fly it now?"

"Not just yet, sweetie. Right now it's just a prop."

Carefully Skye arranged Chelsea cross-legged on the grass, the kite propped on the ground diagonally to her; the child held it upright and slightly to the side. Behind her, sailboats moved slowly past on the water. Moving quickly, ever cognizant of the light, Skye set up her camera and tripod. A slight breeze kicked in and she sent Jared to pull a strand of hair off Chelsea's face.

Shooting quickly, Skye took several frames of that pose, working with different lenses and filters. Jared stood quietly in the background, watching. After a while, she forgot all about him.

Chelsea was the perfect subject, posing just as Skye

asked and holding it without complaint. "A real ham," said her father proudly.

"Chip off the old block," mumbled Skye. He chuckled.

At one point a bobbing mass of ducks came over to investigate, and Skye, working without the tripod, got several shots of Chelsea feeding them bits of a candy bar.

It was a dream shoot and Skye knew it. A little pit of excitement formed in her stomach. Somehow she realized that there was a future for these photographs beyond making a proud father happy. For now, though, she just enjoyed the rush of creativity and the warmth of the sun on her back. She even sneaked a shot of Jared.

At last she folded away the tripod and camera case.

"*Now* you can fly the kite," she told an exuberant Chelsea.

With Skye comfortably planted beneath a tree, Jared and Chelsea argued and fussed over the kite together. They were at total ease with each other. Underneath the bantering and teasing, Skye sensed a powerful cord of love stretching between them.

Soon they took off across the meadow, Chelsea's skinny little legs pumping double time to Jared's long strides. Snatches of squeals and shouts came to her, carried on the wind. The new grass cushioned Skye and gave off a cool fragrance that reminded her of her own childhood, her own kites.

For a moment she drifted, her thoughts undisturbed, for once, by flashes of a swollen face.

"*Skye!*" Jared's shout broke the reverie. "Your turn."

"I can't," she called, gesturing toward the cane.

"Bullshit," he answered with a smile. Handing the string and winder to Chelsea, he ran toward Skye and reached her, panting.

"You don't have to run," he assured her between gasps. "And you don't need this." He gave the cane a scornful little kick.

"But . . ."

"No buts. Here, take my hand." He extended it toward her.

She hesitated.

He reached further and clasped her hand, pulling her easily to her feet.

"You can do it. I can help you out to where Chelsea is, then you're on your own."

Skye's cheeks grew hot, but she didn't protest as he supported her elbow in a firm but gentle grip and led her to the center of the meadow.

"Hi, Skye! This is so neat!" Chelsea scampered about, nearly dropping the string.

"Now," Jared said, taking her hand. His hand was large and surprisingly rough for a man who made his living with a typewriter. He placed the winder in her hand and curled her fingers over it.

"The trick is to give her a steady base, but allow her all the freedom she needs at the same time." He squeezed her hand. "Just don't let go."

His hand was warm and he held her with his eyes. Looking up at him with that cowboy hat cocked at a rakish angle over his eyes, she wondered . . . The string gave a sharp tug and Skye grabbed the winder with both hands and gazed up at the tiny red diamond dancing in the blue high above.

Jared stepped back a little to give her room to work the kite. He was right; she didn't need the cane. Gradually she got into the rhythm of the wind and gave herself up to it. She felt her heart soaring with the kite, and knew, in that moment, that everything was going to be all right.

A cold wind off the lake caught them both by surprise. It was getting dark. With a weary sense of peace they brought in the kite and prepared to leave.

On the way out, they crossed White Rock Creek where it feeds the lake near Lawther Drive. Police cars huddled together not far from where they crossed the creek, and at one point, a traffic cop waved them around a detour. They passed a WFAA news van.

"Wonder what happened here?" Skye mused. "It doesn't look like an accident."

"Could be a drowning," said Jared.

"How awful," she said, glancing anxiously in the rear-view mirror at Chelsea, dozing in the back seat. She drove thoughtfully for a while, trying to shake the uneasy feeling that had settled over her like a cobweb.

"Water really alters a body," said the field agent from forensics to Carmen Ruis. "Whatever evidence there was has probably been washed away by now."

"How long do you think the body has been here?" she asked.

"Not long—say, a day or two—but long enough, like I say, to do the damage. Putting her facedown hasn't helped us much, either." He stood knee-deep in water, oblivious to the cold or his ruined shoes. A good man, Foster.

The pack of kids who discovered the body earlier that day had worked over the banks of the creek well enough to obliterate whatever helpful tracks might have been left.

"You can see by the marks, here, that she didn't drown. She was strangled. Probably dead before she was dumped; we'll hope to find out for sure from the autopsy."

The woman appeared to be fairly young—early thirties, Ruis guessed, with long dark hair. Although water-damaged, the clothes were obviously good quality. She wore an impressive wedding set. Ruis didn't figure it would take long to get an ID, if she was local.

The field man turned over the body. Something incongruous seemed to jump out at Ruis. This woman was classy, with expensive clothes. So why was she wearing that cheap little lapel pin of a cat's face?

"Holy baloney!" said Jared, glancing at his watch.

"What is it?"

"I promised Lisa I'd get Chelsea back home by six-thirty. She's supposed to go to a slumber party tonight."

"What time is it now?"

"Six."

"Where does . . . she . . . live?"

"My ex-wife, you mean? Over on Hillcrest."

"Well, that's not all that far from my studio, Jared. Why don't you let me drop her off there on the way back. We should just make it. Then I can take you back to your car at the studio."

He straightened in his seat, grinning from ear to ear. "Perfect! Then I can take you out to dinner."

She looked sideways at him. "Forget it, cowboy."

He put on a contrite face. "I'll change clothes and everything."

"No . . . really. I'm kind of tired."

"You don't have to think of it as a date, you know," he said. "I'm not trying to stomp on Paul's memory."

Her cheeks burned furiously. He'd read her mind, and it frustrated her. "That's not it."

"It's just food, Skye," he said gently. "We all gotta eat."

"Some other time, really." She felt confused. The truth was, the bottom line was, she wanted to go. So why was she sabotaging herself?

For the rest of the drive, he stopped singing along with the radio, which made her even more miserable. Why was she doing this?

Jared's ex-wife and her husband lived in a beautiful home surrounded by big trees. Lisa, a lovely woman with Chelsea's turquoise eyes, and soft, shoulder-length brown hair that swung forward in a blunt cut, came out to the car when they drove up.

"I'm surprised you're not running late," she said, smiling broadly.

"Lisa, this is Skye Meredith, the photographer who took some fantastic shots of Chelsea today at White Rock Lake."

"I've heard so much about you," she said warmly,

extending her hand to Skye through the rolled-down car window. "Jared showed me one of your books. I can't wait to see the proofs."

"*Mama*, Skye brought a *kite* and we got to go to the *lake* and it was so *neat* and I got to feed the *ducks* and Skye took lots of pretty *pictures* of me and it was so much *fun!*"

Lisa laughed while Jared pulled the chattering child from the back seat. "I can't thank you enough, Ms. Meredith. Clearly you have made a hit with my child." She kissed Jared on the lips and touched his cheek with her hand, then bent down to speak to Skye. "Don't let this guy's sweet-talkin' charm fool you. He's totally incapable of taking care of himself."

Grinning, he got back in the car. Chelsea and Lisa waved as they drove off. Skye looked over at him, wide-eyed questions all over her face, but she didn't know quite what to say.

"So go ahead and ask. You want to know what in the world I could have done to blow it with such a terrific lady."

"She is terrific," Skye admitted.

"It's simple," he said without rancor. "She told me that if I didn't quit drinking, she would leave me. By the time I sobered up enough to realize she was gone, it was too late."

Skye nearly ran the car over a curb. "I didn't know . . ."

"That I'm an alcoholic? Not to get excited. I've been sober for four years, ever since Lisa left."

"She didn't want to . . . give you another chance?"

He shrugged. "Said she loved me too much to watch me fall off the wagon if something went wrong someday."

She drove in silence for a moment. "Do you think you will? Fall off the wagon, I mean?"

"Not if I and AA can help it."

"So you do go to meetings."

"Absolutely. Don't miss your turnoff."

"Oh, Jared," she said after a moment, "I didn't mean that remark I made about all writers being alcoholics . . ."

"Don't worry about it." They pulled up in front of the

studio. Most of the stores in the shopping center had closed. "I make jokes about it all the time. It's good therapy."

He hung around while she let herself into the studio and put all the camera equipment away, then walked her to her car.

"Sure you won't reconsider about dinner?"

She wanted to say, *Yes, let's go out.* Instead, she said, "Some other time, honest."

All the way home, Skye lectured herself. "What is the matter with you? He's a nice man. You like him. He likes you. He even knew Paul and liked him. So what is the problem? What's wrong with a little dinner? Nobody said you had to fall in love with the guy."

By the time she got home, she was thoroughly disgusted with herself. Her mail was bundled up on the hall table with a rubber band. Lots of big envelopes from photography wholesale houses. She tucked it under her arm and made her slow way up the stairs and into the apartment. She was tired. That was true enough.

She crawled out of her clothes and into a shimmering blue silk caftan that Paul had given her one Christmas. It always gave her a luxuriant, catlike feeling to wear it and perked up her mood somewhat.

A knock sounded at the door. Wary of another surprise visit from Tommy, she called, "Who is it?"

"Pizza," came a muffled voice.

Pizza? She hadn't ordered any pizza.

She opened the door as far as the chain would allow. Grinning like a schoolboy caught in a prank, Jared stood there, holding a pizza.

"Never knew a woman who could resist pizza and a smiling face."

"You are incorrigible!" She had to laugh.

"So, encourage me." He stepped into the room and gave her a low, admiring whistle. "I see you were expecting me."

"*Jared!* I was not. I . . ."

He was laughing. "Did you know that you have this enchanting blush whenever you embarrass yourself?"

"You are the most . . . maddening . . . man!"

"Or when you get mad? It's great fun watching you."

She yanked the pizza from him and turned her back. She didn't want him to see that she was smiling.

Intending to break out a bottle of wine, Skye thought better of it and dug out a couple of soft drinks from the refrigerator instead. Jared was singing a nonsense opera at the top of his lungs, making up words as he went along. Shoving the bundle of mail over to one side of the bar, she placed a couple of paper plates on the bar.

"Our finest china," she said.

"And only the best crystal," he intoned, popping a pull tab on one of the drinks. "God, is that your mail? What is this, are you on the junk-mail hit list or something?"

"I subscribe to several trade publications, and all these film labs and whatever get hold of my address." Taking a stringy bite of pizza, she flicked off the rubber band with her thumb and scattered the mail over the counter.

A plain brown envelope lay in the midst of the others. It was addressed to her in block print with no return address. There was no stamp. Apparently it had been placed in her mailbox by someone other than the postal service. There was a little bulge in the bottom of the envelope just big enough for a roll of film.

Chapter Eleven

THE PIZZA SLICE fell from her hand. "*No, no, not again!*"

"Skye, what is it?"

Her voice rose to the keen of grief. "Not another one, please God, not another one!" Slipping off the barstool, she staggered into the living room, bumping blindly into furniture. Only dimly aware that Jared was coming after her, she knew that she was losing control, but couldn't seem to stop herself.

He reached for her and she slipped from his grasp, moving from the sofa to the chair to the fireplace like a wild animal trapped, crying, "What have I done? What have I done?"

"*Skye!* For God's sake, what is going on?" Jared took her arm in a firm grip. She tried to pull away but he grabbed the other arm and shook her roughly. "*Stop it!*"

Shaking her head back and forth, she struggled against him.

He shook her again, harder. "*Get hold of yourself.*" He forced her to look into his eyes. "I'm here. Let me help you." Then he enfolded her in his arms and held her tightly until she had exhausted herself.

"Sit down and tell me what in the name of God is going on with you. Every time I come over here, you seem to get involved in some crisis or other, and I want to know what it is." He pushed her gently onto the sofa and sat next to her, one arm firmly around her shoulders, holding her hand with the other.

After taking a deep, shaky breath, Skye told him. Everything.

When she was finished, Jared got to his feet and crossed to the cold fireplace, leaning into his hands against the mantel. For a while, he didn't speak, and Skye worried about what was on his mind. Would he think she was crazy? She'd certainly acted like it tonight.

Finally he turned to face her. "I think we need to see what's on that film," he said.

"Oh, Jared, I can't . . . shouldn't I call Investigator Ruis?"

"Wouldn't you rather make sure that this really is another woman's body in these pictures first? You'd have to develop the roll to find out."

With a feeling of deep weariness, Skye struggled to her feet. "Okay," she said. "I'll do it."

"We'll do it together." He took her elbow, helping her toward the darkroom. Ripping open the envelope himself, he shook out the film. "Same kind?"

She nodded, dread descending on her like a black cloak.

There was no feeling of warmth and security this night as Skye went through the mechanical movements of developing the film, although she was greatly relieved to have Jared with her. There was little to tell by the negatives, which appeared to be similar to the last ones, but her hands shook so badly that Jared had to prepare the contact sheet while she guided him verbally.

As they dropped the prints into the washer, Skye sank onto the stool. An icy hand had closed over her heart and she was having trouble breathing. When Jared flicked on the overhead light, black spots danced before her eyes. He took the contact sheet from the washer and held it out to her.

"Skye, I'm afraid it's like it was before. Is this the same woman as the last time, or someone different?"

She looked at the photograph he held in front of her.

Mrs. Sanders. The mother of the twin babies.

There was a great rushing in her ears. The ceiling tilted, and everything went black . . .

. . . Jared's voice was coming from far away, but his face was very close. Skye was lying on the floor of the darkroom. The stool lay next to her. With numb apathy, she realized that Jared was picking her up in his arms. That was good, because her legs had turned to rubber. She wondered vaguely what had happened.

He carried her into the bedroom and placed her gently on the bed, then hurried into the bathroom for a cold wash-cloth, which he placed on her forehead. He took her hand in his.

It all came back. Mrs. Sanders . . . *All I want to do is love them,* she'd said. Now she would never be able to again.

Skye rolled over, clutched the pillow to her face, and wept. Jared let her cry herself out, pushing her hair back out of her face. After a while, he got up wordlessly, ran off a long section of toilet paper in the bathroom, gave it to her, and sat on the edge of the bed.

"Blow your nose, sugar bear, then tell me who that was in the picture."

She did as he said.

Leaning his chin against his knuckles, he placed his elbows on his knees and thought for a long time. Skye, stupid with fatigue and grief, was glad to let him.

"We'll go to the police—Investigator Ruis—tomorrow and show her the photographs. Then, my sweet, we are going to find out who is doing this to you."

"But I wouldn't know where to start or who to ask . . ."

"Not to worry. You don't do investigative articles for *Texas Monthly* and the *Times Herald* and a few others, like

The Wall Street Journal, by writing up recipes. I've learned a few tricks and made a few contacts through the years."

Relief washed over her like a tropical ocean wave. She sat up and flung her arms around him. He held her tight, his big hand in her hair. She felt the chemistry between them changing and pulled away slightly. He lowered his lips to hers and suddenly she was hungry for him, channeling all the power of the night's emotions into passion.

They fell back on the bed, his hands firm and hard on her body, and she was filled with the scent and taste of him. Abruptly he pulled away from her and sat up.

"What's wrong?" she whispered anxiously. "I want you to stay, Jared. I really do."

"I know you do." His smile for her was tender. "Believe me"—he took her hand in his—"I've never wanted a woman more. But not this way. Not like this."

"What do you mean?" Her cheeks were growing hot.

"You're vulnerable right now. Scared and alone and upset. I'd be lower than a worm if I took advantage of that. That's not how I want it to be between us, anyway."

"I don't understand . . ."

He touched the back of his hand against her hair. "I've loved you ever since you came limping out from behind that counter, chin up and full of courage, telling me of your loss, showing me how you'd built a new life for yourself—"

"Full of courage?" She shook her head. "I don't know how you ever got that impression. I'm a quaking mass of little fears. It's a wonder I get through the day."

He regarded her, his head cocked. "Ah, but you more than get through it, Skye, you *triumph* through it!"

She gave him a weak, doubting smile.

"Courage isn't lack of fear, Skye. Courage is doing what you are afraid to do, *in spite of* the fear. That's one thing Vietnam taught me."

She sighed. "I'm afraid to be alone tonight," she said in a small voice.

"Don't worry. I'm not going to leave you alone." Pulling

off his boots and dropping them to the floor with a thunk, he stretched out on the bed beside her, pulling her back against him, spoon fashion. Bartholomew joined them and Jared laughed, wrapping his hand around the cat's middle and arranging him against Skye.

Surrounded thus with love, Skye fell instantly, deeply asleep.

Hours later, the car across the street pulled away from the curb.

So. What he had suspected all along was true. She was a slut, and she hadn't learned her lesson. She'd received the film, and what was the first thing she did? Shacking up, rubbing her body all over . . .

A slut. A tramp. A bitch in heat, that's what she was. She would never have loved him. She would only have teased him, led him on, used him, deceived him, like all women everywhere.

Bitterness curled within him. What a fool he'd been, living in a fantasy world. Should have trusted his instincts from the start. Now he would mount his campaign in real earnest. He'd wipe them all out, smear them from the face of the earth.

He fingered the roll of film in his pocket. He would love to see how the pictures had turned out, but knew better than to turn the film into a lab. Too bad he didn't have his own darkroom, like *her*. It would have to be stored in the refrigerator, he decided, until time for the Great Revelation.

When that time came, the whole world would know about his greatness. His book would be a number one best-seller. He'd be on all the talk shows. It was almost too exciting to wait, but he could do it.

The eyes, they told him that he could. They were there, in his room, all the time. They didn't speak, of course, but they didn't have to. It was the way they looked at him. There used to be one pair of eyes and now there were two, urging him on, believing in him.

At first, he had been frightened by the eyes, but not anymore. He welcomed them now, even slept without a light so that he could see them. They comforted him. He *knew* he was on the right track. The eyes would guide him. They would show him what to do next.

He wondered if he ought to write about the eyes in his book, then shook his head. Nah. He wouldn't want people to think he was crazy.

Chapter Twelve

JARED WAS GONE when Skye awoke. Her dreams had been disjointed and confusing, and she carried those feelings into wakefulness. There were no signs around the apartment to indicate that she had slept with a man.

Slept with, but not made love to, and for that, she was grateful to him. Jared was right. The "desire" she felt for him the night before was simply a desperate plea not to be left alone. At least, that's what she told herself as she hurriedly dressed and made the bed. He had handled the situation well, she thought; some men would not have.

Skye considered herself sexually inexperienced, having had only one lover before Paul, and that a brief college romance. Never had she awoken next to a man she hardly knew. Sex, to Skye, meant commitment, and she was far from being capable of committing to anyone yet.

Bartholomew loved bed-making and leaped onto the center of the bed for a play fight while Skye struggled to flatten the bedspread.

"Get off, you silly cat." Stretching out onto the bed stomach-first, Skye flipped back the covers to surprise him and was rewarded with a raking claw across the cheek.

"*Ow!* Keep that up, you wretch, and I'll hand you over to Tommy." She touched her cheek. It was bleeding. The guilty party, thoroughly unconcerned, followed her into the bathroom as she cleaned and doctored the wound.

"So this is the thanks I get for buying you that expensive new cat food," she told him as he hurried ahead of her into the kitchen, meowing lustily.

The place seemed strangely empty without Jared. Paradoxically she resented that. It had been hard, learning to live without a man. She wasn't ready to start missing another one. It didn't help when she discovered hot water in the pot under the coffee maker, and realized she'd forgotten to add coffee.

The contact sheet with Mrs. Sanders's picture lay facedown on the bar. Skye edged around it as long as possible before her conscience pushed her into picking it up. She had to look for similarities. The police would want to know.

Poor Mrs. Sanders. Her lovely chignon had come undone. Skye tried to avoid looking directly at her face. Like the other woman, she seemed to be lying on a carpeted floor of some kind, with her head raised. There was something else about the photograph . . . something that nagged the edges of her thoughts . . .

A heavy pounding at the door brought a gasp and a jerk of her hand, spilling coffee onto the counter.

"*Room service!*" shouted Jared, embarrassing her. She moved quickly to the door.

"Not so loud! Mrs. Thomas can hear you."

Jared laughed as she opened the door. He'd changed clothes and shaved. "Is she your chaperone? Do I have to get her approval to—hey, what happened to your face?"

"Ask Bartholomew. You brought doughnuts."

"It's my specialty. That and pizza." He touched her cheek. "You all right?"

At his touch, something shivered deep within, and Skye grabbed the doughnuts and turned away so that he wouldn't be able to see her blush. How she hated that trait; it was so easy for people to read her mind, especially when she didn't want them to.

They drank coffee and ate the doughnuts right out of the box. Skye let Jared do most of the talking; it was easier that way. Neither of them seemed inclined to bring up the night before, and it lay between them like an unresolved argument.

"Have you called Investigator Ruis?" asked Jared finally.

"It's Saturday. I thought she might not be in."

"You can't put it off, Skye, you know that."

Twin babies, romping gleefully on a white rug, flashed into her mind. Laughing mother. *I can't wait to see those proofs.* The black cloak of despair descended again on Skye. "I know," she whispered.

Carmen Ruis replaced the telephone in the cradle and lit a cigarette. Somehow it did not come as a surprise to her that Skye Meredith was coming. The woman had been evasive on the phone, but Ruis knew it had to have something to do with the latest murder.

At her request, forensics was rushing the autopsy report. An ID had already been made on the woman in the creek: Theresa Sanders, a lawyer married to a lawyer, age thirty-two, two kids. Her husband was said to be deeply distraught and under sedation.

According to the report of investigating officers, Mrs. Sanders had gone to the supermarket about 7:00 P.M. for disposable diapers and milk. She was expected to return shortly, but when two hours passed with no sign of her, her husband had bundled up the two sleepy babies and gone in search of her. He found her car and called the police. No one had seen anything.

As far as Ruis could tell, the MO was the same as in the Sharon Smith case. It appeared that the woman had been strangled with a cord of some kind, moved to another location, the creek, and dumped. She'd be willing to lay a wager that the woman had not been raped. It would be an unusual rapist who would kill the victim, then put her clothes back on before dumping the body. Unless . . . She made a note on a pad: *Have forensics check for the presence of semen in the mouth.*

Her clothes would also be checked for semen, Ruis knew, even the shoes, and especially the panties. There was an unending variety of weirdos out there.

Ruis rubbed her temples. It was awfully early in the day to be getting a headache. *It could be worse*, she thought. *She could have been tortured, like Maria was.*

She could have had her nipples clamped off with a vise grip and burning cigarettes stuck into the wounds; she could have had a broken bottle shoved up her vagina; she could have had her clitoris . . . Ruis got up abruptly and crossed to the coffeepot. She wished Doc were here, to keep her on track. It was his turn for weekends off.

Paperwork proved a distraction of sorts, and she had just opened a new pack of cigarettes when Skye Meredith walked in the door with Jared Martin.

"I'll be damned," said Ruis to herself.

Jared spotted her right away and came toward her with that winning smile.

"Been a long time," she said, shaking his hand.

Skye looked from one to the other. "You two know each other?"

"Jared used to work the police beat for the *Times Herald*," explained Ruis. "He worked downstairs in the pressroom. The worst kind of ambulance-chasing." She grinned at him.

"You were over in PES then, as I recall."

"PES?" asked a bewildered Skye.

"Physical Evidence Section," said Ruis.

"You were a real go-getter," said Jared.

And you were a drunk, thought Ruis, though she had to admit he seemed sober enough now. *I'd have gone out with you in a minute, drunk or sober, if you hadn't been married.* She wondered how in hell he'd wound up with a little mouse like Skye Meredith.

"What can I do for you, Skye?"

"We need to talk someplace private," answered Jared. He seemed to have taken charge. She led them without comment into the interrogation room and tried not to show surprise on her face when they showed her the contact sheet. In spite of all her theories about this case, she really had not been expecting it.

"Do you know this woman?" she asked Skye, making a quieting gesture toward Jared.

"It's a woman who brought twin babies into my studio for a portrait last Friday," said Skye in a voice so small Ruis had to strain to hear her. "Mrs. Sanders."

Ruis regarded the photograph. "Did you receive this in the mail?"

"No. I got the film again. Only this time, it came with the mail at my home. I mean, someone must have put it in the mailbox."

Ruis looked up sharply. "You should never have handled the film, Skye. You may have destroyed fingerprints or other valuable evidence."

Skye looked stricken. "I'm sorry."

"My fault," interjected Jared. "I should have known better."

"Did you bring the envelope?"

"Yes. I brought everything—the film canister, negatives . . ."

"If this happens again," said Ruis sternly, "I don't want you to even open the envelope. Bring it straight to me, understand? And don't touch it any more than you have to. Use a handkerchief or gloves or something."

Skye nodded. She looked like a child being scolded.

Ruis studied the contact sheet some more. "Are there any similarities between these photos and the others?"

"Yes. That carpet that she's lying on—it's the same, I think."

Ruis nodded. "Anything else?"

Skye looked as if she were about to say something, thought better of it, and shook her head. Ruis watched her for a moment. Was she hiding something? "What happened to your face?"

"My cat scratched me."

Ruis got to her feet. "I'm going to send this stuff over to the lab now. Then I'm going to talk to my sergeant and we'll be getting back to you, probably, with some more questions. Don't leave town or anything."

"No, of course not."

"Who's your sergeant?" asked Jared.

"Moses Malone. We worked together before, on a Vice assignment."

"I knew Malone when he was on patrol," said Jared. "He's a good man."

"The best."

"Ms. Ruis?"

They both looked at Skye.

"Could I be . . . mistaken . . . or anything?"

"About what?"

"About whether or not that really is Mrs. Sanders."

Ruis shook her head. "We've had an ID on this one already, Skye. Her husband positively identified her last night."

Skye covered her face with her hands. Jared put a protective arm around her.

Things are getting more interesting all the time, thought Ruis.

"Why didn't you tell me you knew Investigator Ruis?" Skye asked Jared as they got into the car.

"You didn't ask."

"I hate that kind of answer."

"I don't know her all that well, anyway. We worked in the same building; I spoke to her now and then when I needed more information than I was getting through channels."

"And did you get it?"

"What?"

"The information."

He looked over at her. She sat with her arms crossed over her chest. "What are you so mad about?"

Her cheeks·again. "I'm not mad."

He chuckled and shook his head.

"What's so funny?"

"I think you're jealous."

"*Jealous!* You are the most conceited man!"

"And you, my dear, are completely out of touch with your feelings." He started the car and began singing along with the radio to the Beatle's song "Try to See It My Way."

"What do you do . . . program that thing? Every time we ride in your car that stupid radio plays some song you can make a point with." She was smiling in spite of herself. Jared Martin had the most uncanny way of making her laugh no matter how impossible the situation or what her mood was.

"We need to start this afternoon." It was a change of subject, and with Jared's simple statement Skye felt a chill. She was aware of what he meant but didn't want to think about it.

"How?"

"I think I know how Ruis thinks. She's going to be looking for some sort of connection between the two murders."

"What kind of connection?"

"Isn't it obvious, Skye? A connection with you."

She pulled her coat a little closer, even though the car was warm. "But I didn't know Sharon Smith."

"Maybe not, but she had to have some connection with you."

Skye shook her head. "I only met Mrs. Sanders once, when she brought the babies in. She made the appointment over the phone."

"But you did photograph them."

"Yes."

"Then that's where we'll start."

"I'm sorry, Jared, but I'm so tired I'm stupid. I'm not following your train of thought at all."

"Okay. We are going by the studio before I take you back to the apartment, to get your appointment book. We're going to try to find some connection between Sharon Smith and one of your clients."

"Like what?"

"Like maybe you did a portrait of her niece, or something. I don't know. That's what we'll try to find out."

"How are we supposed to do that?"

"We'll go straight to the source. Her parents."

Forensics came through with the autopsy report on Theresa Sanders late Saturday afternoon. As Ruis had expected, there was no evidence of sexual assault, nor was there any water in her lungs, which meant she was dead before she hit the water. As before, death was caused by ligature strangulation.

Ruis lay down the report for a moment, thinking of her afternoon interview with John Sanders. It had not been easy. His shock and grief seemed genuine enough and he had an iron-clad alibi; a neighbor had dropped in on him just before Mrs. Sanders left for the supermarket and had gone with him to check on her when she didn't return.

She picked up the report. One point stood out. In spite of the water damage, forensics had been able to pick up a trace of skin tissue underneath Mrs. Sanders's fingernails. In the miraculous way of forensic science, they'd managed to type the blood of the individual whose tissue was present under the nails: AB positive.

Mrs. Sanders's blood was type O.

Ruis's pulse quickened. This was a break, indeed. Now they knew the blood type of the killer. The woman must have reached behind her as the cord tightened around her neck and clawed at the killer's hands . . . or face.

On an impulse Ruis knew would probably get her into

trouble, she picked up the phone and dialed Skye Meredith's number.

After a brief exchange of pleasantries, Ruis took the plunge. "Skye, I need to know one thing here that would help with the investigation."

"Anything."

"Could you tell me your blood type?"

There was a long hesitation. Ruis wondered if Jared was in the room.

"Why do you need to know?"

"As I said, it would help with the investigation. If you would rather not answer the question, you would be entirely within your rights."

"But you could probably find out, anyway, couldn't you?"

"If we had to, yes."

"I want to cooperate, Investigator Ruis, it's just . . . it sounded like a strange question."

"I understand. We could work through a lawyer, if you'd rather."

"Why would I need a lawyer?" Sharp panic in the voice.

Crap. She was blowing it. Doc would be furious. "Don't worry. I didn't mean to imply that you need a lawyer. It's just that, in a case of this sort, some people prefer working that way."

Silence. She wasn't going to find out. At least not now.

"All right. I'm sorry. I guess I'm getting paranoid or something. My blood type is a little unusual, so I used to give blood a lot before the accident. It's AB positive."

Bingo.

Chapter Thirteen

IT WOULD BE dark soon and he was glad. There was so much he needed to ask the eyes, and they only came to him in darkness. Strange. All his life he'd been afraid of the dark—at least, ever since he was twelve. Ever since that time he had to spend three days in the closet, when Mr. Peterson . . .

Curling his hands into fists, he shoved them deep into his pockets. It wasn't Mr. Peterson's fault. None of it was Mr. Peterson's fault. Mr. Peterson *loved* him. Mr. Peterson was his *friend*.

His hand closed over one of the cat's-head pins he kept in his pockets. He pulled them out and arranged them on the table in front of him. It was *her* fault. The bitch. If it hadn't been for *her*, everything would have been all right. She was the one who ruined everything. She always ruined everything, took away everything he loved . . .

When he was great, when he was famous, she would come begging to him, begging him to forgive her. And he would laugh in her face. He would smear her face in it. But he would not kill her, not like Skye Meredith and the other ones. No. He couldn't. If he killed her, she would take away the eyes. He knew it.

The eyes were his salvation. They kept him from being

afraid. They helped him decide what to do. They *guided* him. They were his friends, and nobody was going to take them away from him.

With deliberate movements, he lined up all the pins in a neat row. He had the power now. He laughed aloud. The thrill was almost too much to bear. *He had the power over the eyes!* He could have as many eyes as he wanted, to keep him company in the dark. When he lay in his bed at night, he could see them, watching over him. First there were two and now there were four. Soon there would be six.

By the time he was through wiping out all the evil against the children, he could have a whole *room* full of eyes!

Leaning back in the chair, he smiled at the arrangement of pins. In a way, he was grateful to Skye Meredith. If it hadn't been for her, if it hadn't been for the evil she was, if he hadn't decided to destroy her and her accomplices, he would never have discovered the eyes.

He would be gentle with her. She would never have to know anything. And in the end, she could be with him always, in his room at night, with the other eyes.

As soon as Skye hung up the phone from talking to Investigator Ruis, she called Jared. They'd spent most of the afternoon going over her appointment book, then he'd left, saying he had some things to do at home. He was supposed to come for her in the evening, so that they could visit Sharon Smith's parents together, whose address they got from Sharon's recent obituary. Jared answered on the fourth ring. He seemed surprised to hear from her.

"I thought you were going to rest for a while," he said accusingly.

"Jared, can you think of any reason why Investigator Ruis would want to know my blood type?"

There was a long silence.

"Jared?"

"I'm here." Another pause. Something about his silence

worried Skye. He must know something he didn't want to tell her. She waited, almost afraid to prod.

When he spoke, his tone was guarded. "I guess maybe she wanted to make some comparisons."

"What kind of comparisons?" Another silence. "Jared, I need to know. She just called and I want to know why my blood type could possibly be important to her."

"All right. She probably wanted to know if your blood was the same type as the victim's."

"But why? What difference would that make?"

"I'm not sure," he answered, and she knew he was lying.

"Jared . . . do you think I should get a lawyer?"

"A *lawyer*? What for?"

"Investigator Ruis mentioned that I might want one, that's all."

"She's just covering her bases. I wouldn't worry about it."

"You mean, it was just something she was supposed to say?"

"Something like that."

She felt better, at least partly. The blood-type question still bothered her. "If you know something, Jared, I wish you would tell me."

"If I knew something, sugar, I would."

I'll bet. "Are we still going to the Smiths' tonight?"

"I think we should. Don't you?"

"I don't know. I feel like a vulture, or something. Maybe we should just leave them alone."

"But if you can help them find their daughter's killer, don't you think you should?"

"I guess so."

"Then I'll see you around seven."

By seven o'clock, Skye's stomach had tied itself in knots. Jared took one look at her when she opened the door and took her in his arms, holding her close. His worn leather coat against her cheek made her think fleetingly of her father and she gave herself up to the feeling of being protected. Jared kissed her forehead and led her to the couch.

"I can go alone," he said. "I'll be doing most of the talking, anyway."

She leaned her head back against his arm. It was a powerful temptation. She could just turn the whole thing over to him and forget all about it, bury her head in the sand, pretend it didn't happen.

At least, until the next roll of film came in the mail.

"No," she said reluctantly, "this is my fight, really. I shouldn't have even involved you in it. It's just . . . I didn't know what to do."

"Two heads are better than one, as the saying goes. Besides, it's a challenge."

She straightened and looked at him. There was a gleam in his eyes. "*You're enjoying this!*" The idea horrified her.

"C'mon, Skye. It's like putting together the pieces of a puzzle, or solving a whodunit."

She pulled away from him. "Two innocent people have been murdered. Doesn't that *mean* anything to you? And it could be my fault."

"You're being ridiculous."

"Am I? I don't know of anyone else receiving undeveloped photographs of murdered women in the mail." She got up and moved over to the fireplace. "I don't really know you at all, do I?"

"*Now* what are you mad about? Everything I do pisses you off."

"I'm mad because you don't seem to care about these women's lives. I'm mad because you think this is some kind of adventure." Turning away from him, she said, "I'm mad because I'm scared."

He came up behind her and put his hands on her arms. "Of course I care about those women, Skye. I'm sorry if I seem . . . hardened. It's all those years covering police news, I guess. It toughens you. Takes away your innocence. Not that I had any to take away, after Vietnam."

With a heavy sigh, she nodded. "I'm sorry. I guess I'm just too close to the situation to be objective about it."

"Objectivity is my job. Let's go now, before it gets too late."

Mr. and Mrs. Riley Smith lived in a worn-down house in a tired neighborhood, the kind of neighborhood where people stopped dreaming years ago. The street was poorly lit, and they nearly missed the house.

"Like I said, let me do the talking," said Jared.

The woman who answered the door was obese and wore a mumu in a glaring floral print. Her hair frizzed out of her head in a bad perm.

"Mrs. Smith? I'm Jared Martin of the *Dallas Times Herald*. Maybe you've read my column?"

Her stare was blank.

"This is my photographer, Skye Meredith. We are doing a story on unsolved murders for the *Times Herald,* a sort of Crimestoppers thing, in hopes of gaining information from the public that might prove helpful in solving the crimes."

Skye glanced at him, trying not to show shock on her face.

"I know you've just been through a terrible tragedy, and I was hoping that if you would give us an interview, we might assist the police in finding your daughter's murderer."

Tears welled up in the woman's eyes. "Thank God," she said. "This is what I've prayed for. The police haven't been any help at all, and there my baby's killer goes free. *Vengeance is mine, saith the Lord,* but I don't hardly see how He can get vengeance when a man like that goes free. Please come in."

Skye followed Jared into the small frame bungalow. A television blared from the corner of a dark living room. The woman went to turn down the volume. It was *The 700 Club.* "My husband isn't here right now, but I'd be glad to talk to you."

There was a portrait of a pretty, dark-haired young

woman on top of the TV. Skye took a deep breath and stared at the floor.

While Jared took notes, the woman poured out her story of the night her daughter disappeared. Tears streamed down her face as she spoke. Jared asked careful questions. Skye hardly heard any of it. Afterward, she took them to her daughter's room.

"Aren't you going to take any pictures?" she asked Skye.

"Uh, I . . ."

"She's just looking around for now, Mrs. Smith. We'll come another time for photos." The woman nodded. Skye felt sick to her stomach.

Mrs. Smith picked up a teddy bear from a huge pile of them on her daughter's bed. "She loved teddy bears all of her life, ever since she was little. She was just a big ole kid herself. That's why all them kids at the Kiddie Shack loved her." Wrapping her arms around the bear, she walked Skye and Jared to the door.

"When will this story be out?" she asked, dabbing at her eyes with a tissue.

"I'll let you know."

"Will you be callin' me, Miss Meredith?"

Skye looked into the woman's eyes. She'd seen eyes vacant with grief before. "Mrs. Smith . . . I have to tell you—"

"That we've got to be going. We'll be in touch." Jared placed a firm hand underneath Skye's elbow and propelled her toward the car.

"How could you lie to that woman?" she blazed as soon as they settled into the car.

"Do you want to find out anything or not?"

"Yes, but not like this. Not by lying."

"Oh? And what do you propose to do, Skye, tell her that you saw photographs of her murdered daughter before the police even found her body?"

Dumbfounded, she could think of no response. He started

the engine. "We do want to find Sharon Smith's killer. That's true enough, isn't it?"

"I guess so."

"Then leave the rest up to me."

"But she was so . . . pathetic, Jared. It doesn't seem right. You took advantage of her."

"If we can find out who did this to that woman's 'baby,' and get him behind bars, then we would be doing the right thing, as far as I am concerned. The end justifies the means."

"So why do I feel like throwing up?"

"You're new at this."

They drove in silence for a while. "So what do we do now?"

"We go by the Kiddie Shack on Monday."

"Same lie?"

He looked sideways at her. "Gimme a break."

She started to say, *I'm sorry*, but thought better of it. She wasn't, entirely.

"We're still looking for a connection between you and Sharon Smith. The film with her pictures on it came to your business address. Since you didn't know her, we'll start from the business end of it."

She looked out the window at the glittering lights of Dallas. "I don't think I can take much more of this."

"Yes, you can. You can take a whole lot more than you realize."

Moses Malone and his wife, Sally, lived in a rambling brick house that had been home to five children, three of whom were grown and gone. He had put two kids through college and had two more nearing high school graduation. Carmen often wondered how he and his wife managed on police officers' and schoolteachers' salaries, but she never heard him complain.

She had spent many pleasant hours with his rambunctious and loving family, and knew he would not mind if she dropped in on him after duty, even if it was a Saturday night. He answered the door in his favorite camouflage pants, which he wore hunting, and a holey Dallas PD sweatshirt. No one could get grungier than Doc when he set his mind to it.

"I wish you'd get you a man, Carmen," he said without preamble, "to keep you busy on Saturday nights so you'd leave me alone."

"What makes you so sure I don't have a man?" she asked, grinning, as he let her in.

"You're too damn restless, that's why."

"I guess that's one word for it."

"Now, now, I won't have no dirty talk in my house."

"Since when?"

Sally looked up from her chair as they entered the den. She was a beautiful woman with milk-chocolate skin and not a strand of gray in her hair. She smiled.

"It never ceases to amaze me," said Carmen, "how an ugly guy like you wound up with such a lovely woman."

"She must want something from you, Moses," Sally said. "She's flattering you again."

"She *always* wants something." Moses sat in his chair and Carmen took the couch.

"How about a beer, Carmen?" Sally got to her feet.

"You read my mind." Carmen knew that Sally would stay out of the room while they talked shop. The violence they faced on the job every day upset her.

"You remember the Sharon Smith case, when that woman, Skye Meredith, came in and told us about seeing photographs of the woman before her body was discovered?"

"Sure." He pulled his chair into the reclining position, but his eyes were keen.

"Well, we got an ID on the body at White Rock Creek."

"I heard."

"Anyway, Meredith comes in to see me this morning, and she's got a black-and-white contact sheet of photos of the victim. Don't you think that's a little too close for comfort?"

"Maybe. What else have you got?"

"First, she knew this latest one . . ." She consulted her notes. "A Theresa Sanders. Said she did portraits of the woman's kids a week ago yesterday."

"Okay."

"But I've made a connection between Meredith and the first victim. Sharon Smith worked at a day-care center called Kiddie Shack. One of the little girls who stayed at the Kiddie Shack each day was also photographed by Meredith a few weeks ago."

Sally brought two beers and disappeared.

"*And*, forensics typed some blood from tissue found underneath Sanders's fingernails that was different from her own. It matches Skye Meredith's blood type."

"How'd you find that out?"

"I asked."

There was a question on his face, but she hurried on so that he wouldn't have time to ask it. "Also, there was a scratch on Meredith's face when she came in this morning. Said her cat did it."

"Same MO both times?"

"Yes. Strangulation from behind with a cord of some kind. Body dumped elsewhere. And—I think this is important—*there was no evidence of sexual assault.*"

He ignored her self-satisfied grin. "What's the report from the crime lab?"

"PES found carpet fibers on the first victim's coat. I don't have the report in on Sanders yet, but in the photographs, she seemed to be lying on a flat, indoor-outdoor type of carpet. Meredith says it's the same as the first one." She took a big swig of beer. "I glanced around her folks' home—"

"Whose folks?"

"Sharon Smith. They had orange shag carpet in the living room. Kiddie Shack isn't carpeted, and Skye Meredith has hardwood floors with scatter rugs. Offhand, I'd say the photographs weren't taken in any of those places."

"Anything else?"

"Two things. This Theresa Sanders was classy. Good-looking, well off, nice clothes. But she was wearing a little lapel pin like something a kid would wear. It was shaped like a cat's face—you know, a lot like those smiley-faces that used to be so popular—like that. The cat's face was yellow, and smiling. It just seemed out of place to me." She took another swallow of beer.

"And?"

"And? Oh, yeah. That carpeting and all, in the photograph. The victim's head seemed to be raised, like on a staircase, only it wasn't a staircase."

Doc didn't say anything for a while, which was fine with Carmen. She was tired of thinking and glad to let him do it for her.

Suddenly he got to his feet. "C'mere."

She followed him without question as he led the way through the sliding glass panel door in the den, across the patio, through the gate in the fence, and out to the garage, where he took a set of keys out of his pocket and opened the trunk of his car. A little light in the trunk door illuminated the space in the darkened garage. The interior of the trunk was carpeted, up and over the wheel well.

"Like this?" He smiled broadly.

"You goddamned genius," she said. "That's it exactly."

"So. Now we know how the killer works."

"The victims' cars weren't used, either. Sharon Smith didn't have a car and Sanders's car was left behind in the parking lot of the supermarket."

"If we can get a match on the carpet fibers, that'll go a long way toward getting a conviction," he said.

She nodded thoughtfully. "Doc, I want to bring Skye Meredith in for questioning."

He slammed the lid of the trunk. "You don't have a damn

thing on her, Carmen, and you know it. Just a bunch of circumstantial stuff."

"Doc, you've got to admit that this is a hell of a coincidence."

"I don't have to admit anything that a judge and jury wouldn't accept."

"I just want to question her."

"You can question her, Carmen, as a *witness*, not a *suspect*. There is a difference and you know it."

"I still say she is the closest thing to a suspect we have."

"That may be, but you've got to get a lot harder evidence on her before we can take any formal steps. The last thing I need is a goddamn wrongful arrest lawsuit against us."

They headed back into the house. "Have supper with us?" asked Doc.

"Thanks, but no. I've got some more work to do."

"Just don't you forget what I said about objectivity. I'd hate to have to pull you off this case." He put his hand on her shoulder. "Go out tonight, pick up some guy, party down. Get away from it for a while. Life's too short to burn out on the job. Whatever's eating at you will keep."

Carmen heard every word her good friend was saying, but she wasn't listening to any of it.

Chapter Fourteen

THE LIE WORKED as well the second time as it had the first. While Jared spoke to Sharon Smith's supervisor at the Kiddie Shack, Skye wandered around the nursery school, watching the children play.

Two little girls were building a castle with blocks in the far corner. Skye instantly recognized the one with ginger hair, brown eyes, and freckles.

"*Amber!*"

The little girl looked up from her play, broke into a huge gap-toothed smile, and shouted, "Hi, Skye!" in a resounding voice.

"You lost a tooth."

"I fell off my swing set. The tooth fairy brought me *two quarters*!"

"Why, you lucky girl." Skye smiled at the child. She looked even cuter without the tooth. "Did your mama like the pictures I took of you?"

"Oh, yes. She shows everybody, even the mailman!"

"You'll have to come see me again sometime."

"Mama says we can't afford any more pictures for a while."

Skye laughed. "No, silly, I don't mean that. I'd just like to see you."

The child concentrated on her blocks. "Is that why you came here today?"

The smile faded from Skye's face. "No, we just needed to talk to your teacher for a while. I didn't know you came here."

"My mama brings me here every day on her way to work." Amber laid down the block she was holding and her voice grew quiet. "I don't like it here anymore."

Skye knelt beside her. "Why not, sweetheart?"

"Because I miss Sharon," she whispered.

Putting her arms around the little girl, Skye shot Jared a significant look. He came over to her.

"Who's this?"

"This is one of the prettiest little girls I ever photographed."

Amber smiled shyly.

Jared looked into Skye's eyes. "There's the connection."

She nodded.

There were no more questions after that, and as Jared drove Skye to the studio where she had appointments lined up all afternoon, she stared out the window in morose silence.

"It doesn't make sense to me," she said finally. "How can one man *know* all this? Amber was brought in by her mother. I had no idea what nursery school she attended. It's creepy."

For once, Jared made no comment.

"And why would he pick Sharon Smith? I didn't know her, but if kids loved her . . . and all those teddy bears . . . she must have been a sweet person." She ran her fingers through her hair. "Why *her*?" She looked over at him. There was a furrow between his brows, and he drove without the radio. "I don't even know why I'm asking. It would be like trying to figure out why a man would fall in love with someone he has seen only in the movies, and try to assassinate the President of the United States to impress her . . . or why a man living in Hawaii would hear a song by John Lennon on the radio and track him halfway across the world to murder him. There *is* no answer. It's insanity, that's all."

"You're getting angry," he said. "You ought to see those cheeks—they match my car."

"Damn right I'm angry! A sick, sick person has destroyed the lives of two innocent families, left two babies motherless, stolen life from two kind and loving people, and . . . and . . ."

"And what?"

"And ruined what little life I had."

They pulled into the parking lot of her studio. "We've got to do something, Jared. I can't just sit around and wait for those rolls of film. I've got to figure out who's doing this and stop him."

He stopped the car but she didn't get out.

"I think I know where to start, too," she said thoughtfully.

"Where?"

"I've got to close the studio."

"What?"

She turned to him. "It just came to me, just now, and it's the only thing that makes any sense. If these women are being killed because they have some connection to my studio, then the only tangible thing I can do to stop the killing is close the studio."

"Now wait, Skye. Don't you see? You're playing right into the guy's hands. I think the important thing for you to do is carry on your life like nothing is happening."

"But something *is* happening, Jared! Women are dying. I would be terrified to think that, with every child who comes in for a portrait, a mother or baby-sitter or whoever is going to die. I can't take that chance anymore. I've made up my mind." She got out of the car.

"But Skye—"

Leaning down into the car window on the driver's side, she said, "You told me on the way to the Kiddie Shack that you were working under a tight deadline for a story. Why don't you go on home and finish it? I've got some phone calls to make." Then she kissed him on the cheek and walked away.

Not looking back was one of the hardest things she'd ever done.

He found the address easily enough and parked two houses down, in front of a house that had a For Sale sign in front. Stretching out in the front seat, he leaned his head on the armrest, so that only the slightest part of his head would be visible to anyone who bothered to look. In spite of the cold, he kept the windows rolled down so that he could listen for cars coming or people talking.

While he waited, ponderous, sagging gray clouds collected, shoved together by a fierce and angry wind. Turning on the radio very, very low, he learned that the temperature had dropped twenty degrees in two hours and was still dropping. Sleet, ice, and snow flurries were expected. It had been a typical February in Texas.

Shivering, he was tempted to leave, but it was too close to the dinner hour. Everyone would be returning home. He would watch, learn some things, then go home and consult the eyes. They would know when and where he should make his next move.

A car pulled into the driveway of the house he was watching. A man got out and entered the house. Half an hour later, another car parked next to the first one and a woman went in.

It was getting dark, hard to see. He blinked and rubbed his eyes. It was freezing. The wind slashed through the open car windows like a wet whip. He wouldn't be able to stay much longer. Hands numb with cold, he rolled up the windows. It helped some. His neck ached and his legs were cramped. The little car rocked in the wind.

He was going to have to leave. Come back tomorrow. Rubbing his hands to loosen them up for driving, he sat up in the seat. No one would be able to see him now, or would likely be watching. A car passed; he ducked his head as the lights flashed into the car.

Parking at the curb, a woman got out, her movements hurried against the cold. Opening the other door, she helped a little girl out, slammed the car door, and raced against the wind for the front door of the house. The door opened for them and they went in.

Squinting, he studied the car parked ahead. There was movement, jostling, within. *More kids.* Only moments later, the front door opened and the woman came out, laughing and waving. Pulling her collar up against the cold, she got back into the car and drove away.

Watching the taillights, he counted houses as the car passed them. One . . . two . . . three. Then he started the engine and followed the scarlet points of light.

"Investigator Ruis? This is Skye Meredith. I'm sorry to bother you at home, but they said you were off on Mondays and Tuesdays."

"How'd you get my number? It's unlisted."

"Well, Jared helped me. I hope you're not angry."

"Not at all. I've been wanting to talk to you, anyway. What can I do for you?"

"I really need to talk to you about . . . the things that have been happening. I thought, if you didn't mind, I'd come over tonight."

"Here?"

"I'm sorry, I guess that's not possible. I've just got all this stuff on my mind, and . . ."

"Tell you what. Why don't you come into the department tomorrow morning, say around ten? Doc—Sergeant Malone—will be there, and I'll come in."

"I hate to disturb you on your day off."

"No problem."

"I really appreciate it, Investigator Ruis."

"See you tomorrow."

Ruis hung up, gathered the towel more tightly around her wet hair, and lit a cigarette. Was Meredith going to confess?

Probably not. That would be too easy.

She got up, went into the bathroom, pulled off the towel, and began combing her hair with a fat, wide-toothed comb. The whole apartment was cold. She could feel a draft down the back of her neck even with the windows closed. Ruis turned up the little gas heater in the bathroom.

What was going on with this Skye Meredith? Ruis had done a little checking. Meredith was widowed. Grief could do crazy things to some people.

She turned on the hair dryer. The heat of it felt good on her cold, wet head. What motive could a woman like that have to kill those other women?

The kids. It had something to do with the kids.

Working the comb and the hair dryer simultaneously, Ruis thought of Doc. Maybe he was right. Maybe she had nothing but a lot of conjecture, worthless in the courtroom. Maybe somebody else *was* murdering these women and sending Meredith their photographs. But why? It didn't make any sense.

Ruis was more inclined to believe that Meredith was taking the photographs herself.

So why would she bring them in to the police? Why not just keep them, or sell them for pornography?

Her luxuriant, heavy hair was warm and dry. Ruis unplugged the hair dryer and stretched out on the bed, pulling a comforter over her and plumping the pillows.

The cigarette . . . where had she left it?

She found it on the edge of the sink. "I'm gonna burn this place down someday," she mumbled, reaching for the ashtray beside the bed and rearranging the covers.

Some way or another, Ruis was convinced, Skye Meredith was involved in these murders. All she had to do was figure out how.

And then prove it.

* * *

It was late and Skye couldn't remember when she'd last eaten. She took a can of soup from the cupboard but the electric can opener balked, and though she searched throughout the drawers, she couldn't find a hand-operated one. A quick survey of the refrigerator reminded her that she'd forgotten to shop for groceries, so she settled, glumly, on crackers and peanut butter.

Munching on a cracker, she moved restlessly into the bathroom to run a bath. Bending over to reach the faucet, she bumped into a small bottle of Paul's cologne that she'd been unable to part with. It fell to the floor with a crash.

The room reeked of her dead husband.

As she grabbed a towel to clean up the mess, she put her foot down on a piece of glass. Wrapping the towel around her foot to staunch the blood, she limped into the bedroom. The stench of Paul followed her.

He smiled at her from the photograph beside the bed.

"No," she cried. "*No!*" Snatching the small frame off the table, she whirled and smashed it against the wall, smashing, smashing, smashing, ignoring shards of glass that flew across the room, splintering bits of frame, chips of paint from the wall. Bartholomew sprang from the bed and vanished.

When the frame was demolished, her rage was still not spent. Seizing the closest thing to her, a pillow, she battered it against the wall, the door, the closet, screaming "*No, no, no,*" until the seams of the pillow split open, spilling out clouds of feathers.

Her own voice was a stranger to her, a demonic thing separate from her being. It bellowed out gibberish words that had never invaded her consciousness before. "*I hate you!*" she shrieked. "*I hate you for driving so goddamned fast all the time. I hate you for refusing to wear a seat belt. How could you leave me alone like this? How could you?*" With each word, she struck out blindly. "*Everything that's happened . . . is . . . all . . . your . . . fault!*"

The pillow slammed against any hard object she could

find, releasing a blizzard of white around her, but still she did not stop until, from the outer edges of her mind, she heard a sound. Knocking. A voice other than the demon's.

"Skye? Miss Meredith? Are you all right? Let me in."

The pillow fell limp from her hands. It was Mrs. Thomas.

Shakily she mustered an answer. "I'm all right, Mrs. Thomas. Sorry to have disturbed you. I . . . I was trying to kill a mouse."

"I thought that's what you kept that cat for," came the suspicious response.

"It's all right, really," she called, and waited, holding her breath, until she heard footfalls moving away from the door.

Then she looked around in disbelief at the bloody wreckage of her life.

Chapter Fifteen

WITH A GLEEFUL sense of anticipation, he rolled a clean sheet of white paper into the typewriter, taking care to align it just so. The eyes had come to him in the night and indicated that it was time for him to start his book. At first, he'd been reluctant. He wasn't ready yet. After all, the work wasn't finished. But then he realized that his work would *never* be finished. In fact, the more he thought about it, the better the whole idea sounded; this way, he could record his pathway to greatness *as it was happening*.

The photographs would make good illustrations, he decided, right in the middle of the book. He was keeping the film safe in his refrigerator. Someday it would all come together. He could hardly wait. It was tempting to daydream about what he would do with all the money the book would make, but for now, it was more important to get started on it.

A title. He needed a title. He toyed with a few on a piece of scratch paper, but none of them sounded right, so he simply typed "Chapter One" at the top of the page.

How best to start? His own childhood? It seemed the way he should go, but the more he thought about it, the more uncomfortable he became. Forget it. None of that stuff mattered.

For a long time, he sat in front of the typewriter, staring at the blank page. Finally, seized by inspiration, he typed furiously. Then, heaving a great sigh, he pulled the sheet from the carrier and settled back in his chair to read.

Satisfied, he placed the page next to the typewriter and put a book on top of it. Then he stared into space, smiling, thinking of what he'd written, the perfection of it. He liked the way the paper remained so clean and white, marred only by one single sentence in the middle of the page:

The dark sky laughing children seeing blindness is the joy.

It was all so clear to him.

The apartment was bitterly cold when Skye awoke. It was one of the drawbacks of living in an older building, she reflected as she scurried about from room to room in her heaviest robe and fluffiest slippers, turning up heaters. She had expected to open her eyes to the same black pall of depression that had settled upon her months before and had gotten so much heavier with recent events. Especially after last night.

Instead, her mind was as clear as the ice that sheathed barren tree limbs in the front yard. It was as if she'd gone through a whole year with a backpack over her shoulders, day and night, loaded with large stones, only to awaken one day and find that someone had removed all the stones in her sleep.

She felt confident, in charge, like a football coach pepping up the team before a big game. Whatever it took to beat this thing, Skye was certain that she had it.

Her newfound strength was tested first thing when she learned that the old water pipes had frozen. Careless of her. She should have left the faucets running in the night, but she'd been too busy cleaning up feathers and glass to think of it.

What a job that had been; then she'd had to win over

Bartholomew anew, just as she'd had to do when she first came upon him, a scrawny, starving street kitten.

Before leaving for the police department to meet with Ruis, Skye had to finish all the phone calls she'd started the day before. Calls to Metroplex Messenger to cancel deliveries indefinitely, calls to photo labs to mail remaining proofs to her at home, calls to clients, telling them that an unexpected family emergency would keep her away from the studio for a while. It would mean losing a lot of customers and a lot of money, but Skye was determined to stay away from the studio until the man they sought was behind bars.

It was almost time to leave. Paul's picture, unframed and somewhat wrinkled, lay beside the phone next to her bed. For a long moment she held it in her hands, studying his handsome smile and graying temples. A lump formed in her throat and she put the cool photograph against her cheek.

"Good-bye, my darling," she said, and placing the photo carefully, lovingly, into the bedside drawer, she closed it.

With brisk, determined movements she bundled into her warmest clothes and headed downstairs, moving as swiftly as the cane would allow. Her eyes fell on the little round table at the foot of the stairs, beside the banister.

An expensive 35-millimeter camera, extra lenses, and several rolls of film lay on the table.

Coming to a breathless halt, Skye stared at the camera and film. Slowly she reached for one of the rolls. It was black-and-white film.

In a stumbling rush Skye took the hallway to Mrs. Thomas's room, shouting for her. When there was no answer, she headed toward the kitchen. Mrs. Thomas, a tiny, birdlike woman with carefully sculpted gunmetal-gray hair, met Skye in the parlor.

"What in the world is the matter, child?" She wiped her hands on her apron.

"Whose camera is this?" Skye was too upset for pleasantries.

"Why, it's Tommy's, of course. Why do you ask?"

"He's never had one before, has he?"

"Well, sure he has, but never one this nice."

"When did he get it?"

Mrs. Thomas eyed Skye as if she were holding up a bottle of snake oil. "I don't know right off, Skye. A month or two, I guess."

"Since when did Tommy get interested in photography?"

"Well, why don't you ask him? He's out back, working on the pipes."

Skye pushed past the bewildered woman, through the kitchen, and out the back door, slipping and almost falling on the icy porch. He was right outside the back door and leered at her. "I see you've changed your original opinion of me. Can't wait to get a look at me now, can you?"

She ignored his look, his tone, and his words. "What are you doing with that expensive camera, Tommy?"

"Nothin' right now." He grinned at his little joke.

"I mean, why did you buy one?"

"Because I wanted it, why else?"

"Since when have you been so interested in photography?"

Raising himself to his full height, Tommy was eyelevel to Skye on the porch. He met her stare. "What business is it of yours?"

She stepped back slightly. "I'm just curious, that's all."

With slow deliberation, he raked his gaze over her body, stripping her with his eyes. "Maybe I like to take pictures of pretty ladies taking their clothes off at night. You know, through their windows."

Her cheeks flamed. With as much dignity as she could muster, Skye made her way back into the house, slamming the door behind her.

In spite of slippery roads and numerous traffic accidents blocking the way, Investigator Ruis made it to the department hours before Doc reported for duty. It had been one of those mind-racing nights, filled with replaying mental tapes of all that had transpired since the first day she met Skye Meredith. At four in the morning, she gave in to her own inability to let it—or her—rest, and came in to work.

The biggest insanity of all, she thought as she made room in a crowded ashtray for yet one more butt, was that she wasn't getting paid for it. Budget cutbacks had put a crimp on overtime. This was her day off in every sense of the word. Still, she couldn't leave it alone.

Maybe Doc was right; maybe Maria's death had warped her ability to be objective on similar cases. None of the other officers were this obsessive about solving a case; they couldn't be: burnout came too soon as it was.

Her training had taught her, *drilled into her,* that a criminal investigation was the simple gathering of information. The gathering of information was supposed to be even more important than the gathering of evidence, in a way, because it was nonprejudicial. She was supposed to be just as open to information or evidence that worked *for* a suspect as that which worked *against*.

Perhaps that was why she'd been unable to sleep, why she'd come in at the crack of dawn on her day off in the middle of winter, for Christ's sake. She wanted all the available, impartial information in front of her.

The case files on the Sharon Smith and Theresa Sanders homicides were admittedly slim. The murderer, if one and the same person—and the *modus operandi* indicated that it was—appeared to fit what the profile of the FBI's Behavioral Science Unit referred to as an "organized" killer. The bodies were transported from the scene of the crime and hidden, weapons used and other evidence were absent, the offense seemed to be planned—as opposed to the so-called crime of passion—and the victims appeared to be either unknown to the assailant or casual acquaintances.

Although the discovery of the bodies aroused attention, investigating patrol officers could find no witnesses. Subsequent interviews of family members and neighbors to the victims revealed no obvious domestic disturbances which could lead the investigation in that direction.

Apparently the killer struck with such speed and surprise that it was unnecessary to bind the victims, for there was no forensic evidence of it on the victims' wrists. That might be the killer's undoing, she thought, now that they had his or her blood type.

But the most interesting aspect, to Ruis, was the absence of sexual violation of the victims, either before or after death. The choice of sudden strangulation as a method of death was also less violent and certainly less bloody than other murders she had investigated.

There was the cat's-head pin, for what it was worth. Mr. Sanders claimed to have never seen it before. Ruis had ordered it kept as evidence, though she wasn't sure why.

The contact sheet, envelope, and film canister had been thoroughly examined by the crime lab, so smudged over by several sets of fingerprints that none were clearly visible. Probably belonged to Skye and Jared. Nothing else distinguishable appeared even under the lab's microscopic scrutiny.

Then there was Skye Meredith herself. Ruis lit one cigarette with the butt of another and stared out the window at heavy, gray skies. Was Skye Meredith a killer or a victim?

Ruis's knowledge of psychology, other than the street kind, was limited, so she was winging it in that field, but she wondered about the phenomenon of multiple personalities. To her understanding, one "personality" could do and say things of which the other would be totally unaware.

Could that be the missing link? Could Skye be murdering these women for her own secret, agonizing reasons while in one personality, then striving in some deep, guilt-ridden way to turn herself in?

Ruis's hands were shaking. Too much coffee, too many cigarettes. Her head was aching, too. She swallowed two aspirin and wandered up and down the hall for a while, rolling her neck around and loosening up her shoulders. Should have brought some sweats and worked out in the basement exercise room. Get the kinks out.

Doc arrived, his eyes widening in surprise at seeing her. She told him about Skye's phone call from the night before.

"If she's coming in," he said thoughtfully, "we should be more prepared. Ought to have searched her apartment and the studio."

"I thought you said I could only question her as a witness and not as a suspect."

"That still holds true, basically, but I want you to videotape the interview, all the same, and give her the *Miranda.*"

"Won't she get spooked?"

"Maybe, but if she's thinking of confessing, we've got to cover all our bases. If she starts backtracking and looking around for a lawyer, we'll know we're on to something."

"So you think she might be a suspect."

"I've seen that case file," he said, gesturing toward the random reports, photographs, and carefully bagged evidence on her desk. "There's not much there. This Skye Meredith is the only lead of any kind we've got on either case. She may have some information that could break it wide open. I want you to be prepared. Have you collected your notes, written down your questions?"

Ruis nodded.

"Just remember what I said earlier."

"I will."

"Uh-huh. Now, tell me what that was."

"That I should retain my objectivity at all times, that she is not yet a hard suspect, that I'm not out to get anybody, but that I'm supposed to be a truth-seeker." She grinned.

"Don't get smart with me." His voice was teasing, then serious. "Just do your job and keep your personal opinions to yourself."

"Or you'll take me off the case."

"That's exactly right."

"Do you want to come with me to the interview?"

"Nah. We don't need any of this good-cop, bad-cop crap you see on TV. Just be prepared, get it on tape, then have her wait around while the statement is typed, so that she can sign it."

"Wait a minute while I get my Big Chief tablet and fat pencil. I need two witnesses, right?"

"I have to take you through this kindergarten stuff so you won't run off on some cockamamie tangent and get us sued, Ruis." In the little gesture of support that was quintessentially Doc, he squeezed her shoulder and headed off in search of coffee.

Ruis reached for another cigarette and discovered, to her dismay, that she was out. It was going to be a tough day.

Chapter Sixteen

MAKING HER WAY down slippery, sloppy roads, Skye allowed herself enough time to make one stop before heading on to the police department to see Investigator Ruis. There were no cars parked in front of Playtime Toys, and Skye wondered why Clyde bothered to keep the store open on such a miserable day.

Glancing around as she entered the store, she didn't see Ro-Tex and had to file up and down several aisles before finding Clyde.

"Well, look what the cat dragged in." He smiled at her. "I've gotten all the entry forms printed up for our promotion. I thought next Monday would be a good time to start. I've already talked to the *Times Herald* and the *Morning News* about an ad."

"Clyde—"

"This ought to really perk up business around here. This has been the slowest month in my memory. We should do it once or twice every year; what do you think?"

This was going to be harder than she thought. "Oh, Clyde, I'm so sorry about this . . ."

He straightened and his eyes became shrewd. "About what?"

Clyde's whole expression had changed. There was a

wariness, a tenseness about him that made Skye uncomfortable. She hated to have to let him down. "I've had a, well, a family emergency, and . . . I'm having to close the studio for a while. I can't do the promotion. At least not now. But when I reopen—"

"A family emergency, huh? What's the matter, did you find a hangnail or something?" He shook his head and turned away from her. "Just like a woman. I never found a woman yet I could depend on."

"I assure you, Clyde, this is terribly serious. I would never, never have done this to you otherwise. But I promise that, just as soon as I reopen, we'll do it then."

"Sure, Skye. And in the meantime, I go out of business. Forget it."

A veil had dropped over Clyde's eyes that excluded Skye, and she knew instinctively that he would never trust her again. With a helpless sense of resignation, she moved away from him with heavy steps. As she passed the counter on her way out the door, she spotted a small wire basket beside the cash register.

It was filled with little yellow cat's-head lapel pins.

Skye Meredith looked more nervous than usual when she entered the Crimes Against Persons office, Ruis thought. Smiling to put her at ease, she got to her feet and met Skye halfway.

"Have any trouble getting here?"

"Some, but the traffic is melting most of the ice. It's not as bad as it was earlier." There was a tasseled woolen scarf around Skye's neck, and she fingered the tassels as she spoke.

Doc came up and shook Skye's hand. "Good to see you, Ms. Meredith. We appreciate your coming in like this to give us a hand."

Doc's presence seemed to relax Skye somewhat, Ruis noted. "Will you be joining us?" Skye asked politely.

"Not this time. I think Carmen can handle it."

More tassel-fingering.

"Would you like some coffee?" Ruis asked Skye as they entered the interrogation room.

"Please."

"How do you like it?"

"Sugar. No cream."

Ruis fetched coffee for them both and bummed a couple of cigarettes off another officer for herself. Just before entering the room, she signaled for Doc to turn on the remote control for the video camera that was mounted in the upper corner of the room.

After they were settled, she said, "Twenty February 1990, ten o'clock A.M. This is Investigator Corporal Carmen Ruis, Badge Number 4576, Crimes Against Persons Division, Dallas Police Department, questioning Ms. Skye Meredith, 1852 Prestonshade Road, Dallas, concerning homicides of Sharon Smith and Theresa Sanders.

"Ms. Meredith, is your statement voluntary?"

Skye nodded.

"Please speak aloud, Skye."

"Yes, it is." Skye had taken off her coat and scarf. The scarf lay on her lap and she worked the tassels through her fingers.

"Skye, I must tell you that these proceedings are being videotaped, and that you may stop the interview at any time. Is that clear?"

Skye looked around, then up at the camera. She pointed at it. "You mean . . . that thing is on?"

"Yes. It's more accurate that way, when the formal statement is typed up. We don't have to rely solely on my notes. Is that okay with you?"

Skye's cheeks had turned a deep rose. "Yes," she whispered.

"Please speak up."

"*Yes.*"

"Thank you. Now, Skye, due to the seriousness of the matters we will be discussing, you should know that you have the right to remain silent, that anything you say today could be used against you in a court of law, that you have the right to have a lawyer present during the interview, and that if you can't afford one—"

"You mean I'm *under arrest*?" Skye's face was contorted with horror.

"No, no. You are not under arrest. However, your statement could be used as evidence in either of these murder cases, and if you incriminate yourself, it could be used against you."

"If I incriminate myself? How could I incriminate myself? I haven't done anything wrong!" Skye's voice had risen to a shrill pitch.

"It's all right, Skye. Nobody said you've done anything wrong. I just want you to fully comprehend what we are doing here so that you may change your mind about the interview if you wish."

Skye looked down into her lap, where she was slowly shredding one of the tassels on the woolen scarf. "No, I want to go ahead with it," she said. "I want to do whatever I can to stop the killing."

"Fine. Now, Skye, I want you to tell me, in your own words, your connection to these murders, and why you are making this statement."

Skye took a deep breath. "Okay. A couple of weeks ago—"

"Excuse me, Skye. Could you be more specific? A date, a day of the week, whatever?"

Her cheeks turned scarlet. "Um, I don't know . . . it was . . . I'm sorry. I'm confused right now. I can't seem to remember the exact day."

"That's all right. Go on."

In a slow, careful monotone, Skye related the events to date. "At first I didn't have any idea why *I* was getting the film. It didn't make any sense. Then Saturday . . . last Saturday . . . that would be February the seventeenth . . . Jared and I—"

"Jared who? Could you give us his full name, please?"

"Jared Martin, the columnist for the *Times Herald*. Anyway, we learned that Sharon Smith worked at a day-care center where one of my clients, a little girl named Amber Dawn Salerno, stayed. It still doesn't make any sense. I mean, I didn't know where she stayed. Her mother brought her in. I don't know how anybody else could know, either." She stopped and took a long gulp of cooled-down coffee. Ruis waited. "So I figured that if it has something to do with my studio, then I didn't dare do any more portrait work for a while. I didn't want anybody else . . . well, I decided to close the studio for a while."

"And the name of your studio is . . ."

"Skye Meredith Studios, located on 115000 Preston Road, in the Preston Haven Shopping Center. Next to Playtime Toys."

"You specialize at your studio, do you not?"

"Yes. I specialize in children's portraits."

"And how long has your studio been open, Skye?"

"Let's see, now . . . I opened on January second . . . I'd been open about a month when I got the first roll of film."

"And what were you doing before then?"

"I was in a bad car wreck on November 20, 1988—over a year ago—and my husband, Paul Schofield, was killed. He was a professor of photography at SMU. We worked on books of photography together, and I did some free-lance photography, mostly children's portraits. My pelvis was crushed in the accident and both legs were broken. I spent most of the next year in hospitals and rehab clinics, learning to walk again." She held up the cane. "I still have to use this. Then I spent a couple of months living with my folks, James and Melva Meredith, in West Texas, on their ranch, recuperating. I moved back to Dallas in early December last year, sold our house, moved into my apartment, and opened my studio."

"So you've been under a tremendous amount of stress

lately. The death of your husband, selling your home, opening your own business, recovering from serious injuries."

Skye shrugged. "I'm getting stronger all the time." She looked up, and Ruis detected a glint of a challenge in her eyes. She gave an answering nod and went on.

"I have to ask you, Skye, if you know of anyone, anyone at all, who could possibly have a grudge on you, or who would have a motive for murdering these women?"

"I hate to say anything," said Skye. "I don't want to get anybody in trouble, especially if they are innocent."

"That's understandable. But we would not necessarily run out and arrest someone just because you gave us a name. We would simply talk to them. Maybe they could give us some information."

"I don't know . . ."

"If we found out later that you had some information that could have proven instrumental in obtaining an indictment or a conviction, you could be indicted yourself for withholding that information."

Skye rubbed her hands over her eyes. "This is getting so complicated."

"This is not a simple case, Skye. It's not a case of wife beating or a barroom brawl. We are dealing with a very clever and cunning murderer who may murder again. Whatever information you have could prevent that."

Skye looked up at the camera. "Could you turn that thing off?"

Ruis suppressed a sigh. "Are you terminating the interview?"

The young woman's cheeks were flaming. Her lap contained little tufts of blue wool from the scarf she'd been fingering. She was obviously extremely nervous, but she surprised Ruis with a lift to her chin. "I do not want to mention a person's name in the presence of a video camera and have it written down in a formal statement, but I would be glad to discuss it with you in private. The newspaper people call it off the record, I think."

"The names you give me will automatically become material witnesses, Skye, possibly even suspects, whether it's written down formally now or later." Ruis was exasperated with the woman because she felt she was losing control of the interview to Skye. She had more questions she had intended to ask and was afraid that the next time she saw Meredith, she'd have to work through a lawyer, which would be even trickier.

"Tell you what, Skye. Let's leave that question alone for a while, shall we? Why don't you tell me about Jared."

"What about him?"

"He's obviously involved in this case to some extent, and I'd like to know how that came about."

The mention of Jared's name had two effects on Skye. Her eyes lit up, and then, in a millisecond, she glanced at Ruis with a look of . . . suspicion? It was curious.

"Jared brought his daughter in for a portrait session a couple of weeks ago—"

"Before or after you received the first roll of film?"

"Before. No . . . now that I think about it . . . I had just gotten the first roll of film the day before and had developed it that night. In fact, I canceled the session with Chelsea because of it."

"Who's Chelsea?"

"His daughter. I thought you knew that."

"Should I?" Ruis had the distinct impression that the conversation had taken a subtle turn, that she was now dealing with Meredith, not as a police officer, but as a woman. When Skye didn't answer her question, she went on. "Why did you cancel the session?"

"I was upset about the photographs—of Sharon Smith, though I didn't know that was her name then—and I had a bad headache."

"Had you met Jared Martin before then?"

Skye shook her head. "No. He knew my husband,

though. He'd taken a night class in photography under Paul once."

"So you and Jared became . . . friends?"

The blush and drop of the eyes told Ruis everything she needed to know. Skye Meredith was in love with Jared Martin. There was a quickening of disappointment within Ruis at that realization, but she ignored it and proceeded with the interview.

"You said that you and Jared had learned of Sharon Smith's connection with your client . . . Amber Dawn Salerno. How did you learn this?"

Skye's expression closed. "I'd rather not answer that question," she said.

Ruis was willing to let that one go. She knew Jared Martin well enough to have some idea of how he worked. Still, she made a mental note to go by and talk to him soon. He owed her a few. Besides, it would be a good excuse to see him.

She switched subjects. "We've been able to pinpoint dates for the deaths of the two victims from autopsy reports. Sharon Smith was apparently murdered between seven and ten P.M. on Tuesday, February sixth. Theresa Sanders was killed on a Thursday night, February fifteenth, again, between seven and ten P.M."

"Investigator Ruis, do you think there is some significance to those dates?" Skye interrupted.

Ruis shook her head. "Probably not. But I have to ask you if you can account for your whereabouts on those two nights."

"Me? But why? Are you accusing me of murder?"

"I'm not accusing you of anything, Skye. Surely you can see our position. Twice now, you have brought our attention to the murdered women—one even before we *knew* she'd been murdered. Once, you provided photographs of the victim. So far, we have no other leads on these murders. We have to ask you this." Ruis kept her expression carefully guarded, so that Skye would not feel threatened.

"I'm home almost every night of the week, Ms. Ruis. What do you think I'm going to do, go dancing?"

Ruis was surprised at the bitterness in Skye's voice. Those telltale cheeks of hers were fire-engine red again. "Could your landlady verify that you were home on those nights?"

Skye slumped in her chair. "Mrs. Thomas plays bingo on Tuesday and Thursday nights," she said quietly. "But I assure you I was there."

Although Ruis had some other questions in mind, she decided to bring the interview to a close. Meredith was getting tired and defensive. She wanted to keep the lines of communication open with the woman, maintain her trust, so that she would be approachable in the future. "I think we've got about all we need for now, Skye," she said gently. "Why don't you go on home and get some rest? I'll be in touch."

Skye nodded, defeat rounding her shoulders.

Ruis opened the door and signaled to Doc to turn off the camera. When she came back in, Skye said simply, "Tommy Thomas and Clyde Winslow."

"What?" Ruis scrambled for her notepad.

"Tommy Thomas is my landlady's son. He doesn't live with her anymore and I'm not sure of his address. He's been making hostile remarks toward me lately, and he recently bought a new Canon camera with lens attachments and some black-and-white film."

Ruis wrote it down. "And Clyde Winslow?"

"He runs the toy store next door; I'm not sure whether he is the actual owner."

"Playtime Toys?"

"That's right."

"And?"

"And . . . something has been bothering me about the similarities between the pictures of the two women, only I couldn't remember what it was. Today, in Clyde's store, I found these, and it all came to me in a rush."

On the table between them, Skye spread out four yellow cat's-head lapel pins. "Both women were wearing these on their coats when the photographs were made. It just seemed like too much of a coincidence to me."

Staring at the lapel pins, Ruis felt a tingle at the back of her neck. She'd felt that tingle before, when they were closing in on a bust, when everything started to come together, when their hard work paid off.

Sometimes one little coincidence was all they needed.

Chapter Seventeen

CRAWLING INTO THE driver's seat of her car, Skye slammed the door and leaned her head onto her arms against the steering wheel. She felt completely drained and wondered how she would find the strength to drive home. She'd missed lunch, waiting for the statement to be ready, and during that long, lonely waiting period, the uneasiness she'd felt from the beginning of the interview with Ruis had grown to a gnawing fear that she had somehow made a terrible mistake.

All she had wanted to do was talk to Investigator Ruis about the connection she and Jared had found between her and Sharon Smith. She had thought it would only take a few minutes. But from the moment she entered the police department, something had seemed wrong. Then the videotape, then Ruis reading her rights . . .

What was going on?

"I haven't done anything," she whispered, and yet, increasingly, she was being made to feel that she *had*, or that someone thought that she had. How could this be happening? She'd never even had a speeding ticket. She'd gone to the police because she was afraid, and she thought they could help her. Now she was beginning to feel afraid of the police.

Home. She just wanted to get home, take a long, hot bath, and go to bed with a good book. Forget everything. The cold and stress were getting to her; the pain in her legs was deep. She ground the key in the ignition. Nothing. Again. Nothing.

Come on, you stupid piece of—

The engine coughed slowly to life. Babying it, she eased the car out of the slick parking lot and into what little traffic existed in the middle of a bitter cold afternoon. Driving twenty miles an hour slower than usual, she got all the way to the LBJ off-ramp before remembering that she still needed groceries. The idea of pushing a cart up and down endless aisles and standing on concrete floors waiting to be checked out made her want to cry—nothing was harder on her legs—but it had to be done.

Parking in front of the closest supermarket, she hurried through the chore, throwing things into the cart at random as she thought of them, knowing she was forgetting half of what she needed. By the time she made it back out to the car, her legs were numb with pain. Whimpering slightly under her breath, she put the key in the ignition and turned it. Nothing. Again. Nothing.

No. Please.

Again. Nothing. Again. Nothing.

Pounding on the steering wheel and cursing, she tried everything she could think of to start the engine, but it was all futile. For a moment she sat, fighting back tears. Into her frustrated fog came a name: *Jared*. She seemed to remember that he lived near here. She dug through her purse for the card he'd given her once, found it, and hauled her weary body back into the supermarket to the pay phone.

Please, God, don't let it be the answering machine.

"Kelly's Pool Hall."

"Jared?"

"Skye! To what do I owe this pleasure?"

"My car broke down, and it's full of groceries, and I've been at the police department all day, and I'm cold, and—"

"Wait, wait. Start from the beginning and tell me where you are."

She did, and as she hung up the phone, felt a tremendous lift of relief. It was nice not to be so alone anymore.

The red '66 Mustang pulled into the parking lot almost before she had time to think. Jared fiddled under the hood of her car, pronounced it impossible to fix before morning, loaded Skye and her groceries into the Mustang, and headed toward his apartment with such breathless efficiency that she didn't even bother to offer an objection.

"This is nice," said Skye as they entered Jared's apartment, looking around with pleasure at the exposed brick, wood-burning stove, and hanging plants. "I didn't think men's apartments were usually so . . . warm."

"I guess living with a woman gets a guy spoiled to that stuff."

She wandered over to one wall, filled with framed magazine covers. *Texas Monthly:* "Legal Illegal Aliens, by Jared Martin"; *Sports Illustrated:* "Hang Gliding in Three Easy Lessons: A View from a Hospital Bed, by Jared Martin"; *Fortune:* "T. Boone's Pickens Ain't So Slim, by Jared Martin." Not all the cover stories listed Jared as the author, but Skye knew he'd written them or they wouldn't be framed. He came up beside her.

"Impressive."

"You ought to see the bathroom. It's papered with rejections."

She smiled wanly, felt her knees go weak, and plunked down in a nearby chair.

"You look awful," he said.

"Thank you."

He dragged an ottoman over to her chair, lifted her legs, and set them upon it. "Make yourself comfortable. You are about to get a bowlful of Jared Martin's Big Batch Blowout Beef Stew." He took her coat. "This scarf's seen better days, hasn't it?" Holding up her tattered blue scarf, he grinned.

"My worry beads," she called as he disappeared into the kitchen, and Skye wondered why he didn't question her about her day at the police department.

The chair was comfortable. Skye let her head fall back on the headrest. A clanking at her elbow brought open her eyes. Jared had set a cup of steaming herb tea beside her. She took a bracing sip, feeling the warmth spread throughout her cold limbs. The pain began to seep away. Limp, she gave herself up to the luxury of being cared for, and the last thing she remembered before she fell asleep was Jared singing "Yesterday" in the kitchen.

When she opened her eyes, it was dark outside the window. A fire crackled in the wood-burning stove. The table was set with candles, as yet unlit. Wonderful smells came from the kitchen. There was a muted sound of typing from a back room. She stood up and stretched, embarrassed with herself for having fallen asleep, but feeling greatly refreshed. There was a soreness in her legs, but most of the pain had abated. She followed the sound of typing to a room down the hall. The door was cracked open.

Jared was sitting at a battered wooden institutional desk, crowded with books and papers, typing. His concentration was intense and he didn't hear her. The room was stuffed with books. Against one wall stretched a lumpy old sofa. The wastebasket was overflowing, with wadded sheets of paper littering the floor. The room was a direct opposite to the other rooms in the apartment, which were neat and well kept.

Curious, Skye moved into the carpeted room and peeked over his shoulder. Something next to the typewriter caught her eye. A stack of papers was held down by a book. She glimpsed one word, "Chapter."

"You're writing a book?" she said.

In one fluid movement, Jared sprang from his chair in a whirl, bringing his arm back in full swing. It caught Skye just underneath the cheekbone, lifting her feet off the floor, and slamming her against the wall.

"For Christ's sake, Skye, even Chelsea knows better than to do that!"

"What," she asked, touching her cheek gingerly, "did I do?"

"You snuck up behind me when I was working." He squatted down in front of her, where she sat on the floor against the wall. "Oh, Christ. I can't believe I did that." He touched her cheek.

"I was not sneaking up on you." She pushed his hand away.

"Just don't ever come up behind me like that, you understand? Especially when I'm working."

She struggled to get up. "What the hell are *you* mad about? I'm the one that got knocked practically across the room."

He took her arm and lifted her up in that effortless way of his. "I know. God, I'm sorry. It's just a reflex, I guess, left over from the Army." She felt herself being propelled out of the room, like a child who's caught a grown-up in some embarrassing act.

"For heaven's sake, Jared." She pulled her arm away. "What is the matter with you?"

"I just don't like people messing around in my office. I don't like them reading over my shoulder. And I don't like them asking questions about my work."

"Well, excu-u-use me," she said in a parody of Steve Martin. "I didn't know I was disturbing the *great man at work*. Believe me, I'll know better next time." She dug around in her purse for a mirror. Her cheek was swelling.

"Oh, shit. I seem to be screwing this worse every time I open my mouth. Here, sit down. Let me get you an ice pack."

"Forget it. I'll live."

"Aw, c'mon, Skye. Don't make me feel worse. I feel like a worm as it is." As he talked, he busied himself with a dish towel and ice.

Suddenly Skye felt, of all things, laughter, bubbling its way to the surface. She tried to hold it in and failed.

A look of alarm crossed Jared's face. "Are you crying?" He came closer. "You're *laughing*! What the hell's so funny?" His expression changed from alarmed to wounded.

She guffawed, held her sides, wiped tears away. "I was just thinking," she gasped, "that every time we get together we wind up fighting. I guess now we're going to start slugging it out."

"That's not very funny."

"Yes. It is."

"If you could see that shiner you're getting, you would know that it is not funny." But he was smiling. He handed her the ice pack.

"*Ouch*. No wonder Rocky talks the way he does." She looked into his eyes and was startled at the intensity of his expression. She couldn't fathom it, exactly, but she felt almost consumed by it. Jared's eyes had an energy all their own that was almost hypnotic. Her cheeks grew hot and she tore her gaze away.

Only one thing bothered her as she watched him dish up the steaming stew and sing along with *The Big Chill* sound-track album.

Why was he so secretive about that book?

"So, tell me about your big day at the police department. What were you doing there?" Jared splashed a generous amount of hot sauce into his bowl of stew and took a big spoonful.

Skye struggled to bring her thoughts under control. "I thought it would be a good idea to tell Investigator Ruis what we learned about Amber and Sharon Smith and all. But no sooner had I gotten there than the next thing I knew, she had a video camera going and was reading me my rights."

"*Reading you your rights?*" Jared's spoon stopped half-way to his mouth.

"Isn't that what it's called when they start telling you that you have the right to remain silent, that anything you say can be used against you in court later—that stuff?"

He placed the spoon back into the bowl and rubbed his hand over his chin. "What did Carmen say about it? Did she tell you why?"

"Just that the statement could be used as evidence and that I could incriminate myself with it." She toyed with her stew. It was delicious, but she had suddenly lost her appetite. "Jared, I think the police are beginning to think that I killed those women."

The statement, said aloud, was even more preposterous to her than when she'd thought it.

Jared ate quietly for a moment, then said, "I think you should proceed very carefully from now on, Skye, until this guy gets caught. He's obviously extremely smart, because the police apparently haven't found anything on him yet."

She stared at him as the horror of his remark sank home. Jared avoided her eyes.

"You're saying I could actually be arrested if . . . if the police had reason to believe that I did it?"

He shrugged. "So far, you're all they've got."

"*But I haven't done anything!*" Skye got to her feet and began to pace behind the table. "I'm innocent! Doesn't that count for something?"

"Calm down." He came around the table and put his arms around her. "They won't arrest anybody until they have strong enough evidence to get an indictment. What kind of evidence have they got on you?"

"Maybe they think the photographs are evidence."

"If they honestly thought that, Skye, they'd have arrested you by now. Here, sit down and eat. You haven't eaten all day." He nudged her into her chair and sat down himself.

She forced down a bite or two, then said, "What about that blood-type thing?"

Pretending not to hear, he continued eating.

"Jared, don't do this to me. You know something you're not telling and I have a right to know."

"Okay." His spoon clanked into his empty bowl. "Sometimes a victim will claw an assailant during the attack. Forensics can detect the blood type of the assailant from skin tissue found underneath the victim's fingernails."

She took a sip of water. "Well, then, our blood types must not be the same, or they would have said something, or arrested me by now, wouldn't they?"

"Sure," he said, and she felt, again, that he was lying.

She couldn't eat any more. "So what do we do now?" she asked.

"I'll talk to Carmen Ruis, see if there's anything she's willing to tell me about the investigation. Beyond that . . . we wait."

"What are we waiting for?"

"The killer's next move."

Chapter Eighteen

IT WAS WORKING. The plan was working, and he could hardly contain his elation. He had put her out of business, pure and simple, and he had saved the children.

He smiled. Already, his cleverness was astounding. Even though he'd left his signature pin on two bodies, the police still had no idea it was him. Boy, would they be surprised.

When the Great Revelation was made, the world would be clamoring to know his methods. Of course, he would never reveal everything, but he had to be thorough. Genius did not allow sloppiness.

But he would have to move quickly. Skye was getting too nosy for her own good. He didn't like what she was up to, talking to the police, and the rest of it, telling them her lies.

His plans from now on would have to be made very carefully, each step laid out for a reason. After all, he had the power, and he intended to keep it.

He hadn't seen the eyes much lately, because he'd been working very hard on his book, but he *felt* them, felt their restlessness. They were ready for him to act, he knew it.

He didn't intend to keep them waiting for long.

It was getting late and the day was catching up to Skye. Even though it had been over a year since the accident,

Skye still fatigued early. Pain had a way of tiring a person.

It was awkward, being at Jared's. She was beginning to regret the impulse that had brought them this far. She longed to be at home in her own uncomplicated bed. While Jared washed the dishes, Skye cleared the table. When she put away the hot sauce in the refrigerator, she had to make room for the bottle beside several rolls of film.

"You should show me some of your work sometime," she said, indicating the film.

"I'd be too humiliated." He reached out his foot and kicked the refrigerator door shut.

Other than that, Skye said little, and Jared didn't seem to mind. It was the afterward that bothered her. It had been a long time since she had to think about how to handle herself after dinner at a man's apartment.

"You look beat. Why don't you go on back and crash on my bed? This sofa makes into a bed. I'll turn in later." Jared seemed to have read her mind, and Skye was touched. He never seemed to press her; a paradox, considering his enigmatic, overbearing personality.

"I didn't bring anything to sleep in."

"That's okay with me." There was a mischievous glint to his eyes.

"Jared . . ."

"Okay, okay. I'll get you one of my flannel shirts. I don't sleep in pajamas." He made a mock-leering face and headed down the hall toward the bedroom.

Skye followed him. A large four-poster king-sized water bed dominated the room and she almost laughed. It suited him. The room was done in earth tones. Some very good pen-and-ink drawings of wild animals native to the state of Texas hung on the wall in attractive frames. Jared handed her a red-and-black-checked flannel shirt she'd seen before, made another leering face, and left.

She went into the bathroom to change and laughed out loud. It was, indeed, papered with rejection slips. The shirt was very large on her and hung almost to her knees. Rolling up the sleeves, she went in search of him to say good night and found him sitting on the darkened sofa, lost in thought. She'd never seen him look so serious and wondered if it was a part of his nature that he never showed anyone.

"Jared?"

He looked up as though he didn't recognize her, but the expression was fleeting and quickly replaced by the old smile.

"That shirt has never looked so good."

She sat beside him. "Are you all right?"

"I was just thinking. It's a lot of work for me, you know."

"I wanted to thank you for helping me out, and all, today."

He touched her face, his fingertips feather-soft, against her bruised cheek. "Does it hurt? Don't tell me, I feel guilty enough as it is."

"It's all right. I know you didn't mean to hurt me."

He brushed the hair out of her face, cupped the back of her head in his hand, and kissed her.

The shock of his lips on hers electrified her body, as if bringing the dead back to life. Melting against him, she parted her lips and tasted his mouth, exploring it with her tongue. He responded, welding his body against hers with hard, masculine force, pressing her back against the couch.

His hands moved over the flannel shirt, discovered her breasts, cupped them. She gasped, thinking fleetingly about her lack of available birth control, then not caring as his tongue flicked around her ear and down the side of her throat. She moved her hands underneath his shirt, working her fingernails over his back, and parted her legs, feeling the thrust of his hard jeans against her panties. Moaning, she arched her back against him.

He kissed her once, twice more, then pulled away, leaving her disheveled, panting, and confused. Running his hands through his hair, he sat up. "I didn't bring you here for this, honestly I didn't."

It took her a moment to collect herself. "I know you didn't, Jared. It doesn't matter, anyway. I'm a big girl. I can make my own decisions."

He caressed her leg. "I know you can. I just want to make sure that they are the right decisions for you. I don't want you to have any regrets."

"Why don't you let me worry about that? It's been a long time for me, Jared . . ." She caught her bottom lip in her teeth; she didn't want it to seem as if she were begging.

"I know it has, Skye. That's why I want it to be right for you when . . . I just don't want to push anything. Things have been moving very fast for us and you've been under a lot of strain. I don't want to add any more."

Suddenly Skye had the feeling that Paul had walked into the room and sat down on the couch between them. Although Jared didn't say as much, she knew that's what he was getting at. It was a sobering thought. She wondered what it would take to make things "right."

I was afraid to love again at first, she thought. *Now he's afraid to let me.*

Maybe the idea of being her first lover since Paul's death was a little daunting to him. Whatever his reasons, it was not in her nature to push sex. Maybe he was right. Maybe they needed a little more time.

"I don't think I would have any regrets, Jared, but it has to be right for both of us. I wouldn't want you to have any regrets, either." She kissed him and, before he could answer, walked down the hall to the bedroom.

The heated water bed proved a delight to her tired legs, sensuous, like a whirlpool, and comforting, like her grandmother's feather bed. She stretched out, catlike, under the single comforter. The flannel shirt grew too hot and she dropped it on the floor. She fully expected for Jared to slip into bed beside her at any moment, but before long, the sounds of typing drifted across the hall. The monotonous rhythm finally put her to sleep.

Drifting on the edges of wakefulness, she became aware

of Jared's firm, warm body against hers and she pressed it close to her. Neither of them spoke. She felt drenched in his kiss, kicked off her panties hurriedly, and wrapped her legs around his body. In spite of her fatigue, Skye felt no pain. It was as if her legs were weightless. His hardness entered her and she cried out, thrusting upward to meet him . . . and opened her eyes.

She clutched the pillow close, her pelvis arched against it. Bewildered, she rose up on one elbow. She was alone. It took a moment to realize that she had only been dreaming.

Sweating, she fell back on the bed and kicked the covers off. *An erotic dream. I'll be damned.* Maybe it was a good sign: the first one she'd had since Paul's death that didn't involve him.

This was ridiculous. Why should she have dreams about Jared when the man was right here in this apartment? All she had to do was march down the hall and climb into bed with him. She glanced at the clock. Two A.M. She'd give him a little dream of his own.

Struggling a little with the unfamiliar, water-filled mattress, she sat up, then caught her breath.

It was the sound of typing. Though she hadn't heard it at first, it hadn't stopped. She listened for a moment. Every now and then she could hear mumbling remarks, the sound of paper being wadded, then the typing would start again.

Touching her cheek, she winced. *I don't like people messing around in my office. I don't like them reading over my shoulder. And I don't like them asking questions about my work.* Apparently he didn't like being interrupted, either.

With a heavy sigh, she plumped the pillow and lay back, arranging the comforter just so, trying to get settled. Even so, it was a long time before she got to sleep.

Skye's car was not that hard to get going, after all. The battery simply needed recharging.

"You ought to get a new one," said Jared as he slammed down the hood.

"Are you kidding? I just closed the studio indefinitely. I can't afford a new car right now."

"How about a newer used one? The payments would probably run about the same." He came around to her open window.

"I don't make car payments. This was part of the insurance settlement after the accident."

"Oh. Well, as long as you're happy with it—"

"Actually, I'm not," she said reflectively. "Mother picked it out for me while I was in the hospital. To tell you the truth, I've never liked it. We've never had similar tastes on anything, and then . . ." She glanced sideways at him. "Every time I look at it, I remember how I came to get it. I guess I was predisposed to hate the thing."

He squeezed her arm. "If you change your mind, I have a friend who is an extremely rare bird—an honest used-car dealer. He could fix you up with a nice trade-in. Think about it."

She put her hand on his. "You worked awfully late last night."

"I was on a roll. Couldn't stop if I wanted to. I had all this stuff running through my mind. Might as well get it on paper."

"But . . . so late?" Her cheeks burned. He didn't know how close she had come to seducing him. Just the memory of it made her feel shy.

"I like to work late at night. No interruptions."

She glanced away. "I guess I'd better be going."

"Want to do something this weekend with Chelsea and me?"

She felt foolishly happy. "I'd love to."

He leaned in the open window and kissed her. "I'll call you."

The weather had warmed up considerably since the day before, and though it was still cold, the streets were no

longer icy. Skye made it home in good time and Bartholomew met her at the front door, yowling. Both his food and
water dishes were empty and she refilled them. The cat box
needed changing, too, a loathsome chore, but a necessary
price to pay for his company.

She emptied the used litter and her other garbage into a
large plastic bag and made her slow way downstairs,
through Mrs. Thomas's kitchen, and out the back door to
the dumpster in the alley.

A pale, watery sun was emerging and the cutting wind of
the day before had died down. Skye sensed that the last
bitter cold snap of winter was over and that the season was
dying with dignity. For a little while she stood leaning
against the dumpster, cane hooked over her arm. Something about the coming of spring put new zest in her blood,
made her feel that all her wounds were healing and that,
before too long, she would be well.

Time to get back. Turning, she almost collided with
Tommy Thomas, and yelped in surprise.

Everything about his body—posture, expression, stance—
was set against her. What had she done now?

"Where do you get off sending the police snooping
around me, asking questions, acting like I done committed
some crime?" With each word, his finger poked painfully
into her chest.

"Stop it." She shoved his hand away.

"I want to know what's going on and you're gonna tell
me."

"I don't have to tell you anything." She started to brush
past him, and he grabbed her arm.

"*Ow*. You're hurting me, Tommy." She tried to pull
away, but was caught fast.

"You're gonna tell me what I want to know and you're
gonna tell me now." His eyes squinted into hard black slits.

Skye looked around. Most of the houses were deserted
this weekday morning. Her heart began to pound. "Let go
of me."

His fingers squeezed harder. Her arm was going numb. She began to tremble. Had to think fast. A bluff. She needed a bluff. "Get your hands off me, or I'll file an assault charge on you so fast it'll make your head swim. Then you *will* be talking to the police." Lifting her chin, she forced herself to look him in the eye.

Slowly he let go and stepped back. "I hope you enjoy that cute little apartment of yours," he said, his lips hardly moving, "because you ain't gonna be in it for long."

Leaning heavily on her cane, she turned and headed for the house, careful not to hurry or look back. Once upstairs, she closed the door and locked it, then sank into the nearest chair. Her hands shook so badly she had to clasp them together in her lap. She took deep, long breaths to calm the jackhammer in her chest.

What if Tommy was the murderer?

For the first time since Paul's death, she was very much afraid to be alone.

Maybe she should talk to Investigator Ruis about police protection.

That was a laugh.

Maybe she should call Jared.

And what could he do about it?

Her shoulders were knotted and she felt another headache coming on. A long, hot bath would help her relax, clear her thoughts.

As she got up to head for the bathroom, she noticed a large brown envelope on the coffee table.

A large brown envelope with one word on the front in block print: *Skye*.

Chapter Nineteen

JARED'S FACE SHOWED all-over surprise when he opened the door to Carmen, and, she liked to think, a little pleasure.

"Why, it's Investigator Corporal Carmen Ruis," he said with a big smile. "What brings you out to our humble, if crime-ridden, neck of the woods?"

"I was in the neighborhood," she said in a sarcastic drawl, and he laughed.

"Come on in. The coffee's hot. You still like it black?"

She followed him into the apartment. "You bet. Great digs you got here, Martin. I was expecting something a little more, shall we say, primitive."

"Oh, it isn't mine," he shot back. "I just come here twice a week to clean."

"Well, somebody does, anyway." She'd forgotten the easy rhythm of banter with Jared. She'd always enjoyed dueling wits with him. He walked into the kitchen for the coffee, and Carmen spotted Skye Meredith's ragged woolen scarf on the counter. She glanced around, momentarily panicked that the woman was here, then decided it was a false alarm. Still, she had been here, probably last night.

He brought the coffee. "Let's sit down here in my comfy cozy living room."

"Said the spider to the fly."

"Quick as ever I see, Ruis."

"Got to be to survive Capers."

"How do you like working that division?"

"It's interesting," she said. "Never boring."

"That's important to you, isn't it?" He turned the magnetism of his eyes upon her. He'd always had that ability to concentrate the full force of his attention on whatever interested him at the moment, and to block out what didn't.

"Isn't it to you?" she asked.

He inclined his head in agreement. "It's one reason I like free-lancing. I can pick my own areas to write about."

"So you're not on the *Times Herald* staff anymore."

"They fired me a long time ago. You knew that."

"Yeah, I knew it. I was just being polite. How'd you talk them into taking your column?"

"Easy. First I sobered up. Then I begged."

She looked around at the framed magazine covers. "You seem to be doing all right now."

"You ought to see my bathroom. I paid my dues."

"Your bathroom?"

He grinned. She couldn't resist the challenge and wandered down the hall in search of it, then broke out laughing. "How apropos for you to express your opinion of these rejections in such a graphic and, dare I say, shitty way." She rejoined him on the couch.

He set his coffee cup down on the table. "But you didn't come here to discuss my interior decorating. It's about Skye, isn't it?"

"Direct and to the point, as always. What's going on with her, Jared? Is she genuine?"

"I'd stake my life on it."

"How much do you know about her?"

"Enough."

"Oh, come on, Jared. Give me a break here."

"Okay." He stared into space for a minute. "I knew her husband before he was killed. He was a lot older than her, maybe twenty years, I'm not sure. He told us once—I took a photography class under him—that she took one of his classes the last semester of her senior year at SMU. They had a whirlwind courtship and got married as soon as she graduated. He was crazy about her." He leaned back and crossed his legs. Carmen lit a cigarette. "I think their relationship was kind of father-daughter, in a way, but I also think that it was Skye's talent and ambition that got those books published."

"What books?"

He got up and fetched *Cowboys: The Last American Heroes.*

She flipped through the book. "Beautiful."

"Yes. Schofield was a good photographer, technically. He was an expert with a camera and skilled in the darkroom. But Skye . . . Skye had the *vision,* the imagination. See, he'd been teaching twelve, maybe fifteen years before he met her. He'd never done a book before. He would never have had the nerve to open his own studio, as she has done."

Carmen sneaked a glance at him. His eyes had a focus that excluded her.

"I've tried to get her to do a book on children, but she won't." He shook his head.

"Why not?"

"No confidence. She doesn't recognize her own talents."

But you do, thought Carmen. She was beginning to understand.

"What's she like?" It was a leading question, timed just right. He would fall into answering her before he knew it.

He smiled. "She's gentle as a kitten, so people think they can push her around, but she's got a spine of steel. It's like everything else, though: she doesn't realize it yet."

She tapped ash into an ashtray. "If she's as sweet as you say, then why would anybody send her undeveloped film containing photographs of murdered women?"

He stood and walked away from her. "I wish to God I knew."

"Jared . . . if, as you say, she has this low self-esteem, and then her father figure and beloved husband is killed suddenly, tragically; and she was nearly killed herself and, crippled, she's struggling to run a new business—"

"Don't get sneaky with me, Ruis. I know what you're getting at. You think Skye murdered those women."

"What else can I think, Jared?"

"You tell me."

She took a long drag on her cigarette.

"Are you going to arrest her?"

"This is an ongoing investigation, Jared. I can't answer that."

"Don't give me that crap."

"All right, then, I'll put it this way. I won't make an arrest until I've got enough evidence to back one up."

"And so far you don't."

She shrugged.

"You're good, Carmen," he said, "real good. If a loved one of mine were murdered, I'd want you on the case."

"Why, thanks, Jared." She was surprised and flattered.

"I just think it's possible, sometimes, to be too good. Do you know what I mean?"

She nodded slowly. It was something to consider.

Cotton-mouthed, Skye stared at the envelope. *How did it get there?* She'd left the apartment unlocked while she carried out the trash. Was the killer that close to her?

Her knees turned to jelly and she sat back down in the chair. The palms of her hands were wet. She wiped them on her jeans. There was a rushing in her ears and she gulped air.

The envelope was not the same as the others. It was larger, and there was no bulge that might be film. Had he developed the photographs himself this time?

Ruis said not to touch the envelope, to bring it straight to her. But it drew from Skye a morbid fascination by its very differentness. *What was inside?*

Heart pounding, she found her hand reaching for it even as her mind objected.

Don't touch it. Fingerprints. She had to think straight. Gloves. She had some bulky knit gloves in the pocket of her coat. The coat was on her bed in the other room.

Oh, God. Could the killer be in the apartment right now?

Holding her breath, she strained to listen. No sound.

As before, she kicked off her shoes, got to her feet, and moved as silently as possible across the floor to the darkroom. Even in daytime it was pitch-dark inside. What should she do? Should she turn on the light and take her chances? What if he had a gun?

Not a gun. A cord to strangle her with.

She shuddered, the noise in her thumping heart echoing in her ears.

Protection. She needed some protection. A wooden block on the kitchen counter held a collection of knives. Withdrawing a large, sharp one, she held it tightly in front of her and snapped on the darkroom light, fear grinding her teeth together.

Nothing.

It was too late to worry about noise. She hurried into the bedroom, clutching the knife in front of her like a battering ram, holding on to the furniture with one hand for support.

No one.

That left the bathroom.

There wasn't much room between the bed and the bathroom door. She could be thrust back upon the bed by someone stronger. Taking her bottom lip between her teeth, she thrust herself into the space and switched on the wall light.

Empty.

A movement caught her peripheral vision. Clothes swaying.

The closet.

She whirled, a scream on her lips, and saw Bartholomew strutting out, tail held high.

Skye collapsed onto the bed. The knife fell to the floor. She covered her face with trembling hands.

Could the envelope have been left in the night, while she was gone?

That idea was even more chilling. If that was true, it meant that the killer could get into her apartment with the doors locked.

"*God help me,*" she said aloud.

Bartholomew sprang to the bed and she jumped, needles of fear pricking all over her body.

She couldn't take much more of this.

Numbly she groped in the pockets of her coat for the gloves and took them into the living room.

The envelope lay in its place, spoiling her coffee table, destroying her peace, assaulting her life.

Slowly she drew on the gloves and approached the envelope like it was a coiled snake.

Maybe I shouldn't be doing this. Maybe I should call Investigator Ruis.

She picked up the envelope. It had a brad clasp.

Maybe I should call Jared.

She pulled open the brads.

I don't have to do this. I'm playing right into his hands. He wants me to do this.

She reached inside and drew out the contents.

It was a magazine, cheaply printed, with lurid colors and a cover photograph of a beautiful little girl with long blond hair and big blue eyes, naked, posed with her legs apart. The title of the magazine was *Alice in Funderland.*

Skye Meredith, photographer of children, was getting her first hard look at child pornography.

Chapter Twenty

TURNING THE PAGES was difficult with gloves. Although the cover was glossy, the pages were of cheap paper with black-and-white photographs. The faces of the men were not shown; they were either depicted from the waist down or wore frightening black hoods over their heads.

"Alice," who was about five, was shown performing every act of sexual perversion Skye had ever heard of, and some she hadn't. In one photograph the little girl sat astride a man on a bed, backward. She was too small for the penis to penetrate all the way. In another, she performed fellatio on him. There was Alice with a pony, Alice with a little boy, teasing him to erection. In one picture, a man masturbated her and she writhed on the bed, her face contorted with . . . pleasure or pain? Skye couldn't tell.

In every picture, the child was solemn and unsmiling, the hardness of a streetwalker's eyes looking out from the softness of her little-girl face. Beside each photograph was italicized text, written from "Alice's" point of view:

And then he kisses me between my legs on my little wee-hole—that's super! Sometimes he lets me suck his willie. I like that! But my favorite part is when he puts his thingummy in my love-place. That feels so-o-o-o good! I can't wait until he comes to see me again.

By the time she reached the end of the magazine, Skye felt very old. All her life she had been sheltered and protected by the men who loved her. She'd grown up a happy child, cherished by her parents, treated well by her friends. College had been a positive experience, full of parties and interesting people. The six years she lived with Paul had been full and rich. Skye moved in a world of love and security, not without tragedy or struggle, but always with the comforting sense that she would never be harmed by the people around her.

A world of innocence.

That world had been invaded by brown envelopes, spewing forth their contents of death and misery.

But nothing she had seen before could have possibly prepared her for this.

There had been an unreality about the murdered women. Even at the forensics institute, the face had seemed . . . almost asleep. She had learned to block the faces out of her mind, put them in a separate mental closet she kept locked. In that way, she could divorce herself from the reality of it. It was survival, of sorts.

But the brutal ravaging of a child's innocence was something else. The men in their black hoods seemed like evil incarnate. It was destruction in its basest form.

Until a few minutes ago, until the arrival of the third brown envelope, Skye had never even realized that such destruction existed. She'd seen the church groups on TV, ranting and raving about "pornography," waving their copies of *Playboy* and *Penthouse*.

Obviously they didn't know what they were talking about.

The sight of the magazine sickened her. She shoved it back into the envelope, stripped off the gloves in two sweeping movements, hurried into the bathroom, and threw up.

* * *

So far the morning had been unfruitful. Carmen had found Tommy Thomas living in a seedy neighborhood near Fair Park, in a run-down two-room flat. It was unclear how he made his living, but the camera equipment Skye had described would have cost hundreds of dollars. There was no sign of it in the apartment and the man was hostile and closed to her questions. She decided to run a computer check on him.

The visit with Jared Martin had been a pleasant interlude, but he told her little that she didn't already know and nothing that she could use. He seemed smitten with Skye, Carmen thought ruefully. It was about the way her luck with men usually ran.

She planned one more stop before lunch, then back to the office computer for more searching through suspects. A sense of urgency dogged her heels, for she knew that, the more time that passed after a crime was committed, the colder the trail got.

Skye Meredith Studios was, indeed, locked up; curtains were drawn across the windows and the glass door. After a cursory check, Carmen headed next door. A tall man in a robot suit and cowboy hat stood near the door when Carmen entered Playtime Toys.

"I'm looking for Clyde Winslow," she told him. Without speaking, he turned on his heels and headed for the back of the store. She followed, wondering if the man was mute.

They found Clyde in a back storeroom. Carmen showed him her badge and introduced herself.

"Do you sell these pins in your store?" She held out one of the cat's-head pins in the palm of her hand.

"Up next to the cash register," he said. "What of it?"

"Could you give me a description of any adults who have bought these pins in recent weeks, especially if they bought several at once, or came in frequently to buy them?"

"You've got to be kidding." He led the way out of the storeroom to the counter. A wire basket filled with the pins sat next to the cash register with a sign that said, "25 cents." "See this? People come into the store, they buy stuff, they get to the checkout, and they pick up extra junk that they find while they are waiting to be rung up. It's called impulse purchasing. No way could I remember who all bought one of these pins."

"Wouldn't you remember if an adult came in and bought a handful of them? Wouldn't you find that unusual?"

"Not necessarily. Folks give their kids birthday parties, they pick up cheap favors for the guests. So what? I don't pay attention to each item that each customer buys."

Carmen stared at the wire basket. There was something macabre about seeing so many of the pins in one place. Digging through her purse, she pulled out a photograph of Theresa Sanders.

"This woman ever come into your store with twin babies, about a year old?"

He peered at the picture, put on his glasses, smiled. "Yeah, I remember her. Skye Meredith borrowed a couple of toys from me for a session with those kids, and the lady brought them back and bought a couple for herself. I remember her because she was real pretty and she had this big stroller with those kids in it."

"Did she buy any of these pins?"

He frowned. "I don't remember, really."

"It's very important, Mr. Winslow. This woman was murdered wearing one of these pins from your store."

He took a step back and went pale. "I didn't know. Geez . . . I didn't . . ." His face assumed a sly expression and he stepped closer to her. "You want to know an adult that bought a bunch of these pins, ask Skye Meredith. She bought a whole handful."

With careful precision, he drew the pocketknife blade along the edges of the newspaper clipping until it came clean. This would make a new collection. He had a collection from California, a collection from New York, and now he would have a collection from Texas.

The evil was everywhere, reaching out long tentacles like the root system of a large tree. He had so much work to do. Sometimes, he was overwhelmed by it.

Still he was comforted by the fact that, after the Great Revelation, after his book was published, he would have a network of assistants to help him wipe out all the evil everywhere and save the children.

He pictured himself, like the Pope or Jesus, seated on a throne in flowing white robes in the middle of a vast field, like Woodstock or Central Park. The countryside would be covered with thousands and thousands of children, all of whom had come for his blessing. They would all want to kiss his hand, and he would never turn anyone away. He would love everyone and everyone would love him.

At night he would be surrounded by crowds of eyes, watching over him, protecting him. He had even found a passage in the Bible that clearly showed his destiny, Hebrews 12:1: *Therefore, since we have so great a cloud of witnesses surrounding us, let us lay aside every encumbrance, and the sin which so easily entangles us, and let us run with endurance the race that is set before us.*

Skye Meredith was sinful. She had this sweet way about her, but he knew better. He knew what she did with her body by night, what she did with her camera by day. She entangled others with her sin. But not for long.

He thumbtacked the clipping to the crowded bulletin board. The plan was all coming together. Pulling out the calendar with large squares, he drew a red circle around one of the dates. There were two other red circles on the calendar: February 6 and February 15.

At the sound of Jared's knock, relief warmed through Skye's body. It had taken all day long to reach him. Night had crept up, almost unnoticed by her. Fear and worry had a way of stretching time to the breaking point.

It was all she could do not to fling herself into his arms when she opened the door. All she could think about was that Jared would know what to do. Jared would take care of things.

"I nearly wrecked my car getting here," he said. "From the sound of your voice, I thought you'd gotten another roll of film."

Closing the door behind him, she held out the magazine. He reached for it. "Don't touch it without gloves," she warned. "Jared . . . I found this on my table this morning when I came back from taking out the trash."

Jared's expression convulsed. He drew back as if the magazine were steaming hot. To Skye's mind, it appeared as if he aged right in front of her. Deep lines cragged his face. He glanced up at her and his eyes were changed. She did not know this man.

"I don't have to touch it," he said, turning away from her. He walked across the room and leaned against the fireplace.

"But . . . I want you to see it."

"*I don't have to see it!*" he snapped. "It's obviously kiddie porn. Oh, Jesus." He wiped his hand across his eyes.

Skye hadn't given much thought to Jared's reaction, but she hadn't expected this. She put the magazine on the table, drew off her gloves, and went up to him. He didn't look at her. She didn't know what to say.

What could she say to this stranger?

Finally she said, "You've got to help me."

"What do you expect me to do?" He walked away from her again and sat on the couch.

"Well, for starters, help me figure out what is going on here."

"That's obviously a job for the police."

"How can you say that?"

"*For Christ's sake, Skye!* Can't you see? This thing is getting way out of control."

"Oh, you mean . . . as long as only women are getting killed it's not out of control. It's a great big adventure. Now it's getting nasty and that makes it out of control?"

"That's not what I meant and you know it."

She stared at him. "I don't know anything anymore."

With revulsion, he pointed toward the magazine. "That little girl is about the same age as Chelsea."

Her legs felt leaden. She sat down in one of the chairs in front of the fireplace. "I know. It's all I've thought about all afternoon."

"I can't deal with this, Skye." His voice was uncharacteristically soft. "I just can't deal with it. It's gone too far."

"I just want to know what this has got to do with me!" she flared. "My brain is tired from trying to figure out *why*."

"Come and stay with me," he said suddenly. "Let me protect you."

There was a note of pleading in his voice that surprised her. "Oh, Jared. The thing is . . . for how long?"

"Until this is all over."

"That's just it. It may never be over."

His face hardened with anger. "So you're just going to quit photography, and hang out here all alone in this apartment until the killer is ready for you? He knows where you live, Skye. *He can get in*."

"I've got a life, Jared. I have to live it."

"Oh, you call this a life?" He got to his feet, frustration and disgust framing his posture.

She stood as well, wincing in pain, glaring at him across the room. "What is *with* you? I don't understand why you're acting like this."

"If you had a child, you would understand," he said quietly.

Skye felt as if she'd been slapped.

Too late, he realized what he'd done. Reaching toward her, he stepped forward. "Hey, I'm sorry. That was out of line."

Mustering a thin shred of dignity, she said, "If all we are going to do is fight about this, then I guess you'd better go."

"Skye . . . I didn't mean to hurt—"

"It's okay," she said, but her tone belied the words.

"*Don't make me leave you here alone!*" His voice rang with exasperation.

But she did, in the end. As she shut the door firmly behind him, she realized, finally, that this was the way it was going to have to be. Maybe the killer already knew that.

It was her wits against his.

Chapter Twenty-one

SKYE STAGGERED INTO the apartment, her arms laden with library books, and collapsed onto the sofa. The librarian at the main branch downtown had told her that until recent years, not much material on the sexual exploitation of children was available. It was only after accusations of child abuse by various day-care centers gained national attention that the public began to demand information on a subject from which most people naturally recoiled.

To her growing horror, Skye read that one out of every four children was victimized by sexual molestation, by family members or strangers, and that at any given moment in the United States, some 300,000 persons were engaged in activities of the sexual exploitation of children.

During that morning research, Skye found that she could not stand, emotionally, to read for more than a couple of hours before she had to get up and roam restlessly about the apartment, doing sporadic housework or some other mindless chores. She would burst into tears at odd moments.

All those suffering children. It was almost too much to contain.

A section in one book on "chickenhawks" caught her attention and she sat up straighter, causing a mew of protest from Bartholomew, who, as cats will do, had draped himself right smack in her way as she worked. A chicken-hawk, she read, was a man who preyed on boys. The boys were called chickens. A chickenhawk would single out some lonely kid, generally one from a broken home or dysfunctional family, and befriend him, showering him with gifts and money. The molesting would start sometime after, but the bewildered child often confused the attention and even the molestation itself for love. With shame and embarrassment all mixed up with affection, the child would seldom testify against the molester.

But how did the chickenhawk get away with it? And where were magazines like this published and how were they distributed? There were a lot of questions the books didn't even address, much less answer.

And the biggest question of all was, of course: Why had the killer wanted Skye to see this pornography? What was he trying to tell her?

Her eyes were burning. She leaned her head against the soft sofa cushion and closed them. There had to be a way to find these answers. Even more important, it had to be fast.

There was no way of knowing when the killer would make his next move, and Skye wanted to be ready.

"Youth. Sergeant Pendleton speaking."

"Um, Mr.—uh, Sergeant Pendleton? My name is Mary Thornton. I'm a reporter for the *Dallas Times Herald,* and I'm doing an in-depth, journalistic study on child pornography. I wonder if you could put me in touch with an officer who has been on the force for a long time, or who may be retired, who can give me an interview on how the business has grown through the years." *Smooth. Very smooth. Jared would be proud.*

"Oh, sure. That would be Sergeant Hendricks. Worked this division for twenty years. Just retired last year."

"Thank you so much. Could you give me his number?"

"I'm sorry, we don't give out the home numbers of our officers, but I think Hendricks is listed in the phone book."

"Thanks. I really appreciate it."

"No problem."

Skye's hands were shaking so hard she had trouble replacing the receiver. What if they checked out her story? What if they called the *Times Herald* and found out there *wasn't* a Mary Thornton? What if Investigator Ruis got wind of it?

Hell, it was too late to turn back now.

Skye was amazed at how easy it was to gain entrance into some places with the credentials of a big-city newspaper behind you. Like most retired cops, Hendricks was flattered to be asked about his work and eager to talk to her. He gave her directions to his house.

In order to look more convincing, she took along a notebook and a camera. She couldn't remember ever being more frightened. And yet . . . at the same time . . . there was a certain exhilaration. For the first time since this ordeal began, Skye was feeling more in control.

She was *doing* something, instead of sitting back and letting something be done to her. She was fighting back.

Sam Hendricks was big, barrel-chested, and bald, with a paunch. As his meaty hand engulfed Skye's, she pegged him as a former football player. She didn't figure he'd ever had a problem keeping prisoners in line.

"Pleasure to meet you," he boomed in bass tones. Skye glanced around the cozy living room. On every table and wall she saw photographs of children growing up, children grown, grandchildren.

They made a little small talk. Skye did her best to deflect his questions about the newspaper, thinking up short answers based on things Jared had told her. He was genial, but had a cop's eyes, sharp and wary, yet he seemed to suspect nothing. "When I first got into this . . . story," she said finally, "I didn't even know stuff like this existed."

"Most people don't," he said. "In fact, there are police officers who put in a career on the force without ever seeing any. I've seen guys take a look at kiddie porn for the first time and throw up."

That made her feel better.

"Kiddie porn's a big business," he went on, "but now that it's a federal offense to traffic or possess it, it's become very exclusive. You have to belong to the inner circle to get any, and it takes months. Undercover cops try all the time to break in. Most of them fail."

"The inner circle?"

He nodded. "A group of committed pedophiles. Well, there's not just one group. There are hundreds of them all over the country, thousands worldwide. They collect this stuff, trade and sell it."

"And do it?"

"Yes. And do it. There's a group of parents interested in using children for sexual purposes, called the Rene Guyon Society. Their motto is 'Sex Before Eight or It's Too Late.' They're reported to have some five thousand members."

"You've got to be kidding!"

He shook his head. "Then there's the Society of Pedophilia and NAMBLA, the North American Man-Boy Love Association, and the British Pedophile Information Exchange—they want to lower the age of consent to four."

"But why aren't these groups . . . busted . . . or something? Put behind bars?"

"Because they are almost impossible to penetrate. And because obscenity charges are so vague and hard to stick. You have to have some sort of proof that an *individual* has performed an act of sexual assault on a child to get any kind of conviction."

She stared at him. It was all so hard to believe.

"Usually what they do in Juvenile—well, it's called Youth nowadays—what they usually do is put a guy under surveillance once they have reason to believe he's into this stuff, then get a warrant to search a location where they think the goods are stashed. These guys spend an unbelievable amount of money on their collections. You really can't imagine. What the officers look for is proof of sexual assault—and anytime you get a child to pose for pornography, an act of sexual assault has been committed. It also helps if they can get the kids to turn the guys in, but that's even harder."

"Because they consider the guy their friend. I did some reading before I came."

He nodded approvingly.

"How old are these children when this happens?" Skye asked.

"There have been babies six months old who have been penetrated by a grown man's penis."

"Oh, God." She felt sick.

"Most pedophiles have a sex preference and an age preference. With chickenhawks, there are three different age groups: under eight, eight to twelve, and twelve to, oh, about sixteen."

"And what about the children? What happens to the children?"

"Well, obviously they are screwed up for life. First of all, child pornography is almost always deviant sex: sodomy, sadomasochism, what have you. So these kids are exposed to perversion before they even reach puberty. The little girls, especially, are *trained* to be seductive in the photographs. If they don't cooperate, they're drugged." He paused, regarding some of the pictures around the room.

"Poor kids," said Skye. "I can't imagine what becomes of them when they grow up."

"That's just the thing," he said, earnestly leaning forward in his chair. "When they become adults, they can't possibly have any kind of normal love life. At least half of all kids used this way grow up to become suicidal, and they are all neurotic, depressed, alcoholics, drug abusers—you name it. Some of them are downright psychotic."

Skye found herself scribbling furiously, as if she were a real reporter. "How do they . . . circulate . . . this stuff?"

"Well, in some ways it's harder now, because of the new laws, but modern technology has caught up to the problems."

"What do you mean?"

"Well there used to be ads in the backs of adult sex magazines that said things like, 'If you love children and are interested in a career in photography, write to this box number.' They also had bulletin boards in adult book stores where folks thumbtacked index cards with box numbers to contact. In fact, you could buy kiddie porn in adult book stores. They kept it under the counter.

"But nowadays all that's too dangerous for them, so they've taken to using computer bulletin boards, for one thing. Impossible to trace that way. And it's easier than ever before to go into business for yourself as a pornographer."

"Why?"

"Home video cameras and VCRs." His tone was matter-of-fact. "See, before, they had eight-millimeter stuff that had to be developed someplace. Now all they need is a video camera and a couple of VCRs. A chickenhawk can hang out someplace like a bus station, find a likely kid, offer him, say, two hundred dollars and all the food and drugs he wants to make a movie. Then they rent two adjoining motel rooms, put the food and drugs in one room, the camera in another. All weekend they film, then make as many copies as they want, which they can then sell for, say, two hundred apiece. The kid hits the road and disappears. They can carry a whole 'studio' that way, in the truck of their car."

"What about the magazines? How do they publish those?"

"A lot of magazines are published in Europe. Germany, for example, is one of America's biggest suppliers of child pornography. Then, too, you can tell by the quality of the paper that you don't need a lot of expensive equipment. Any legitimate printing business could put out kiddie porn on the side."

Skye's shoulders felt weighted down, as if everything that Sergeant Hendricks was telling her had suddenly become a burden for her to carry around.

"What about the small children? Where do they get them?"

He shrugged. "Sometimes their parents provide them. Sometimes their parents don't even know—remember the case in California of the day-care center?"

Skye nodded. "But I thought pornographers were sleaze bags—you know, the kinds of people who do hang out at bus stations."

He shook his head vigorously. "That's the thing everybody thinks. But there's two things you gotta remember. First of all, not all pedophiles are pornographers, but they nearly all collect it. Secondly—and this is most important, if you ask me . . ." Sam's eyes grew keen. "They are everywhere. There have been suburban soccer coaches and priests found to be chickenhawks, postal workers and police officers . . . in fact, there was a sheriff from a small town near Dallas who was indicted. In my day, I made plenty of busts in nice, middle-class neighborhoods. It's the same with their victims. It could be anybody, Ms. Thornton. *Anybody, anywhere.*"

She could only think in the darkroom. It seemed that it had been years since she developed a roll of film just for fun. Blocking the day—the library books, Sergeant Hendricks, the suffering children—out of her mind, she worked mechanically, developing a nonsense roll of shots she'd taken of Bartholomew one day while he played with a ball of yarn.

She wanted nothing sinister in her darkroom tonight.

The hypnotic *shush* of the washer and the amber glow of the safety light worked their magic on her, and it was into this relative calm that the thought came to her, so stark as to stand alone above all other thoughts:

Someone thinks you are a child pornographer.

Her heart jumped and she caught her breath. How could anybody think such a thing?

"*Anybody. Anyplace,*" Hendricks had said.

According to the killer, it could even be her.

In a glaring, horrifying way, everything that had happened to her was beginning to make sense.

Deadly sense.

Chapter
Twenty-two

SEEING THE PORNOGRAPHY had done something to him. It was as if the anger that had been simmering inside of him for so long had been stirred into a boiling rage. He hated her with a passion that consumed him, body and soul.

Shit-eating fag, she had called him. *Pig.* He would never know what had pulled her from her usual drunken stupor to come searching for him. He would never know how she *knew* to seek him out at Mr. Peterson's, how she got into the house without them hearing her, how she found the Love Room, where he and Mr. Peterson were . . .

That's when she started screaming those names at him. She'd grabbed him by the arm and dragged him, nude, all the way down the street in broad daylight, cursing and shrieking at him every step of the way. Then she slammed him up against the closet door, grabbed his testicles, twisting them until he screamed in pain, beating him on the head and shoulders, calling him shit-eating fag and pig and . . .

That's when she locked him in the closet for three days. A little dark room. No food or water. He cried and begged to be let out until his voice died out, then he pounded until his fists bled.

After that, he was never allowed to see Mr. Peterson

again, and she never looked at him without disgust in her eyes. Once, a couple of weeks later, he found a magazine lying on his bed, with pictures of him and Mr. Peterson. *Animal* was written on the mirror with lipstick.

He didn't know. He'd seen the camera in the Love Room, but he never knew . . .

Sometimes, in the years since, he'd felt cheated, used, by Mr. Peterson, but how could he stay mad? Mr. Peterson was his friend. Mr. Peterson loved him. *She* never spent the kind of time with him that Mr. Peterson did.

"I'm not a bad boy," he said aloud. He would prove it to her, too, after the Great Revelation. After he saved the children, all the children, and the world would be clamoring for more, he would show her how pure and sinless he was, he would show her. She would beg for his forgiveness, and he would take her by that tangled long hair of hers, he would shove her facedown, and he would make her eat shit.

It wouldn't be long now.

Climbing the stairs slowly to the apartment the afternoon after Skye's interview with Sergeant Hendricks, she spotted the silver, heart-shaped balloons before she even reached the top of the stairs. They'd been tied to her doorknob and strained against their ribbons.

"*Surprise!*" Jared and Chelsea popped out from behind the banister as Skye neared the landing. She should have guessed as much.

"Peace offering," said Jared, and as Chelsea squeezed her in a mammoth hug, she melted, just as she suspected he had known she would.

Laughing, she said, "I guess the least I could do is feed you two scoundrels some dinner. Come on in."

"What a pretty house. Oh, a *kitty*!" chattered Chelsea, who sat right down and made immediate friends with the usually shy Bartholomew.

"What's this?" Jared stood by the table, where Skye had piled her stack of library books. He flipped through one.

"It's the connection, Jared. The connection between me and the—" She glanced at Chelsea. "You know."

He pushed the book away as if it were too unpleasant to handle, but said nothing.

Taking him by the hand, Skye led Jared into the bedroom and sat with him on the edge of the bed. Talking quietly, she told him what she'd learned and what she suspected.

He reached over and took her hand. "This scares the hell out of me, Skye."

She looked at his worried face. "Why?"

"Hell, the guy must be following you around . . . watching you . . . Jesus, it gives me the creeps." He got up and began to pace. "You've got to come back with me. Get out of this place. You being alone . . . I can't stand it."

"I'll be all right." Her voice faltered. She wanted to scream to him about how violated she felt, how terrified . . . how guilty. But she said nothing.

There was something more. Something deep within her resisted the idea of giving up her freedom to Jared, even if he did want to protect her. It was almost as if she were afraid, but even as Chelsea's pretty, merry face peeked around the door at them, a little voice inside her said, *Afraid of what?*

"There's something more," he said, getting to his feet and wandering over to the window, where he knelt and glanced nervously out the curtains. Chelsea left. They could hear muffled sounds from the television in the next room.

"What?"

He crossed his arms over his chest. "I've been turning this thing over in my mind, going over and over it. Then this name sort of popped into my mind. I thought it was familiar, so I went down to the newspaper morgue and checked it out." He looked back out the window, as if it were easier than looking at her face. "Some years ago the body of a little boy was found—he'd been sexually assaulted and tortured to death. The evidence strongly suggested that the kid's Sunday school teacher did it, but the evidence was illegally seized and the judge threw the case out of court. The guy walked."

Skye shivered.

"The boy's father went berserk in court. Climbed over the rails and tried to choke the guy to death, but the guards pulled him off. The judge was kind enough not to press charges."

Jared turned around and looked Skye full in the eye. "The father was Clyde Winslow."

"I'm a little teapot, short and stout," sang Chelsea in a falsetto. "This is my han-dle, this is my spout. Tip me o-ver and pour me out!"

Skye and Jared applauded mightily. "What else have you learned in music class at school?"

"I can't remember *everything*, Daddy."

How that child's light has warmed this apartment, thought Skye. She was going to miss the children she saw every day, even though she hardly had a chance to get to know them. Chelsea was a delight. Still, she could hardly concentrate on the evening, after what Jared had told her about Clyde. It would explain a lot of things about his behavior, but it didn't convince her that he could be a murderer of innocent women simply because of what had happened to his son.

Could he?

Stress-induced exhaustion tugged relentlessly at Skye. She found herself staring at Chelsea. Because of the injuries to her pelvis, the doctors weren't sure if Skye would be able to have children or not. At the time they told her, she was in such shock from Paul's death that the news hardly seemed to matter.

Now she felt different.

She looked over at Jared's beaming face and wondered, idly, if he had ever wanted more children.

Out of the blue, a strange feeling came over Skye. She

got up restlessly and wandered into the bedroom. It was like one of those "What's wrong with this picture?" games. Putting all the recent horrors aside, she should be happy. Jared was a good man who seemed to care for her, Chelsea a sweet and loving child. She was no longer alone.

So why couldn't she enjoy it?

Almost against her will, her hands reached into the bedside table drawer and withdrew the snapshot of her and Paul. Her heart quickened and the answer came to her: *It doesn't seem right. If Paul hadn't died, I wouldn't have met Jared*.

Lately she'd been dogged by the feeling that Paul's death was somehow her fault. After all, *her* seat belt had been buckled. Why hadn't she insisted that *he* buckle up? Why hadn't she asked him to slow down?

Recent events only seemed to justify that feeling. If it hadn't been for her, those two women would be alive now. Those babies would have a mother. No matter who was doing the killing, those women were definitely dead, and somehow, someway, it was connected to *her*.

She didn't deserve to be happy, and worse . . . she was *afraid*.

What if, because of her, something happened to Jared and Chelsea?

"So there you are."

Skye jumped at the sound of Jared's voice and turned guiltily, Paul's photograph still in her hands. He saw, and a careful mask fitted over his face.

"I guess we'd better be going now," he said politely.

Fumbling, she replaced the photograph. "I guess so. Chelsea has school tomorrow."

Moving like strangers, they bundled up the reluctant child against the night's cold.

"Will I get to see you tomorrow?" she asked Skye plaintively.

Skye glanced at Jared. "I don't know, sweetheart. We'll see."

Jared turned at the door. "Be careful." He looked as though he was about to say something else but had changed his mind.

It was as if a cold breeze had blown between them. She gave him a chaste kiss on the lips, hugged Chelsea—a little too long?—and closed the door, locking it firmly.

The apartment suddenly seemed so empty.

She moped around, checking windows and doors, apathetic even about her own safety. Maybe it would be better for everyone if he got to her and finished whatever job he had set out to do.

Such glum thoughts weren't very conducive to sleep, and Skye tossed and turned for hours, hearing things in every creak of the old house.

The blackness outside had lightened to pewter when Skye opened her eyes, suddenly and fully awake.

Something . . . maybe a mental alarm clock, but more likely a sound, had awakened her.

What kind of sound? She couldn't even remember. Plumping her pillows, she tried to settle back into sleep when something out of the ordinary caught her vision. She sat up and stared, her heart contracting painfully.

The door leading from her bedroom to the hall hung high on its frame, leaving a gap at the bottom. The corner of a brown envelope jutted into the room from that gap. Someone had tried to push it underneath, but it hadn't fit all the way.

With a dread feeling of certainty, Skye unlocked the door and picked up the envelope.

The block printing said, again, simply *Skye*.

There was a bulge at the bottom just big enough for a roll of film.

Chapter Twenty-three

ACTIVITY. DIVERSION. IT was the only way to keep from cracking up, thought Skye as she dressed methodically. She would not think. She would not feel. She would simply do.

This time she did all the things Investigator Ruis had told her, handling the envelope with her knit gloves, preparing to take it right into the police department. She was going to let them handle it. She wasn't even going to call Jared.

After twenty frustrating minutes of trying to start the car, she decided impulsively that she would later visit the car dealership Jared had told her about. She probably couldn't afford it, but what the hell. It was activity. It was diversion.

It was a little reward to herself for not going crazy.

On the way to the police department, she concentrated on the traffic, blocking out all other thoughts except the here and now. The big gray stone building looked formidable, but she didn't allow herself time for trepidation as she climbed the steps into the front door, past the empty information desk, and up the stairs to the Crimes Against Persons office.

Threading her way through the other desks, she made her way to Investigator Ruis, who was talking on the phone and didn't see her. Without a word, she withdrew the envelope from her bag, plunked it onto the desk, and sat down nearby. The surprise on Ruis's face was genuine.

"Let me call you back later. Something just came up." She hung up the phone.

"When did you get this?" she asked without preamble.

"This morning. I brought it right over. I wore gloves to handle it."

"It doesn't have an address."

"It didn't need one. It was shoved under my door." Skye kept her face and her voice impassive.

For once, Ruis was quiet, drumming her fingers on the desk, studying the envelope. Then she groped around in her desk for a tissue and an X-Acto knife. Holding the corner of the envelope with the tissue, she slit it open with the knife and dumped out the contents. One roll of black-and-white film.

"Same kind of film?"

"Same kind."

"I don't think we've had a body turn up that matches the MO of the other two."

Skye roused herself from her self-imposed stupor long enough to ask a question. "What is an MO?"

"*Modus operandi*. It refers to the methods used by an individual to commit a crime. Repeat offenders usually use the same methods, like leaving behind a calling card. Sometimes it is deliberate. Sometimes it's just habit. The MO for Sharon Smith and Theresa Sanders would be strangulation with a cord of some kind without sexual assault, then moving the body elsewhere without leaving any noticeable evidence."

Skye nodded. "And you say you haven't found anybody who matches that description."

"That's right."

"Don't worry. You will."

Ruis lit a cigarette. "Thanks for bringing this in, Skye. I'll turn it over to the lab and get back to you. I'll probably have some questions, once we know more."

"Fine." Skye made her apathetic way out of the building to the parking lot. It took even longer to get the car going this time than it had back at the apartment. That did it. Without so much as a second thought, she headed in the direction of the car dealership.

It was probably a bad move financially, but what the hell, she thought, you only live once.

It took longer than usual for Investigator Ruis to get the photographs back from the lab. Physical Evidence and Fingerprinting had gone over the envelope and the roll of film microscopically, searching for anything—a hair or clothing fiber—that could give them a clue as to the identity of the sender. She hadn't received the formal report yet, but one of the guys told her that they hadn't been able to turn up anything. They were trying to analyze the ink now.

She spread the eight-by-tens out on her desk. This woman seemed about the same age as Theresa Sanders, although not as pretty. The cat's-head pin was in place on the lapel of her coat.

Her coat. Why was it that they were all wearing coats? The killer must stalk them outside. She made a note of it. What else was similar?

Her hair. She had long dark hair. Not as long as Mrs. Sanders's hair—she'd worn hers in a chignon. More like shoulder-length. Was that significant? So far, none of the women were blonde or short-haired. And none were older women. All were reasonably young—Sharon Smith being the youngest—and all had fairly long dark hair.

They were all photographed after death in what appeared to be the trunk of a car. Apparently it was the same car.

None of the bodies were dismembered or disfigured, and so far none of them had been sexually assaulted. Murdering the women seemed to be the killer's only aim.

And they all had a connection to Skye Meredith.

Wait. That was an assumption. This body hadn't even

been found yet. But then, Skye had brought in the photographs. That made a pretty strong connection.

You can't commit a murder by strangulation, Carmen
knew, without making some bodily contact. With two
bodies pressed together in a struggle, an exchange would
have to be made. Skin chemicals. Clothing fibers. A loose
button.

She prayed that, when the body was found, there would
be some sort of tangible evidence that would give them the
murderer's head on a platter. More and more, Ruis was
convinced, that head would belong to Skye Meredith.

Who else could it possibly be? They didn't have a single
hard suspect in the case. She'd dredged up computerized
lists, cross-matched with the FBI's, of serial killers from
other parts of the country, serial killings which may have
something in common with these suspects wanted in connection with other strangulation deaths of females. She'd
driven herself nearly blind trying to find someone, anyone,
who could connect to these deaths . . . and the only name
she kept seeing in her mind's eye over and over was *Skye
Meredith*.

Leaning back in her chair, Ruis made a mental list of
those connections: One, the photographs, by far the most
compelling connection of all. Two, the same blood type,
underneath one victim's fingernails. Genetic fingerprinting?
Ruis knew she'd need more hard evidence against Skye
before the department would justify that kind of expense,
unless the DA's office ordered it. (And she intended to get
it.) Three, one victim was a client's baby-sitter, and another
victim was a client's mother, which made a connection to
the victims—though how that fit in with murder, Carmen
couldn't begin to guess. She'd leave that up to the shrinks.
Four, those weird little cat's-head pins. They came from the
toy store next door to Skye's studio, and Skye had brought
in a handful herself. Five, no sign of sexual assault. Most
random murders of women by men were related to sexual
assault. Six, the MO. Ligature strangulation could be done

by one woman to another if her adrenaline was pumping and she was determined. Seven, the photographs. Eight, the photographs. Nine, the photographs . . .

Ruis lit one cigarette with the butt of the old. *Dammit!* She was sick of standing over strangled corpses, then having to confront sweet Miss Meredith's innocent baby blues over a set of film negatives which, they both knew, would show a still-warm body.

But what could she do? They'd had to let Methodist minister Walker Railey walk for the attempted murder of his comatose wife, simply because there wasn't enough hard evidence convicting him to make the case in a court of law. It had made them all sick.

But that was an act that had been *done*. This was still going on. What could she do?

By God, there *had* to be a way to stop Meredith.

Before leaving that night, Carmen paid a visit to the new inverted-triangle building that housed City Hall. The Communications Division of the Dallas Police Department, once called Dispatch, had been moved there.

The big, long well-lit room was divided in the middle by a glass wall. On one side, civilian workers took incoming calls and relayed them, by computer, to appropriate desks on the other side, manned by uniformed officers. Each officer was in charge of dispatching those messages to about fifty officers that cruised a certain section, or geographical area, of the city.

It was like walking into a civilized beehive. The softly clattering computers translated some two thousand calls a night into flesh-and-blood responding uniforms. In order to keep it all straight, the Communications officers had to do five things at once with two hands and think along three different trains of thought.

Ruis didn't know how they did it.

She explained to the watch commander about the unusualness of her case, and asked if she could be notified if someone reported finding a woman's body, which fit the MO, in any part of the city.

He said he would do what he could.

She'd left the same message with the officers on deep night watch from Capers. She didn't want an officer unfamiliar with the case to make any careless assumptions.

Then she went home, ate a quick supper, and lay down on her bed fully clothed to get what sleep she could.

Dazed with shock and anxiety, Skye almost didn't notice Tommy standing by the staircase as she mounted the stairs to her apartment. When she did see him, the day's pent-up anger flared. After looking around to make sure his mother was not near, Skye withdrew the magazine from her bag. (She'd taken it to the police department but had decided, impulsively, not to show it to Investigator Ruis.) She handed it to him. "Did you put this in my apartment?"

At first his eyes widened, then he began to look through the magazine with interest. "Getting kinky, are we, Skye?"

She jerked the magazine from him and stuffed it back into the bag. "I asked you a question."

"So you did."

She wanted to hit him right in his smug face. *"Did you put this magazine in my apartment?"*

"No way," he said, stroking his fingertips down her arm. "I like my women with a little . . . experience."

Yanking her arm back as if she had been burned, Skye said, through clenched teeth, "You'd better tell me, you creep . . . Are you putting things under my door?"

"No, but I'd like to put something under your skirt." He grinned.

Skye turned on her heel and hurried up the staircase. She should have known she'd get nothing from Tommy. Now all she wanted was to get away from him.

She could feel his gaze crawling beneath her clothing as she ducked out of his view and fumbled for her keys. She let herself in, slammed the door, locked it, and leaned against it, shaking.

She wasn't safe anywhere.

"*Sh-sh-sh-sh.*" His eyes opened in the darkened room and he looked around. "*Sh-sh-sh-sh.*" What was that? The eyes were there, and they were looking straight at him. "*Sh-sh-sh-sh.*" He sat up. They were ringed around the foot of the bed, all six of them, at head-height, as though standing at attention.

Whispers. His heart began to pound. The eyes had never spoken before. "*Sh-sh-sh-sh.*" He felt the hair on the nape of his neck bristle. More whispers. He strained to hear.

"*One more.*" One more what? Did she have another assistant that he didn't know about?

"*One more.*" The eyes were getting closer, drawing near to him.

"*Sh-sh-sh-sh.*" Whispers.

What was happening? Why, *he* was supposed to have control over the eyes! When did *they* take control? The new ones. The new ones must be their leader.

The eyes were very close.

"*Which one? Who?*" he cried. He thought he had done the job so well. He thought the eyes were pleased. The time for the Great Revelation was drawing close. The book was almost finished.

Were they talking about Skye Meredith? "Yes," he said, "I know there is one more. Skye Meredith. She's the one."

"*Sh-sh-sh-sh.*" He closed his eyes. He couldn't stand to see them anymore. A hiss by the side of his ear, "*One more.*"

"Okay, okay," he stammered. "You mean one more besides her."

"*Sh-sh-sh-sh.*"

He didn't understand! What did they mean? Who?

He opened his eyes. They were gone.

"Wait. Don't go. Tell me what you mean."

He looked all around the room, then sat on the edge of the bed, waiting for them to come back. The room was pitch-black, and for the first time in weeks, he was afraid.

Hammering noises. "Oh, Paul," she groaned, "why do you have to get into these fix-it jobs so early in the morning? Sunday's our only day off." More hammering. Skye fought her way up from sleep and opened her eyes. The clock read 7:30.

The pounding noises grew louder. Someone at the living room door. Drawing on her robe, Skye pulled open the bedroom door.

Investigator Ruis and Sergeant Malone stood out in the hall by the living room door. Two uniformed officers lurked on the stairway.

Skye jolted into full wakefulness. "What's wrong?"

"We need to ask you some questions, if we could," said Ruis, turning. There were dark circles under her eyes as if she hadn't slept all night.

"But it's so early . . ."

"The woman's body has been found and identified, Skye."

She nodded, the blackness covering her again. "Let me come around and open the living room door."

"Do you mind if I start some coffee?" she asked as she let them in.

"Of course not. I could use a cup myself," said Ruis.

While Skye busied herself with coffee maker and cups, Ruis and Malone wandered around the living room area. Skye wondered what they were looking for. Hands shaking, she reached for a cup and it fell to the floor, shattering. She fumbled for a broom.

"Need some help?" Ruis stood at the bar.

"No, I can get it. Thanks."

Once they were all settled in the living room, Ruis got right to the point. "Did you know a Carolyn Harrison?"

She shook her head. "No."

"Are you sure?"

"My appointment book's in the bedroom," Skye said mechanically. "You can check it out yourself." She fetched it and handed Sergeant Malone the book. "I've never heard the name before."

"All right. Can you tell us where you were last Tuesday night?"

Skye's cheeks flamed. "I spent the night with Jared Martin." She ducked her head and took a sip of coffee.

"Would he be willing to verify this statement?"

"I don't see why not."

"What about Wednesday?"

"I've been here, in the apartment, for the last four nights. Alone."

Ruis raised her eyebrows. Skye dropped her eyes.

"Skye, you told me that you could make a connection between the other two victims and yourself, and yet you say you've never heard of Carolyn Harrison?"

"That's right, but I'm sure one will turn up sooner or later." Her own voice sounded dull to her, dead.

"Is there anything else you can tell us that would help us in this case? Anything at all?"

Skye looked from Investigator Ruis to Sergeant Malone. There was a keenness to their expressions that made her uncomfortable. *They've made up their minds that I did it*, she thought. *That's why they came this morning.* Suddenly she was afraid to tell them anything. She decided not to mention the pornography. It had been a long pause, but still she shook her head in response to the question, mentally cursing the flush she felt spreading over her face.

"Think about it, Skye," said Ruis pointedly. "Anything at all."

She knows I'm lying. "No."

Malone leaned forward in his chair. "You realize that this all looks very bad for you, Skye, don't you?"

"Yes," she whispered.

"I'm afraid I have some more news you may not like."

"What's that?"

"We've got a search warrant which entitles us to search your home, car, and studio."

"*Search?* What would you be looking for?"

He was silent.

"Oh, you mean evidence. You want to search my home and studio for evidence that would incriminate me." She began to laugh. "This is really funny, do you guys know that? There's a crazy person out there murdering innocent victims and stalking me, yet you think *I* did it. That's hilarious." Her laughter grew to a shrill pitch.

They said nothing.

Skye struggled to get hold of herself. "I have nothing to hide, nothing at all. You are free to search every nook and cranny I own. I'll even help you." She stood up and made a sweeping gesture with her arm. "Shall we begin?"

And then, before she could help it, she could hear the sounds of her own laughter careening off the walls of her small, silent apartment.

The officers stared at her. She wondered if she was losing her mind.

Chapter
Twenty-four

THE LEGAL WARRANT presented to Skye gave the officers the right to conduct a "complete search of the premises and property, including all buildings and vehicles, both inside and outside of the property," and gave permission to "take from . . . premises and property, any letters, papers, and materials or any other property or things which they desire as evidence for criminal prosecution in the case or cases under investigation." She understood that they were trying to get in touch with Mrs. Thomas for a similar search of the rest of the house.

Everything seemed unreal. Never had she felt more helpless or out of control. *Don't you see,* she wanted to shout, *I am the victim!*

Investigator Ruis began giving the uniformed officers instructions. Skye sat down on the window seat in the bay window, out of the way, and watched while Malone started riffling through books in the bookcase. In a moment, one of the uniforms joined him. Investigator Ruis and the other officer went into the bedroom.

"Skye, dear, what on earth is happening?" Mrs. Thomas. Skye got to her feet. Sergeant Malone reached the woman first. "Ma'am, we are conducting a police search of these premises. Are you the landlady?"

"Why, yes, but—"

"I'd like to have a word with you, out in the hall, please."

Skye could hear the deep rumble of Malone's voice, the surprised protests of Mrs. Thomas. She sat on the window seat and closed her eyes.

"Skye?" Investigator Ruis stood in front of her. "I need your help in the darkroom, please."

She struggled to her feet and followed the woman. She could hear drawers opening in the bedroom and her cheeks burned at the violation of her privacy. She wanted to go get Paul's picture and hold it, so that no one else could touch it. Instead, she waited passively for instructions from Ruis.

"Now, I don't want to damage any sensitive negatives or undeveloped film, Skye. That's why I called you. I'd like to either take a look at it here or take it back to the department."

"There's really nothing sensitive in here," she said, opening the cabinets. "These are the chemicals for developing, the paper for contact sheets and photographs, instructions from film companies . . ." She opened each cabinet in kind and stood back while Investigator Ruis rummaged through them.

"Investigator Ruis?" One of the uniforms, a young, attractive man, stood in the doorway. "Should we take these?" He held up two letters in Paul's handwriting.

Skye's hand shot out before she had time to think, grabbing the letters from his hand. "If you think letters from my dead husband constitute evidence, you're, you're . . ." Hot tingles of rage surged through her body. Clutching the letters tightly, she stalked into the kitchen, where she collapsed onto a barstool, struggling to untangle the Gordian knot of her emotions.

She felt a cool hand on her shoulder. "He was just doing his job," said Investigator Ruis. "I know this is hard on you. Just bear with us a little longer."

Surprised at the kindness in Ruis's tone, Skye took a deep

breath, then gestured toward the refrigerator. "There are several rolls of undeveloped film in there, in the door shelf. You're welcome to take them and have them developed."

"Thank you." Ruis opened the refrigerator, found the film, and dropped the rolls into her purse. "Skye, I need to ask you something."

"What now? Haven't I told you everything?"

"Yes. But I thought you might be interested in telling it to a lie detector machine. If you are truly innocent, the examination could help to clear you."

To her horror, Skye felt her telltale cheeks flush deeply. She had to look away from those hard, probing eyes. A memory seared into her consciousness . . . her first summer job as a cashier at a discount store. Money had turned up missing at the final evening count and all the cashiers had submitted to a lie detector exam. Skye, a naively honest country girl who felt guilty if anyone even looked at her with suspicion, had been so frightened of all the wires and the stern-faced examiner that she failed the test and was fired. The shame of that day burned into her still. If she'd flunked a lie detector test over something so simple as petty theft, imagine what would happen with a murder charge hanging over her head.

Ruis was watching her.

Skye shook her head miserably. "I'd rather not," she heard herself saying, and squirmed on the barstool. Ruis couldn't hide the expression on her face from Skye. It was *disgust*.

Shortly afterward, Ruis went out into the hall and spoke to Malone. He came back in and continued the search. Skye wondered where Ruis had gone. Her heart was hammering in her chest. It had occurred to her that she might need a lawyer.

Before long, Ruis was back in the apartment, standing over Skye like a disapproving parent. She waved car registration papers in Skye's face.

"You just bought this car," she said accusingly. "Just this week."

"That's right," said Skye. "Yesterday, in fact. I was having trouble with mine, so I bought a newer used one."

Malone and Ruis exchanged a significant look.

"What's the matter with that?" she asked. "Do I have to check with you before I do anything?"

"Where is your old car?" asked Ruis, her eyes narrowed.

"Back at the dealership, I guess. Unless he's sold it by now."

"I'll check it out," said Malone. "When we're through here, you go on and search the studio. We can't search the rest of the house until Mrs. Thomas signs a permission statement, anyway. I'll go to the dealership and see if we can find the other car."

Looking from one to the other, a cold fist closed over Skye's heart, and she was more afraid than ever before.

Moses Malone was angry. As Carmen was finishing up some paperwork, he came up to her desk and slammed down a large brown envelope with *Skye* written on it in block print.

"Check this out. Found it in her desk after you left."

Carmen opened the envelope and withdrew the kiddie porn magazine. She looked at him.

"Same kind of envelope as the others, only larger. Same handwriting. She lied to us."

"I could have told you that."

He paced the floor in front of her desk, his brow furrowed in concentration. "Damn car dealerhip was closed. Can't get in touch with the guy. Must have gone fishin'."

"Well, one thing's for sure. He's not going to sell her car when he's closed. It can wait until tomorrow."

He whirled and put his hands on her desk. "I don't know what kind of game that girl is playing, but we're fixin' to break it wide open." Malone's Texas drawl was always more pronounced when he was upset.

Carmen lit a cigarette. "So now you see I'm not just whistling Dixie where Skye Meredith is concerned."

He ignored the jibe. "A few carpet fibers from the trunk of her old car could damn near make the case, if it matched with the fibers forensics found on the victims. That and any other evidence that might be there. Hell, it all might be here. The cord used for strangling, personal effects of the victims . . . who knows?"

"Not if she cleaned it out before she traded it," said Carmen drily.

"Shit." He paced some more.

"Isn't this supposed to be your day off?" Carmen teased.

He acted as if he hadn't heard. "Goddamn media are having a field day. They're throwing the words *serial killer* around like lawn fertilizer."

"Right," said Carmen, "and this time it's not bullshit."

"Very funny." He ran his hand over his eyes. "I'm halfway tempted to leak Meredith's name to them as a possible suspect."

Carmen shook her head. "Not till we've got harder evidence. You know that, Doc." She didn't mention that the press would go nuts if word became known about the rolls of film and the photographs. Even the DA's office didn't know about that yet.

He rubbed his hands over his eyes. "The goddamn brass are ridin' my ass like you wouldn't believe. We don't get a break on this case soon, they'll stick me over in Records behind a desk till the day I retire. Count on it." He stopped pacing. "Shit, I'm pissed off. Don't even know why."

"Well, I do," she said. "Meredith lied to you." Malone's personal code of honesty was rock-hard. Anytime he knew he'd been lied to, he never forgot or forgave the liar.

"I was willing to give that girl the benefit of the doubt," he said, "then she had to go and lie. That and sell her car. It don't look right, and it pisses me off." He leaned forward on her desk. "I want her under surveillance, starting today."

"You read my mind. Remember, I'm still on duty." She grinned.

"Just be careful, will ya? I don't want to have to fish your body out of some creek somewhere. Call in however many officers you need to help." He turned and stalked off.

He was right. A good surveillance required at least two officers, but she wasn't ready to call anybody else in just yet. She wanted one night to herself to watch that house and think. It wasn't official procedure, but she was willing to get chewed out later. For now, Ruis was glad to have an official excuse for following Skye Meredith around, but one thing bothered her. Something that just didn't ring true. She picked up the child pornography magazine and fingered it thoughtfully.

This was a puzzle piece that didn't fit in anywhere, and for the life of her, she couldn't place it. *But I will,* she thought, *if it's the last thing I do.*

Bartholomew was missing. "Here, kitty, kitty . . . Bartholomew . . ." called Skye, up and down the street in front of the house, up and down the alley behind. He must have been frightened by all the commotion and slipped out of an open door. Still, it wasn't like him not to return in the evening. Skye called until she was hoarse, then dragged herself up to her cold apartment, where she moped around, missing him terribly.

"Silly old cat," she said under her breath. "How could you do this to me?"

Her whole life was out of kilter and she had an awful, skin-crawling feeling, wishing she could be anywhere other than where she was, wishing she could turn back the clock, wishing she could make sense of it all.

She wanted to call Jared, but what good would that do? Chelsea was still staying with him, and besides, she didn't know what she would say.

It was as if someone had upended her life, and shaken her so badly that she could hardly keep her balance. Mrs.

Thomas, furious at the police search, was not speaking to her. *Maybe she thinks I'm a criminal,* she thought. And what else should the woman think? Police officers had searched the entire house, Skye's workplace, and her car. It didn't look good.

It was dark. Skye turned on every light in the place and the television as well. It was bad enough to be alone. She didn't want to have to listen to the sounds of her own loneliness, as well.

The car drove up three houses down and across the street and parked at the curb. He stood in the shadows, watching, as a woman got out and walked toward Skye's place. She, too, moved in the shadows. Once in a while he caught a glimpse of her underneath the glow of a streetlamp. She had thick, dark, glossy hair that swung at her shoulders and wore a pair of binoculars around her neck. Directly across the street, she stopped and melted into the moving blackness underneath a tree.

He could hear the whispers but he couldn't see the eyes. What should he do? He wished he could understand what the whispers were saying.

For a long time he waited.

There was no sign of movement, so the woman must still be there. What was she doing? Why was she watching Skye Meredith's house?

The whispers grew so loud that he was afraid she might hear them, and though he strained to listen, he still could not make out the demands.

Maybe she was one of the assistants. Then why didn't she go in? There had been something familiar about her stride, the swing of her hair . . . something he knew . . . something he had seen . . .

Of course! He knew who she was.

He had to get rid of her now, there was no doubt about it. He had to get rid of her before the plan could unfold. She would get in the way of the Great Revelation, she would mess everything up. Why, she might even take *credit* for it!

Moving soundlessly across the grass, one step at a time, walking so, so slowly that no one would be able to hear, he reached into his coat, withdrew the cord, and wrapped it around both fists.

He moved diagonally across one yard to the side of another house, glancing once at Skye's window across the street. Lights still blazed from both bay windows.

Concentrate. He had to block out even the whispers. Stealth. He had learned stealth and surprise. He was experienced at it.

He was behind her now, moving from shadow to shadow. She heard nothing. Stupid, like most women. She raised the binoculars to her eyes and he waited. They would get in the way. He held his breath.

The binoculars lowered and he sprang, whipping the cord around her neck and tightening it in the fluid motion he'd learned.

She responded with a strength he hadn't counted on, lightning reflexes he hadn't faced before. A sharp elbow jabbed his solar plexus while a heel crunched down on his instep.

Surprised, he doubled over, but didn't loosen his grip. Gagging, she fought to loosen the cord. A dog barked someplace. He felt her weaken, then she reached back a hand and clawed his face, digging into his eyes with long fingernails. With her other hand she grabbed his genitals and squeezed with all her remaining strength. With a yelp, he lost his grip, but felt her crumple into a heap at his feet.

Panting, his heart hammering, he heard the voices screaming, screaming, *No, no, no, no* . . . and he covered his ears, but the noise only grew louder. *Someone would hear them,* he knew it, and why were they screaming? He'd done what they wanted, hadn't he?

What did they want? What did they want?

Clumsily he gathered the inert form in his arms and staggered for his car, dumping her into the trunk, racing around to the front, jumping into the front seat, gunning the engine.

"*What do you want?*" he screamed as the car screached away from the curb, and from some hell, a demon voice shrieked into his ear, and what he heard filled him with excitement and fear.

And then, at long last, he knew what he must do.

Chapter Twenty-five

IT WAS GETTING late. Time for bed. Still, Skye had a restlessness about her, as if something were all wrong but she didn't know what. It was a feeling. Nothing more. The truth was, she was afraid to go to bed.

Strange. She'd gone to sleep the past few nights without any particular fearfulness, in spite of all that had happened. It felt as if someone were watching her, right here in the apartment, watching every move she made as she rinsed out the coffeepot and wiped off the counters. It gave her the shivers down the back of her neck.

Flicking on the darkroom light as she went, she moved into the bedroom, unbuttoning her shirt and thinking about a bath. Almost involuntarily, she looked at the floor in front of her bedroom door and froze, her hand on a button.

A brown envelope, just the corner of it, poking innocently underneath her door.

No, no. Please God, not another one.

There was writing on this one, a message of some kind. With a morbid curiosity, she unlocked the door and picked up the envelope, which also contained a roll of film.

It said, *For Your Eyes Only*.

What did that mean?

She reached for the phone, then stopped. She couldn't

call the police. She was already a suspect. If they knew she had another roll of film, they might arrest her on the spot.

Jared. What good would that do? He couldn't very well drag Chelsea out of bed and come just because she called.

She was going to have to handle this one on her own.

Keep calm. It was the most important thing. She couldn't give in to the terror that gripped her, couldn't let it control her. She had to be in control.

"Courage means doing what you are afraid of, in spite of the fear," Jared had said.

Suddenly, like the scales falling away from the Apostle Paul's eyes on the road to Damascus, Skye could see the situation—indeed, her whole life—in a new, ice-clear way. And it left her cold with fury. Someone was methodically trying to destroy her life. At this very moment, he stalked her, a deer in the telescopic sights of his high-powered weapon.

And what was she doing? She was stumbling from trap to trap in blind panic, providing him, it would seem, with great sport.

Still gripping the envelope, Skye bolted from the apartment, down the stairs, out the door, and onto the lawn.

"*Goddamn you!*" she shouted, holding the envelope over her head in her fist. "*If it's me you want, then why don't you just come and get me!*" Chest heaving, she stopped her tirade and listened. Brittle wind creaked through stark tree limbs. "*You're a spineless, miserable coward!*" she shrieked. "*Come out of the dark and show yourself!*"

Across the street, a curtain parted at a downstairs window. Frustration and fury battling within her, it was all Skye could do not to throw a rock toward the prying window. At that moment, she believed that if the killer did show himself, she could beat him with her bare fists.

Whirling on one foot, she slammed into the house. Mrs. Thomas was out. She was alone. Stomping up the stairs, she stormed into her own apartment and plunked down onto the couch. Only then did she notice the cane, leaning against the coffee table. She permitted herself a small grin.

Eventually her breathing returned to normal and she began to feel sheepish. Her tantrum had accomplished nothing except possibly endangering her more, but at this point, she was too bitter to care. With a deep sigh, she rubbed her eyes. There was still the film to be tended to.

Resolutely she headed toward the darkroom, but was stopped short by a pounding on the door.

Icicles of fear pricked her skin. *The door wasn't even locked*. She looked around the room, trying to think. A sharp letter opener lay on the coffee table. Picking it up, she inched her way over to the door.

"Who is it?" she squeaked.

"Mutt and Jeff Ice Cream Delivery Service." Skye flung back the door. There stood Jared and Chelsea, holding a hand-packed gallon of ice cream from the same gourmet shop they'd stopped at that day so long ago.

"What the hell are you doing here?" demanded Skye. She was frightened to see them. Anyone who got near her, it seemed, wound up in terrible danger.

"We watched a scary movie and Chels got spooked so we went out for a dose of The Treatment," explained Jared, cavalierly sweeping into the room, followed by the giggling child in question.

"You can't stay," insisted Skye, holding open the door with stubborn persistence.

Jared stopped and examined Skye's face. His gaze fell to the envelope she still carried. "Go find some bowls, Pooh Bear," he ordered, still staring at Skye. Chelsea wandered into the kitchen. "What's going on here?" he asked Skye.

"Not here," she said. "We can talk privately in the darkroom." She headed that way. Jared got Chelsea settled in front of the coffee table with her ice cream, the TV tuned to a cable rerun of one of the *Ghostbusters*. "We have some things to do in the darkroom," he told her. "You enjoy the movie. Don't eat too much ice cream, and when we're through, we'll come out and watch the end of the movie with you, okay?" She nodded, already absorbed in the show.

Jared's presence seemed to fill up the tiny room as he shut the door behind him. "This isn't your concern," she told him stiffly. "You should take Chelsea and go home."

"What's the matter with you?" Jared crossed his arms over his chest. "Don't you understand what it means to love somebody?"

Skye blinked and recoiled as if she'd been slapped. "Of course I do," she mumbled, automatically setting out trays and chemicals.

"Can't you accept the fact that I love you? That Chelsea and I are intimately concerned with what goes on in your life? That when you hurt, we hurt?"

"But I don't *want* you to hurt!" she flung at him. "Dammit, Jared, can't you *see* that? I don't want anything to happen to you!"

"And *we* don't want anything to happen to *you*, either, so let us *help* you." His voice, raised in frustration, echoed off the narrow walls.

"You can't," she said woodenly. "This is something I have to face alone."

It was all he could do to keep from screaming. The closet was too small and too dark and he couldn't see the eyes—maybe there wasn't enough room—but he could *hear* them! It was so *loud*! Why couldn't *everyone* hear them?

Was it this way for Jesus? He thought surely it must have been. God spoke to Jesus, so loudly it must have hurt His ears, and yet, nobody else could hear it! And so they crucified Him!

But they wouldn't crucify *him*. No way. No how. The eyes would see to that. The triumphant shouts echoed so loudly he fancied the walls were shaking. (Of course, they weren't. That would be crazy, to think they really were.)

The eyes were shrieking exultant praise for his brilliance! It was so perfect, so pure . . . He couldn't wait until he could add this part to the book. *What an incredible ending!*

They were all here. Just as if he had planned it. In fact, the more he thought about it, the more he believed that, yes, he *had* planned it, it had all been his own brilliant design. All he had to do was *will* it to happen, and it did.

After all, didn't Jesus raise a man from the dead just by willing it?

Since we have so great a crowd of witnesses, let us lay aside every encumbrance . . . That is exactly what he had done. He had laid aside encumbrances. But this . . . this was *better* than bringing some old dead guy to life.

This was a child. A sweet, pure, angelic, innocent *child*.

Not ten feet away from him. Just one closet door away.

And he, *he* would be her savior.

Jared was shaking his head. There was no getting rid of him, so she ignored him instead, and began preparing the film for developing, pushing aside all emotional considerations and concentrating on the job at hand. With each step of the developing process, Skye tried not to think as she waited for the soft *ding* of the timer. Jared's presence in the room was a powerful reminder that, try as she might, Skye could not live her life in a vacuum.

When it came time to turn on the light and wipe off the negatives with the sponge-covered tongs, Skye thought she was prepared. She held them up to the light.

"No. It can't be. It can't be."

"What?" Jared hadn't got a close look.

Fumbling now, dropping things, she prepared a tray of print developer and acidic stop-bath solution. It couldn't be what she thought. It had to be something else. Had to be. Jared lurked at her shoulder.

At first she put the negative in the printing frame the wrong side up, and nearly ruined it, then she underexposed the negatives. It was all right. She'd be able to see enough.

By the dim amber glow of the safety light, the woman's image came to life.

She'd been right.

Skye Meredith was looking at photographs of *herself*, in front of the studio, going into Jared's apartment, coming out of the police department, in front of her apartment.

Her knees went weak and she sank onto the stool.

"Jesus," whispered Jared.

What did it mean?

In the next instant, the light went out.

"What the—Chelsea?" said Jared in a sharp tone. Skye fumbled for the switch.

Nothing.

"It's this old house," she said nervously, reaching for the door.

"Wait." Jared's voice was tense. "I'll go check it out. You stay here."

Something in his tone commanded obedience, and she waited dutifully while the door opened and shut and she felt the emptiness of a room without Jared.

Crash.

The door shook as a heavy weight slammed against it. There was a muffled shout, and another smash on the other side of the door.

Skye gasped. Heart pounding, she fumbled her way to the door, took the knob, turned it, and pushed.

Locked.

No. She shoved against it fruitlessly, then sprang across the room for the other door.

It, too, was locked.

She was trapped.

For the space of a full breath, Skye stood in the pitch-black of her own aloneness and realized what a fool she'd been.

From the other side of the door came a sickening thud, a cry cut short, and another rattling crash.

The doorknob clicked.

"Jared!"

The cry went unanswered, the door swung open, and

Skye backed into the opposite door, groping cabinets for something, anything, she could use as a weapon.

A low, masculine chuckle. "It's time now," said the voice. "Your turn. The Great Revelation is near."

Her heart seemed to swell to twice its size, crowding her throat.

"You are an evil bitch," said the voice, moving toward her. "And I am going to destroy you forever, and save the children."

Jared's voice, drifting up from the kitchen floor, was faint, otherworldly. "Get out, Skye," he whispered. "Get . . . Chelsea . . ."

"You have used the children for your filthy purposes long enough," interjected the voice—a vaguely familiar voice. "But that's okay. I've saved them all. The world will know all about it when the Great Revelation reveals my plan, when the whole world will want to read my book."

"*Chelsea!*" Skye cried. There was no answer.

"I have written it all down, so that everyone can read about my plan as it unfolded. I even have pictures." Another disembodied chuckle.

"*Chelsea! Sweetheart, where are you?*"

"My pictures will illustrate the book. The President will like that."

"P-President?" *Dear God in Heaven, where was Chelsea?* "What have you done with the little girl?"

"What have I *done* with her? I've *saved* her. And now you can't avoid your destiny," he said. "I know all about your wicked games. I'm sick of them, and I'm sick of you. I've played the game before but I'm not going to anymore."

"Please tell me where you put the little girl. If you hurt her, I'll—"

"You'll what? Take her picture? The Great Revelation will never allow it. *I* will take her picture. All the people will like it. Jesus loves me, this I know, for the Bible tells me so."

Jared groaned and retched. The man was so close she

could smell him. She put her hand on the tray, which, she knew from years' experience and feel, was full of the deadly stop-bath solution, and flung it in the direction of his voice.

He shrieked, staggering backward.

Skye shoved past him. "*Chelsea!*" she screamed, running, stumbling through the den, plowing into the coffee table, hands held straight out before her. Desperately she felt along the couch, hoping against hope . . . but she knew, she *knew* that the child was gone.

A madman had taken her.

She could hear him behind her, roaring like an enraged beast. *God help me,* she mumbled, scrambling to the door, flinging it open. Slipping, falling a little, she plunged down the stairs in the dark. Behind her, the apartment door slammed against the wall. He was right behind her.

Where could she go? The keys. She didn't have her car keys.

There was no time to call the police. Staggering, she ran as fast as her legs would allow through the parlor, toward the kitchen, shrieking Chelsea's name, groping over furniture whenever she fell into it, knowing, even so, that it would be empty, fighting panic and despair.

"I've saved the children," he yelled, "and you must die, just as the other one did, just as they all did!"

Her foot hooked onto a chair leg and she fell, hard. Something glass fell beside her with a shatter.

"There you are! I can find you, bitch!"

Whimpering slightly, she struggled to her feet. Into the kitchen. The kitchen. *Where did Mrs. Thomas keep her knives?*

Furniture falling in the parlor. "I saved the little girl. I *saved* her! She is the first one, the first witness of the Great Revelation. Soon she will love me. They will *all* love me. The eyes told me."

Opening drawers, groping, rummaging in the dark. He

was coming, shouting, "Your stud will *die,* just like the other one. The eyes know all, *the eyes know all.*"

The butcher knife. It was heavy. He was in the room and she was backing, backing, until she bumped against the cool, hard wall. She held her breath.

His voice fell to a whisper, a plaintive, begging tone. "Come on. You can join the eyes. You can have the power. Don't you want the power? The eyes have the power, you know." He whimpered. "I'm afraid of them now. They want you. When they have you, I won't be afraid anymore, don't you see?"

A laugh, long, loud, and demented. "I know you're in here, bitch. I don't need the light to find you. I can always find you, just like I found the others. I have a present for you." His voice purred now, syrupy. "A little cord here, so smooth and pleasant. It doesn't hurt, you know. None of the others even cried out. It will be over before you know it, and you can join the eyes."

A black shape, blacker than the darkness. Was she blacker than the darkness, too? Could he see her? Had the stop bath missed his eyes and only burned his face?

He lunged, and she thrust the knife up and out. It met resistance, went deep. He screamed, his voice filling the room like the wail of a banshee.

Chapter Twenty-six

THE MAN'S BODY was heavy on her feet. Trembling violently, Skye, holding on to the kitchen cabinet, disentangled her feet and stepped over him. The phone. She had to get to the phone and call the police.

She stumbled over to the kitchen table. There was a wall phone next to it. She tried the light switch. Still no electricity. Her hand found the phone, pulled the receiver away, held it to her ear. Nothing. No dial tone, nothing.

"Hello? Hello?" She jiggled the connection, then ran her hand down the cord. It had been cut in two.

He must have cut her phone lines, too, before he came into the darkroom.

Jared.

Groping her way over the inert form, Skye hurried through the dark house, stumbling here and there, and lumbered up the stairs, her legs giving way with fatigue and fear.

"*Jared?*" she called.

The sound of a moan. She hurried toward it, stopping once to fumble in a drawer for a flashlight.

"*Jared!*"

He lay in a heap on the floor where they'd left him. A puddle of blood pooled beneath his head.

She fell to her knees in front of him and lifted his head. He cried out. Skye shone the flashlight closer. Through a nasty gash on the back of his head, she could see the white of his skull. When she touched it gingerly, the scalp pressed inward, as if on a baby's "soft spot."

"He . . . took . . . Chelsea . . ." His face was ghost-white in the eerie glow of the flashlight.

"I know. I know." She kissed him. It was a miracle of courage that he had been able to retain consciousness. "It's going to be all right, Jared. I'm going to get you some help." She started to get up, but he grasped her arm with a bloody hand.

"You've got to find her." The words came out in a rush of air. He stopped, panting, his face coated in a sheen of sweat. "I tried to stop him . . . I tried . . ."

"I've got to call an ambulance, Jared. You're hurt badly. The police will find Chelsea."

"*No!*" His grip was surprisingly strong. "It will be too late by then. Skye—" He cried out. She gathered him in her arms, holding him tightly, the warmth of his blood soaking through her shirt. His hands were ice-cold.

"Jared—" Her voice broke. "Hang on, Jared."

"Skye . . . Chelsea . . . my baby . . ." He choked, gagged, and a tear ran out the corner of his eye and down to his ear.

"Jared, sweetheart, he can't hurt her. He's dead."

"Please. Promise me."

"I can't leave you."

"Find . . . Chelsea . . ." His voice was fading. He went limp in her arms.

"Jared . . . *Jared.*"

She put her lips to his ear and said, "I love you."

She had to move fast. Struggling to her feet, she hurried into the bedroom and yanked the spread off her bed and put it over Jared. Led by the flashlight's beam, she found her purse, then hurried down the stairs, through Mrs. Thomas's parlor.

At the kitchen door, she hesitated, revulsion rising with bile in her throat. A wave of weakness washed over her and she broke into a cold sweat. Timidly she shone the flashlight into the room.

He was still there, wadded into himself in an unnatural pose. Taking a deep breath, Skye steadied the flashlight and shined it straight into the man's face.

She gasped, and the flashlight slipped from her sweaty palm, rattling onto the floor and dousing the room in darkness. Skye groped for it. It wouldn't come back on. Willing her mind to think through the haze of shock, she inched around the black form sprawled on the floor, reaching for the back-door knob. She would run next door—no, wait—that would take too much time. There would be too many questions. There was a convenience store down the block with a pay phone. She'd go there. She would call 911. She would ask for an ambulance, and she would ask for Carmen Ruis.

She put her hand on the doorknob—and a cold fist closed over her ankle.

Screaming, Skye lunged into the door and out onto the porch, dragging dead weight with her foot, kicking and screaming, hysteria taking hold, adrenaline pumping.

To the right of the porch leaned a shovel. Skye's fingers curled around it. Whirling, she swung downward, heard the *clang* as metal met skull, felt the vibrations to her elbows, and the clutching hand went limp from her ankle.

She was free.

Skye's new Chevy skidded into the parking lot. She parked diagonally in front of her studio. Fumbling with the keys, she dropped them twice before finally getting the door unlocked. There was something eerie about being at the studio late at night. There were no traffic sounds in the parking lot, no sunlight streaming through the decorative blinds on the front windows, only the jingle of the front bell

as Skye, limping heavily but still caneless, let herself in and
made her way to the counter.

Pawing through her drawers with shaking hands, she
finally found what she was looking for and sat down,
panting, on the stool to stare at the name in front of her.

It was an invoice from Metroplex Messenger Service.

She had never known his name. She'd never even asked
it. Most of the time, she'd hardly spoken to him.

Yet he had murdered because of her, stalked her, kidnapped a child.

Why? *Why?*

No time to think about it. She scanned the invoice for the
deliveryman's name.

Eddie Layton.

A simple, innocuous name.

Don't waste time. Hurry.

Somehow, knowing the enemy made it easier. Having a
name spurred her to purposeful action. No more dithering.

She pulled out the phone book and looked up Eddie
Layton. He lived surprisingly close to her. Her hope was
that he had taken Chelsea to his home, then driven back out
to Skye's.

She tried not to think about what would happen if he had
left the child in a remote or deserted area. Now that he was
dead . . . they might never find her.

Busy. Stay busy. Skye copied down the address, trying
not to think about Jared. Though she'd waited for the
sounds of the sirens before leaving the store, she had no
way of knowing if he would recover from that terrible
wound to his head.

Although uniformed police would probably meet the
ambulance at her apartment, since there had been two
assaults, she'd left an urgent message for Carmen Ruis,
anyway.

Sunday night in Dallas. Midnight. There was a surprising
amount of traffic. Spinning rubber, Skye spun the compact
car out in front of two others and entered a drag race with

life, dodging in and out of traffic like a race car driver on PCP. She prayed she wouldn't get stopped on a traffic citation.

Jared.

Chelsea.

It was all she could think, over and over in a rhythmic chant, all she could see, their faces superimposed on her windshield.

Somehow, these two precious people had become her life.

And she'd been looking the other way.

She hadn't been afraid of death.

She'd been afraid of *love*.

And now . . . Jared . . . Chelsea . . . The string of lights blurred, and she pounded the steering wheel, cursing her own blindness.

Skye threaded her car slowly through the parked cars on the street, looking for the right number on the apartment building, which had an older, tireder look about it than the other buildings in the area, as if it had staked first claim, then been swallowed up by flashier developments and eventually overlooked altogether.

There. The numbers were irregular but the names were on the mailboxes. Still, she almost missed it. The first-floor apartment was tucked into a shadowy back corner of the building, almost hidden from view by a large trash dumpster. It was easy to see how Eddie could come and go at all hours without attracting attention.

The front door was unlocked. It creaked as she pushed it open. The walls in the cramped room were dingy. In one corner, a little pool of light shone from a tiny lamp on a small table, next to a battered old typewriter and a neat stack of paper.

On a shelf, in a shadowy corner of the room, lay Bartholomew's head.

Dumbstruck, Skye froze, too horrified even to scream, too shocked to grieve.

"Chelsea?" She had meant to shout it out, but the shock of finding the poor cat's head had rendered her voiceless. Her heart was seized by fear and dread.

"*Chelsea!*" The cry was wrenched from a place so deep within that it had no name.

A moan, eerie in its lonesome simplicity. She hurried toward it, blocking out everything except the child.

Chelsea sat cross-legged on the bed, her hands tied behind her, adhesive tape over her mouth. Her turquoise eyes were wide with terror, the pupils dilated.

Shaking with relief, struggling not to cry, Skye knelt on the bed and gathered the child into her arms.

Moses Malone stood slope-shouldered in Eddie Layton's apartment, struggling valiantly to believe that somehow, by some miracle, Carmen had made it.

He was not alone in the apartment. Investigators from Capers and Physical Evidence moved about, struck silent by the sure knowledge that one of their own was dead, brutally murdered by the apartment's occupant.

Investigator Hacker, a young man just transferred out of Patrol, who'd had a bit of a crush on Carmen, appeared at Malone's elbow, grim-faced. "The closet," he said, his voice choked.

Malone followed him to a hall closet which contained an assortment of handbags. Hacker dug the wallet from one of the bags and handed it to Malone. The lovely face of Theresa Sanders smiled out from the driver's license photo. Across from it was a snapshot of Theresa cuddling two babies.

He nodded and turned away. An old typewriter on a shaky table across the room drew his attention.

Fascinated, he drew near.

Chapter One

The dark sky laughing children seeing blindness is the joy.

"My God." With a heavy heart, he flipped through the manuscript pages. Sometimes page after page of narrative jumbled together. None of it made any more sense than the first page had.

Next to the table was another closet with the door gaping open. On the inside of the closet door hung a large bulletin board, covered with newspaper clippings. Leaning forward, Malone read some of the headlines: "California Day-Care Center Indicted for Child Molesting," "Angry Mob Surrounds New York Day-Care After Reports of Child Abuse," "Austin Day-Care: Child Porn Ring?"

He wished . . . oh, God, how he wished . . . that he knew what all this had to do with one of the brightest, kindest detectives he'd ever worked with. A friend. No. More like a daughter.

He should have gone with her. He should have realized she was losing her objectivity and was just headstrong enough to act on it, just independent enough to scorn help.

Aw, hell. It didn't make any difference. The guy might have gotten her in her own apartment parking lot, for all they knew.

Either way, she was gone.

His knees buckled and he sank onto a rickety chair, listening to the background murmurings of detectives doing what they did best: scavenging through the remains of death.

Chapter Twenty-seven

AN EARLY SPRING sunlight filtered through the window when Jared was moved from intensive care into a private room. His head was turbaned in bandages, and a tube drained excess fluid from the back of his head into a small plastic bottle which swung whenever he spoke. Though still deathly pale, he had asked Skye to bring him a small radio so that he could tune in to his favorite station. She teased him about being addicted to rock music. The nurses, who all loved him, took special care to see to it that he was comfortable. He ate it up.

Just thinking about how many pints of blood it had taken to save his life gave Skye chillbumps. His weakness made her heart ache. Still, she kept on a cheerful face, which wasn't all that hard, considering her joy at seeing him alive.

"I have a surprise for you," she said, and stepped outside the doorway, gesturing with her hand.

"Hi, Daddy."

Jared's eyes opened wide at the sight of Chelsea in the hospital doorway. "How did you get here, Pooh Bear? I thought kids weren't allowed." He reached out to her.

She stood where she was. "I can't come in the room. But Skye talked to the nice nurse, and she said that, since everything happened, I could come to the door and see you.

But I can't come in." Skye, standing beside the child, squeezed her close. "Do you feel okay, Daddy?" she asked shyly.

"Oh, listen, I feel great now that I get to see you. I wish I could hug you. Do you know how much I love you?"

"This big," she answered, holding her arms wide. "When you get better, the nurse said you could come down to the lobby, and I could hug you then."

"But I can blow you a kiss now, can't I?"

She smiled. Jared hammed it up, smacking a huge kiss and flinging out his hand, and she pretended to catch the kiss with her cheek.

"C'mon, sweetheart," said Skye. "You wait right here across the hall at the nurse's station with the nice lady. I need to talk about some things with your daddy, then we will go get some ice cream, okay?" She hugged Chelsea tightly, and could tell by the bounce in the child's walk how much good the visit had done her.

Jared looked positively transformed. Not until then did she realize how much he had worried about his daughter, in spite of his own problems.

"You're something, you know that?" he said as she took his hand.

"Well, we owe Nurse Jenson a debt of gratitude."

"Which I will repay. Order up a big bouquet of spring flowers for her, will you? No, wait. She sees flowers all the time. Candy. No, wait. She might be on a diet. Let's see . . ."

Skye laughed. "Silly man, why don't you just say thank you?"

"Not my style," he answered, grimacing as he changed positions.

"How is Chelsea, and I mean *really*?" His face grew serious.

"She's doing better than I expected, to tell you the truth. The police department provided an excellent family counselor through the Victim's Assistance Program to help her put it all behind her. I think now that she has been able to see you for herself, she will be fine."

He nodded. "She was always such a sunny child," he said wistfully. "I hope to God she doesn't lose that."

"It will take time." She quirked an eyebrow and said, "Lisa tells me I'm a bit of a hero to her now, for saving her and doing away with the bad guy."

"I think you already were a hero to her. I know you were with me."

She smiled and squeezed his hand. It felt so good to be here, talking with him. She couldn't take her eyes off his face.

"I have something to tell you," she said.

"It's good, isn't it? I can tell by the look on your face."

She gave him a smug look. "I've decided to do the book of children's photographs, after all, and donate the proceeds to the National Center for Missing and Exploited Children."

"*Fantastic!* It'll be great, I know it."

"You're just prejudiced."

His eyes focused on her with their old intensity. "Very." A moment later, he gestured toward her and said, "Where's your cane?"

"Don't need it anymore," she answered. He raised his eyebrows and grinned, but said nothing.

They sat quietly for a while, then Jared asked the question that was on both their minds.

"What about that Layton character?" Grimacing, he adjusted his position in bed.

"Poor man," she said.

"*Poor man?* Are you crazy? After all the things he did?"

"He was just so confused, Jared. They've got him under guard somewhere in the hospital. Turns out I didn't kill him, after all."

"*Here?* You've got to be kidding."

"It's all right, really. I had a chance to talk to one of the psychiatrists who's working with him. Sergeant Malone set it up for me. This stuff's supposed to be confidential, but because of what I've been through, the guy was willing to talk to me as long as he could remain anonymous."

"So, what did the shrink say?"

"He said that Eddie Layton is a classic paranoid schizophrenic with delusions of grandeur."

"Thanks a lot. Now tell me what he said."

She plumped his pillow, fussing over him a little. "Well, one thing he said is that they now believe schizophrenia may be a brain chemical disorder, because it is usually treatable with the right medication."

"Usually?"

"Eddie has several complications. First, he went undiagnosed for years, which means he was not treated. If he'd been on the proper medication . . ."

"You telling me none of this would have happened if Eddie had been a good little boy and taken his pills?" A journalist's skepticism glared from Jared's eyes.

"Nobody can say for sure. Some patients don't respond well to medication, some suffer more from side effects than from the illness itself. Eddie's case is severe enough that he probably would have required hospitalization. Unfortunately his background made it much, much worse."

"Oh, please, tell me you weren't kidnapped by a social worker."

"What's that supposed to mean?" Skye was having difficulty understanding Jared's sarcasm.

"It's just that all these bleeding-heart do-gooders blame everything that a criminal does on his mommy. They don't have to assume responsibility for their actions. Did it ever occur to all these shrinks and doctors and sociologists that some people are just born mean?"

She put her hands on her hips. "I'm not going to argue with you, Jared Martin, in your current weakened condition. But do you want to know the connection between the killer and me or not?"

He looked sheepish. "Of course. I'm sorry."

"I'm just saying this man was very ill, and his illness was

exaggerated by his lousy childhood. Now, do you want to hear it or not?"

"I'm all ears."

"Okay. Apparently Eddie was terribly abused as a child. His father abandoned them when he was very young. His mother was an alcoholic. It was more a case of abuse by neglect than anything else. Anyway, when he was about eight, he was befriended by a Mr. Peterson—a chickenhawk. Do you know what a chickenhawk is?"

Jared nodded.

"This went on for several years, from what the psychiatrist could tell. Then one day his mother caught them in the act."

"Ouch."

"Yes. It was a horrible scene. She beat Eddie and locked him in the closet for three days."

"Poor kid."

"Oh, so now it's poor kid, huh?" She grinned at him. "After that, she treated him like dirt until he ran off when he was sixteen or so."

"So how does that tie in with you?"

"Well, the psychiatrist thinks that Eddie's psychosis lay dormant for four or five years, until this sudden media onslaught recently about child molesting at day-care centers, child molesting in general. Not too long ago, you never heard anything about it. Then there it was on the evening news, *60 Minutes*, *Nightline*, what have you. Magazines and newspapers . . . Everywhere Eddie looked, he saw evidence of his own nightmare."

"I still don't see how—"

She sighed. "The shrinks don't know enough about schizophrenia to blame it on any one thing. Maybe it's genetic—and maybe Eddie's mother was afflicted with the same disorder. Or maybe it's strictly chemical. Or maybe severe abuse can nourish and feed the condition, cause it to sprout—who knows? At any rate, that's about the time he started working for Metroplex Messenger."

"And you opened your studio."

"That's right."

Jared chewed on the inside of his cheek. "So everything clicked at once, and you became the target for all that pent-up rage."

"You sound like a shrink yourself."

He shook his head. "Why did he come after me and Chelsea?"

"I guess he'd been watching me for a long time. In fact, he quit his job a few days before I closed the studio and spent most of his time following me. He figured you were another of my accomplices in this so-called kiddie porn ring of mine. He was trying to save Chelsea, Jared, screwy though that may sound."

He shook his head, for the moment careless of the tube, and looked out the window, his voice grave. "I'll never forgive myself for letting him get away with Chelsea. How could I have been so stupid as to leave her unprotected in your apartment, when clearly the guy knew some way to get in?" He was quiet a moment. "I thought I could protect you, Skye. Look what happened. I couldn't even protect myself." She squeezed his hand. "I tried to stop him. Jesus, I'd have gladly died to keep him away from her . . ." His voice broke.

"Don't blame yourself, Jared." She raised his hand to her lips.

He shrugged. "God! I hope she can forgive me."

"Chelsea doesn't blame you, Jared. She's just glad you are alive."

He sighed and grimaced. "I suppose you are going to tell me there was a method to the guy's madness."

"Yes. There was, really. That's where the delusions of grandeur come in. Eddie set himself up as the self-appointed savior of the children. It was just the starting point, really. He intended to personally wipe out all child pornography everywhere. He had this elaborate plan, see, and he thought that the world would recognize his greatness. In order to be able to take credit for all of it, he set up a pattern. His victims were killed a certain way, and then he left behind his signature."

"The cat's-head pin."

"The cat's-head pin."

Jared was quiet for a while, staring out the window. "What I don't understand is . . . how did he go about . . . selecting . . . his victims? What was the connecting link, and why the cat's-head pin?"

Skye took his hand in both hers. "The police found some family pictures in Eddie's apartment. His mother had long dark hair that hung to her shoulders. Each of his victims resembled her physically, as he remembered her from childhood."

He squeezed her hand. "I guess the shrink would say he was murdering his mother over and over."

"In a sense, I think so."

He looked up at the ceiling. "If it was me, I'd kill Peterson."

"Exactly, but Eddie couldn't see it that way. The victims of pedophiles often have trouble blaming their seducers."

Lacing his fingers through hers, he said, "I guess poor Bartholomew has to fit in here somewhere, and the cat's-head pins."

She nodded, her mouth suddenly dry. It was hard to speak of, just yet. For some reason, the loss of her pet had been one of the hardest things to take about the whole ordeal.

"You know, don't you?" Jared said. "It's just hard to talk about."

"Yes," she whispered, then raised her head to look him in the eye. "Eddie Layton's mother's name . . . was Kitty."

For a long moment, both suffered their own memories in silence. Finally Jared said, "Sergeant Malone came to see me a few minutes ago."

"I'm glad."

"I can't tell you how sick at heart he is about this whole thing."

"Oh, Jared, I'm so very sorry about Investigator Ruis. I heard they found her body the next morning. I feel terrible about it." In spite of everything, Skye meant it.

Jared nodded. "Me, too. The department will miss her. We all will. Anyway"—he roused himself with effort—"Malone said that all the evidence against Layton is clear-cut. They found all the victims' personal effects in his apartment, carpet fibers from the trunk of his car matched microscopically, and would you believe he'd kept extra rolls of film from each victim?"

She nodded mutely. More of Eddie's ramblings were beginning to make sense.

"Plus, they found the murder weapon—the cord. The court appointed psychiatrists to see if he's sane enough to stand trial. My guess is no."

Skye shuddered. "I just want them to put him away somewhere where he can't ever hurt anyone else again."

Jared was getting tired. Chelsea still waited at the nurse's station. Skye knew she should leave, but she couldn't seem to walk out the door. She kept wanting to touch him.

There was a muffled *pop* on one of the other wings, followed by a commotion. "What's going on?" asked Jared.

"I don't know. I'll go check."

She pushed open the door and stepped into the hall. Shouts drifted to her from the other wing, drawing nearer. Two more *pops*. A nurse ran toward her, screaming, "Get out of the way!"

Two more nurses rounded the corner, shouting at everyone to get into their rooms, a prisoner had escaped, but before Skye could move, Eddie Layton, bleeding from a bandage around his middle, his head also bandaged, and waving a gun, came into the hallway and headed straight toward her, bellowing, "You destroyed the Great Revelation, you turned them all against me, now you must die!"

Chapter Twenty-eight

LIKE A RABBIT being stalked by a killer dog, Skye froze. There was nowhere to go that the madman wouldn't follow.

"*Daddy!*"

Before Skye could stop her, Chelsea darted out from behind the nurse's station. She lunged for the child, but Eddie was quicker, snatching Chelsea's arm and jerking her into his body. As he slowly lowered the gun to the little girl's head, Skye felt the blood drain from her face. Chelsea's eyes widened in horror.

"I took this gun from the guard they had on me," Eddie said quietly, "and I killed him with it. I'll kill her, too, if you make one move."

Sounds began to filter in to Skye, bustling, buzzing crowd noises from a distance. Her heart jerked painfully in her chest. Moving awkwardly, Eddie backed into the wall by a door, dragging the terrified child with him.

"I know you don't want to hurt her, Eddie." It was hard for Skye to talk. Her tongue was so dry it stuck to her teeth. "She's just a child. She's innocent, Eddie."

"Shut up! *Just shut up!*" His face waxen, the whites of his red-rimmed eyes stark against the dark hollows under his brows, Eddie pressed the gun harder against Chelsea's head.

"Drop it!"

Skye and Eddie both looked toward the deep bellow coming from the end of the corridor. Moses Malone had rounded the corner from Carmen's wing and assumed the stance of a marksman, legs spread wide, both hands gripping a weapon that looked like a cannon to Skye's uneducated eye.

"I'm a police officer," boomed Malone. "You let go of that child or I'll blow your fucking brains out."

"How do you know the impact won't cause me to jerk my trigger finger?" shouted Eddie back in a reasonable tone, as if they were discussing the proper reel to use for fishing.

Skye shook her head and waved her hands, palms up. "That won't be necessary," she called. "Eddie doesn't want Chelsea, anyway, do you, Eddie?" She faced him. "You want me."

Glancing wildly up and down the corridor, Eddie let go of Chelsea, grabbed the doorknob nearest him, and flung back the door. With the gun still pressed against her head, Chelsea remained perfectly still.

"Get in there," he said to Skye. She hesitated. "*Now!*"

Scurrying into the room, Skye fumbled for a light switch and found herself in a windowless supply room. Before she could say anything, Eddie darted in after her with Chelsea and slammed the heavy door. The room was small and close, lined with overstuffed shelves containing plastic water pitchers, disposable thermometers, various basins and bedpans, the kinds of things necessary to set up a patient's room. Nothing particularly critical was kept in the store room, which probably explained why it had been unlocked. Packing boxes were jammed helter-skelter around the floor.

"Shit," he said, looking around. He picked his way through the boxes to the farthest corner, pulling the child after him. Her face had assumed a plastic quality, as if she'd gone into some sort of coping trance.

"Sure is a small room," he mumbled nervously. "Touch

hat light," he challenged Skye, "and I'll fill the room full
f holes. Can't take the dark . . ." His voice faded.

They were trapped.

Shaking herself from shock-imposed stupor, Skye ran
mental tapes through her mind of the things the psychiatrist
ad told her about Eddie. It had all seemed so clinical at the
ime, so hard to understand.

Common ground. She had to come up with some kind of
ommon ground between them.

"Skye!" Malone's muffled shout came from the other
ide of the door. "Are you okay? What's goin' on?"

"We're fine," she called. "It's going to be all right."

"*Get away from the door,*" screamed Eddie, "*or I swear
'll kill 'em both!*" His chest heaved in a rapid pant. He
roaned a little. Skye could see the red stain on his
andages spreading.

"I know you're scared, Eddie," she said. "I'm scared,
oo. And just look at Chelsea. She's terrified. Why don't
ou let her go? I'll stay. Please let her go."

He shook his head violently. "No. She's safe with me."

"How safe can she be with a gun to her head? What if you
lip? You don't want to kill her."

"She won't die," he said. "She'll join the eyes." A note
f uncertainty crept into his voice.

"What eyes?" Keep him talking. She'd always heard you
hould keep them talking.

His face grew sly. "Wouldn't you like to know? This is
ll your fault, you bitch. Even the eyes know that."

"I never took any pornographic photographs, if that's
vhat you mean."

"*Liar!*" He squeezed Chelsea and she yelped. So she was
ot in a trance.

"Then if you think it is my fault, punish *me*, Eddie, not
Chelsea. You don't want to hurt her. Let her go. Take me
nstead." Skye tried to swallow but couldn't.

There was a moment of silence. Suddenly Eddie let go of

the child and shoved her toward Skye. She stumbled an
fell into Skye's arms.

"You're right," he said. "I can protect her by killin
you."

Skye clutched the trembling child to her, stroking her ha
and murmuring, "It's okay, sugar bun, it's going to be a
right. The man isn't going to hurt anyone."

"Can I send her out?" she asked him.

He shrugged. "Why not? It's you I want."

Skye took Chelsea by the shoulders and looked into he
pinched face. "You go to Sergeant Malone now, honey, an
tell him everything is going to be all right. I love you."

The child flung her arms around Skye. "I don't want t
leave you!" she cried, sobbing. Skye looked over Chelsea'
head at Eddie. He had lowered the gun and was watchin
them thoughtfully. "Listen, Chelsea," she whispered
"Your daddy will be worried about you. You need to te
him you're all right. Don't worry. I'll bet we can still go fo
ice cream later."

At the mention of Jared, Chelsea loosened her arms an
stepped back.

Eddie raised the gun and pointed it at Skye. "No funn
stuff," he ordered. "No trying to run out the door o
anything. I swear I'll kill you if you do, even if that co
shoots me in the process."

Skye smiled and winked at Chelsea, drawing courag
from the child as she watched her stand up straight, squar
her small shoulders, and reach for the door.

"Open it just far enough to squeeze through," said Eddie

Chelsea obeyed, and the instant she opened the doo
Skye saw the flash of a big black hand and the child wa
gone.

She faced a killer.

He didn't look like a killer. At least, not the ones she'
seen on TV. A slender man of below average height, wit
a sallow complexion, thin brown hair, light brown eyes, an
old acne scars. A nondescript man. A man who could wal

through a crowd and never be seen. A man no one would remember as they thumbed through their high school yearbook.

It shook Skye to the core of her being to realize that there did not seem to be a threatening bone in the man's body, and yet he had senselessly murdered several women and nearly one man, kidnapped a child, terrorized Skye for weeks, and now, here she was, a hostage to his gunpoint.

Even as she thought these things, the fear as she had known it slipped away. The fear of the unknown, she suspected, was always greater than facing the adversary.

In a flash of insight peculiar to the heightened sensations brought on by crises, Skye knew that she was not going to die. And with that knowledge came freedom.

Eddie was slumped against some packing boxes. Sweat had broken out on his brow and his complexion was pasty white.

"Eddie," she said, "the psychiatrist can help you get rid of the eyes. He can help you not be afraid anymore."

"You lie," he said, but his voice was weak.

"People have hurt you. Now you are afraid that you will be hurt again. I won't let them hurt you, Eddie."

"You stole the glory from me," he said, gasping. "You are the one who told them I was bad. I'm not bad." He passed a shaking hand over his eyes. "They tried to poison me. They gave me pills to take." He grimaced a smile. "But I tricked them. I hid the pills under my tongue, and then I stuffed them in the Kleenex box." He waved the gun at her. "You told them I was bad and they tried to kill me."

"I didn't tell anyone you are bad, Eddie. I don't think you are bad."

His face grew ugly. "If you didn't think I was bad, then why did you lock me in the closet? Why did you call me those nasty names? It's you, *you*!"

Struggling to his feet, he raised the gun again. "*You are the bitch!*"

"Eddie! I'm Skye! *I'm not your mother!*"

Both hands on the gun, Eddie stopped, blinking, his mouth slack.

"I'm not your mother," she repeated.

A guttural cry escaped him. Racking sobs overtook his body, and he lowered the gun again.

"Let me help you, Eddie."

"I can't stand the pain! It hurts too bad."

"I'll call a doctor—"

"No, no, you don't understand. Nobody understands. I was going to make everybody understand in my book. The Great Revelation would explain everything. Since we have so great a cloud of witnesses, let us lay aside . . . every sin . . ."

"I understand, Eddie, I do."

"No, no, you lie! They all lie. Only the eyes tell the truth . . . the eyes . . ."

He drew up straight. "That's it. The eyes." His face grew peaceful and he smiled. All the times Eddie had come into Skye's studio for deliveries, and they'd chatted, surely he had smiled in just that way, but she had never noticed. She never even knew his name.

He raised the gun and she looked desperately for something to throw or dive behind, but something was different: he was raising the gun too high, he was raising the gun to his own head—

"*No!*"

The explosion in the small room deafened Skye and set up a furious ringing in her ears. Everything happened in dreamlike slow motion . . . The top of Eddie's head disappeared, drenching walls, shelves, boxes, and floor in crimson . . . The door slammed back—noiselessly, in her deafness—Moses Malone grabbed her roughly and yanked her into the corridor . . . People jostled past her . . . Some spoke to her, their mouths moving, but she couldn't hear for the ringing . . . She pressed her face against Moses's scratchy shirt and felt comforted in his big arms . . . Her knees buckled and he helped her to a chair behind the nurse's station . . . And then the sound returned and there was so much noise and confusion—uniformed men in thick vests carrying rifles swarmed around nurses and doctors and other police officers . . .

"Is Eddie dead?" she asked, but nobody answered and she realized that she had only thought the question.

Am I alive? she wondered.

Epilogue

THE NIGHTMARES WERE the worst. Sometimes Eddie chased her down labyrinths of hospital corridors, each one ending in blank walls that she stumbled into like a laboratory rat. Other times it was she who had been shot, and she would struggle to awaken before she died. In one, she looked up from the barrel of the gun and into Paul's face.

Work was difficult for a while. Skye had to rebuild a clientele put off by sensational press. And while the resulting photography was adequate, the creative spark seemed numbed, lacking genius. For each happy, smiling child she photographed, she couldn't help thinking about all the childhoods damaged or destroyed by adults gone out of control.

Though she was able to smooth Clyde Winslow's ruffled feathers easily enough, considering the circumstances, Skye found that she no longer had patience for Tommy Thomas's snide remarks. The decision to find a new place to live was made easier by the fact that her apartment no longer had the cozy, homey atmosphere she had once enjoyed so much. Too many memories.

It seemed only natural, then, for her and Jared to look for a place together. They were married in a quiet little ceremony on a glorious day in May, underneath flickering shade trees on the shore of White Rock Lake. Jared sent Skye a dozen long-stemmed yellow roses, which she twined in her hair and carried in her arms. Chelsea was maid of honor.

Skye and Jared moved into a house filled with rustic wood paneling, large, airy windows, and beamed ceilings. They arranged an amicable and flexible custody agreement with Chelsea's mother, which enabled her to stay with them several days each week.

Only then, with Jared's long, lean body pressed close to hers each night, his hand resting lightly on her thigh, the sound of his breathing soft in her ear . . . only then did the nightmares begin to fade.